What people are saying about …

THEN SINGS MY SOUL

"Amy K. Sorrells struck gold with this timeless story of love, loss, and the beautiful bond of family. I was spellbound as the story mixed history with redemption that comes when we run to the Father."

Kariss Lynch, author of *Shaken* and *Shadowed*

"I really enjoyed *Then Sings My Soul*. It brought to light a little-known and well-hidden period of Ukraine's troubled history. Amy does a great job interweaving the stories of the Stewart family, especially Nel's and Jakob's broken past, and showing how God can redeem even the most broken of hearts."

Ken Ney, MD, board president
of Mission to Ukraine

Praise for …

AMY K. SORRELLS

"Sorrells's words effortlessly rise from the page with a cadence that is remarkably brave and wildly beautiful."

Toni Birdsong, author of *More than a Bucket List*

"Amy Sorrells will break your heart and piece it back twice its size."

Billy Coffey, author of *When Mockingbirds Sing*

"Amy Sorrells weaves an engaging tale in stunningly beautiful lyrical prose. If you are a fan of women's fiction, don't miss this fresh new voice."

Jordyn Redwood, author of the Bloodline Trilogy

"This beautifully well-written book offers hope and healing from tragedy and brokenness."

Birdie Gunyon Meyer, RN, MA,
coordinator of the Perinatal Mood Disorders
Program at Indiana University Health

"Amy K. Sorrells has a lyrical voice that immediately draws you into the complex lives of captivating characters and a powerful tale that will leave you breathless. This is one of those stories that will continue to live on in a reader's mind long after turning the last page."

Tina Ann Forkner, author of *Rose House*

"Evocative, brutal, yet redemptive, it forces you to think long and hard about difficult subjects and pain, but it leaves you with the hope of grace and mercy. Thanks, Amy, for taking me there."

Dave Rodriguez, senior pastor of Grace Church, Noblesville, Indiana

"With poetic prose, lyrical descriptions, and sensory details that bring the reader deep into every scene, Amy K. Sorrells has delivered ... In the end comes redemption, grace, forgiveness, and faith, but not without a few scars carried by those who manage to survive the wrath of hardened hearts. Bravo!"

Julie Cantrell, *New York Times* bestselling author of *Into the Free* and *When Mountains Move*

"I appreciate the author's understanding of trauma as she writes— addressing the level of courage necessary to heal from deep hurts, while at the same time taking great care in gently sharing character experiences throughout her novel. [She] draws readers into another world—a unique time and place where pain and trauma can feel all too relatable—but where readers themselves can taste the same comfort and hope that's woven into this beautiful story."

Nicole Bromley, author of *Hush and Breathe* and founder of OneVOICE

"Author Amy Sorrells writes with tenderness, grace, and the heartbroken voice of experience."

Lori Borgman, columnist for *McClatchy-Tribune*, author of *The Death of Common Sense*, and national speaker

a novel

THEN
SINGS
MY
SOUL

AMY K. SORRELLS

David C Cook®
transforming lives together

THEN SINGS MY SOUL
Published by David C Cook
4050 Lee Vance View
Colorado Springs, CO 80918 U.S.A.

David C Cook Distribution Canada
55 Woodslee Avenue, Paris, Ontario, Canada N3L 3E5

David C Cook U.K., Kingsway Communications
Eastbourne, East Sussex BN23 6NT, England

The graphic circle C logo is a registered trademark of David C Cook.

This story is a work of fiction. Characters and events are the product of the author's
imagination. Any resemblance to any person, living or dead, is coincidental.

Unless otherwise noted, all Scripture quotations are taken from the Holy Bible,
New International Version®, NIV®. Copyright © 1973, 2011 by Biblica, Inc.™ Used
by permission of Zondervan. All rights reserved worldwide. www.zondervan.com.
Scripture quotations marked NKJV are taken from the New King James Version®.
Copyright © 1982 by Thomas Nelson, Inc. Used by permission. All rights reserved.

LCCN 2014948815
ISBN 978-1-4347-0545-7
eISBN 978-1-4347-0893-9

The author is represented by and this book is published in association with the
literary agency of WordServe Literary Group, Ltd., www.wordserveliterary.com.

The Team: John Blase, Nicci Hubert, Amy Konyndyk, Nick
Lee, Jennifer Lonas, Tiffany Thomas, Karen Athen
Cover Design: Faceout Studio, Emily Weigel
Cover Photos: Shutterstock and Robert J. Vukovich (stone photo)

Printed in the United States of America
First Edition 2015

1 2 3 4 5 6 7 8 9 10

122914

THE JOURNEY OF JAKOB AND PETER
ACROSS EASTERN EUROPE

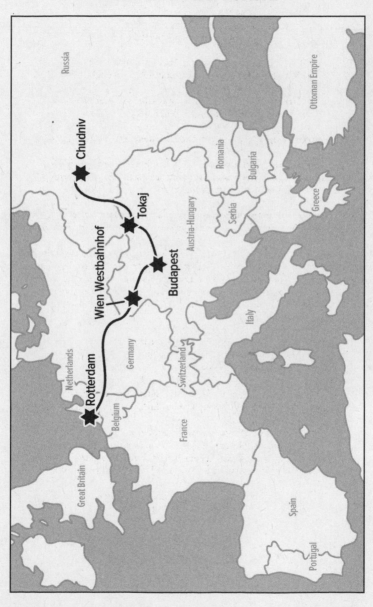

When through the woods and forest glades I wander
And hear the birds sing sweetly in the trees;
When I look down from lofty mountain grandeur,
And hear the brook and feel the gentle breeze:
Then sings my soul, my Savior God, to Thee,
How great Thou art! How great Thou art!

Stuart K. Hine, "How Great Thou Art"

Amid a torrent of sin and sorrow, you may cross the stream of time
upon the stepping stones of the places marked "Jehovah-Shammah."

Charles Spurgeon

JANUARY 21, 1904

---

*Chudniv, a village within the Zhytomyr Oblast
of the Russian Empire (now Ukraine)*

PROLOGUE

Josef Maevski's calloused fingers pressed the brilliant-blue stone against the grit of the turntable as he tried not to rush.

Just the other day, he'd held a half-polished piece of garnet the size of a small strawberry and as crimson red as wine. He had spent hours peering through the loupe, exploring and creating mental maps of the stone's grain, minuscule fractures, and ancient bubbles trapped as the forces of nature formed them. He had only four more facets to create when the stone splintered and cracked clear through, an irreparable chunk flying across the dimly lit room and landing on the edge of the windowsill. A beam of sunlight illuminated the claret sliver so it gleamed like fresh blood on the edge of a cut finger.

I haven't much time, he thought, adding the finishing buffs and polishes to the precious aquamarine, shoving a magnifying loupe against his eye socket and then removing it, angling the stone toward the lantern light and the dwindling sunlight until at last he was satisfied with every facet.

Nobility and villagers alike considered Josef an expert stonecutter. The previous spring, an aristocratic family in Kiev commissioned him to create a one-of-a-kind faceting design for a large, egg-sized aquamarine, chosen for its color, which matched Princess Anastasia's eyes.

Already completed and delivered weeks earlier, Josef's stone would be placed in the center of a gold scepter designed for Tsar Nicholas in celebration of his daughter Anastasia's birthday. The stone in front of him now was one of two smaller versions—still of valuable size—that he'd been working on from what was left of the aquamarine used for the tsar's scepter. Most of the companies whose orders he had received from Kiev shipped him the rough stones, and their coffers were so full that they rarely cared what he did with the scraps.

Josef's father spent years saving enough money to send Josef to Idar-Oberstein, Germany, for an apprenticeship with some of the finest cutters in the world. Because of that, Josef's family could eat and had lived mostly without fear in the bucolic *shtetl*,[1] one of many in the Pale of Settlement. His primary work as a farmer would never have paid the bills. And with four daughters and two sons and a seventh child on the way, peace and dowries were high priorities. At least those had been his priorities until the recent bloodshed in Kishinev, where there had been yet another slaughter of innocent Jewish brothers and sisters, even babies torn to pieces, during the most recent Passover.

"Josef." One breath from his bride still turned his stomach upside down, even after eighteen years of marriage. "Here's your bread and butter. There's not much beef left."

"Thank you. Set it there." He tilted his head slightly in the direction of the table and tattered wingback chair by the fire.

"Josef. You should take a moment and eat something."

"I know, I know." He was more gruff with her than he'd intended.

Eliana started back toward the glow of the kitchen, one hand on her lower back as she lurched unevenly from the weight of the near-term baby within her.

"Eliana, wait."

She turned toward him, her sky-blue eyes melting him with their cool, steady, gentle gaze.

"I'm sorry, *moya lyubov.*[†] You know I have to finish. Peter will need this for his journey. The sooner he can leave the better."

Eliana came back toward him and leaned heavily against the thick wooden worktable as she settled on the stool next to him. Her swollen breasts stretched the scarlet cross-stitching of her blouse. She picked up the aquamarine, which nearly filled the palm of her hand, and a tear rolled down her flushed cheek.

"The color of dawn. Of new beginnings," Josef said, watching as Eliana ran her fingers over the polished contours of the gem, then set it on the table, nesting it into a dingy piece of cheesecloth.

She wiped her face and sighed, appearing impatient. "I thought we'd be safe in the Pale, that what happened in Odessa and Kishinev would not come near us. That if you continued using your trade for the tsar …"[2]

Josef shook his head and ran his fingers through the ends of his thick, black moustache. "We will have to choose a side soon. There is talk in Zhytomyr about the Black Hundreds radicals who are organizing. Among them are those who'd like to kill anyone who even looks like a Jew. It won't matter that we believe in Yeshua Messiah now. I will fight for my village, for Russia, for my family, and for the faith."

"For faith? You would fight for it?" Eliana stood again, breathing hard as she trudged toward the window, where fresh snow swirled against the icy panes. Then she turned toward him, her face red with

---

† *Shh, shh, shh,* my love.

fury. "You heard the reports, Josef. Babies torn to pieces. Babies! Our brothers and sisters stripped naked and herded like cattle into the woods, into great pits, and slaughtered. Who can fight such evil? Not El Shaddai. He doesn't pass over His chosen ones any longer. And Yeshua Messiah, if He were truly Emmanuel …" She held her belly, her interlaced fingers mottled and clenched as if someone were already trying to tear her unborn child from within her.

"The Gospels tell us that even Yeshua Himself felt as if God had forsaken Him, but He hadn't. He won't leave us either." Josef moved toward her, pulling her close, and the two began to sway together as he whispered in her ear, *"Sh'ma Yis-ra-eil, A-do-nai E-lo-hei-nu, A-do-nai E-chad."*‡

She did not answer.

He lifted her chin, wiped her tears with a swoop of his calloused thumb, and locked his eyes with hers. *"Ba-ruch sheim k'vod mal-chu-to l'o-lam va-ed."*§

Eliana pulled her scarf over her head. Her shoulders shook as she cried.

"V'a-hav-ta eit A-do-nai E-lo-he-cha, B'chawl l'va-v'cha."¶

She joined Josef in the Shema, their family's recent conversion to Messianic Judaism not dampening their dedication to offer praise, recite the traditional prayers, and commit to the adoration of God in the midst of fear and pain.

---

‡   Hear, O Israel, the L-rd is our G-d, the L-rd is One.

§   Blessed be the name of the glory of His kingdom forever and ever.

¶   You shall love the L-rd your G-d with all your heart, with all your soul, and with all your might.

In their grief, each syllable felt to Jakob like a forced attempt to believe the words they'd learned as soon as they were able to form words as toddlers; each syllable a vain plea for escape from the new Pharaoh of death bearing down all around them.

"Mama, Peter's coming!" Zahava's shout broke the intimacy of the moment.

Josef and Eliana's oldest daughter had been cross-stitching with her two younger sisters, Tova and Ilana, in the front room by the fire. Now with four-year-old Jakob on his tiptoes at her side, Zahava stood by the window and rubbed a spot of frost off the windowpane. The door to their home slammed open, causing the youngest of Joseph and Eliana's children, Faigy, not yet two, to startle and burst into tears. The wind ushered a swirl of snow and ice into the house, along with a young man, tall but slender beneath his layers of sweaters, sheepskin, and fleece. Ice covered his eyebrows, his beaver-skin hat, and his mukluks.

"Are you a man or a beast, Peter?" Josef's laugh came from the depths of his belly and shook the furniture in the room.

"*Tato*,** it's time."

Josef's smile fell, and Eliana pulled the red-faced and whimpering Faigy closer.

"How can this be?" Josef said. "I heard of the madness in Kiev, but Zhytomyr? Are you sure?"

Peter was only fourteen, but he'd shown enough maturity to help other boys from the shtetl deliver milk and other goods across the countryside, where they often learned news. "There are

---

** Dad.

riders. Madmen. The Black Hundreds are well organized now. More interested in Jewish and peasant blood than in Orthodoxy. They've covered the city, throwing their propaganda leaflets everywhere, gathering more supporters. They've filled storehouses with arms, and barns with horses. They will be in Chudniv by sunset tomorrow, if not sooner."

Josef moved toward his workroom, and Peter followed him, watching as his father picked up the aquamarine he'd been working on and turned it toward the fire, sending reflections flickering around the room. The stone's color reminded Peter of the sky on afternoons he had spent ice-skating with his classmates on the frozen pond behind the village dairy. Josef picked up another stone, identical in cut and splendor to the first round stone on the worktable. He wrapped it and several other stones—some rough and others brilliantly faceted—in cheesecloth and tucked them into a leather satchel. The crinkle of wax paper came from the kitchen, where Eliana wrapped bread and cured beef.

"You must go," said Josef, his enormous hands trembling as he handed Peter the bag of stones. "Take Galya. He is the strongest of the horses. His dapple-gray coat will blend with the birch and the aspen. He will get you across the Carpathian Mountains and foothills and into Hungary. Find your way to the sea as we talked about, and use these stones to buy your train tickets to Rotterdam and your passage to America."

"But, Tato—" Peter tried to protest as his mother pulled him toward her.

Eliana hung the strap of the leather satchel stuffed with food across Peter's chest, then tightened the buckle as he held up his arms while she fussed. When she finished, he stuffed the bag of stones deep into the inside pocket of his fleece-lined coat.

"I thought we'd have more time," Peter said.

"Me too," said Josef. "Try not to worry. We will be fine as long as people still believe I am an artisan and for the tsar, for Russia. Zahava, Tova, and Ilana are strong like their mama, and they'll be here to help. Send letters when you can. Once you find work and a place to live, we will come too. They say there's good work in America. Lots of work for laborers. Factories. Fisheries. The ocean. Can you imagine?"

Peter could not.

"I will finish more stones and use them to pay our way once you are settled," Josef continued. "Faigy will be bigger, and the baby will have arrived and be strong enough to travel. But you must go first."

Eliana put her arms around Peter's shoulders as little Jakob clung to her skirts, his hazel eyes wide with concern.

"Mama." Jakob's chin quivered.

Peter pulled back from his mother's embrace and squatted onto his haunches so he was at eye level with his little brother. He put his hands onto the boy's small shoulders. "It'll be okay, Jakob. I promise."

Peter stood and adjusted the belt across the waist of his *kozhukh*.[3]

"Jakob, come here," Zahava called in a gentle but scolding voice from near the hearth where she and her sisters clung to one another and held the younger ones close.

The wetness of Peter's tears created bright-red splotches on Eliana's faded scarlet head scarf as he held his mother once more. Then he turned to Josef, who helped him fasten the top of his kozhukh and tuck in his woolens as if he were a schoolboy again.

"Let's go, *miy syn*. I'll help you ready Galya."

Eliana didn't bother to wipe the tears flowing down the grooves of her grief-blotched face. She clung to Faigy and leaned into her children, all of them staring at the heavy wooden door after Josef and Peter left.

Jakob ran to the frosty window and used his small fist to clear a spot. He stood on his tiptoes again and strained to watch his father and Peter prepare Galya for the journey.

LATE OCTOBER 1994

South Haven, Michigan

CHAPTER 1

Nel Stewart pushed her bronze, wire-rimmed glasses up on her nose as she peered through the thick window over the wing of the plane and watched the sunrise turn the tops of the gray clouds golden yellow. The color reminded her of the aspens she'd hiked beneath the day before. She'd wanted to soak in as much of Santa Fe as she could, hoping the life she'd found there in nature and the art she loved so dearly would buoy her, if not brace her, for what awaited her in Michigan. She turned a grape-sized, turquoise stone ring around the fourth finger of her right hand. It was one of the first pieces of jewelry she'd made, setting it herself in a wide band of pounded silver.

She grimaced as she bit back the corner of her thumb's cuticle until it bled.

"Coffee?" the flight attendant whispered, leaning slightly over the sleeping bear of a man in the seat next to her. "This is my last pass before we land in Detroit."

"Sure. Black, please. And do you have a bandage?" Nel raised her eyes apologetically.

"I do." The flight attendant—Amanda, her name tag read—smiled as she bent toward the bottom of the refreshment cart. Nel studied Amanda's perfectly coiffed blonde hair pulled into a tight bun, with not a stray hair or split end in sight, and she felt suddenly insecure about her own long hair, loose, untrimmed, and uncolored for months. She'd felt proud of the salt-and-pepper grays at her temple, and the section on the side she'd allowed to form into a couple of dreadlocks, the way many of her artisan friends wore theirs in Santa Fe. Now she felt almost silly.

Amanda finished rummaging in the beverage cart and handed Nel a bandage.

As Nel pulled the beige strip tight around her stinging thumb, she thought about how she didn't feel forty-three. A couple of dread-locks flopped toward her face as she reached forward to pull the tray table down from the seat in front of her.

Her mom loved to say, "You're only as old as you feel."

Amanda handed Nel a napkin followed by a steaming cup of coffee.

Nel returned her gaze to the window and wondered if her mom, Catherine Stewart, had felt eighty-two, or if she'd gone right on feeling young until she died two days ago. Nel thought she'd been aware of how old her parents were getting, but in reality, she hadn't been. She'd failed them both in the worst possible way, not being there when Mom died. Nel pulled the shade down over the window as the sun glared through and made it nearly impossible for her to read and review the latest catalog featuring her jewelry designs. She should've been more cognizant of her parents' senescence, but each time they spoke on the phone—almost daily—her mom's voice had sounded the same as it always had, vibrant and wise, steadfast and kind. Definitely not doddering or declining. And for that reason alone, Nel was glad her mom had died suddenly. Nel doubted she could've handled watching her mom suffer through a long, cruel illness such as cancer or emphysema as so many of her friends' parents had, their faces once taut with joy eventually drooping with despair. And yet as glad as she was that Catherine hadn't had to suffer, she felt heartbroken and angry. She'd never have the chance to say good-bye.

Nel hadn't thought it strange the phone had rung early Wednesday morning. Jakob often called at that time of day, forgetting the time difference between Michigan and New Mexico. But she had been devastated by the reason for his call—that Mom had passed. Not that she didn't adore her father. But she always figured he'd pass first since he was twelve years Catherine's senior. Nel talked to him just as frequently as Catherine. At least once a week she sat at her kitchen table overlooking the Sangre de Cristo Mountains and listened as her parents passed the phone back and forth and bickered about whose turn it was to talk. Nel had noticed that, unlike Mom's vibrant voice, Dad's voice sounded old. Gravelly. As though he had a chunk of chicken potpie stuck in his throat but didn't care and kept talking anyway. That's how he had sounded Wednesday, and before she knew the reason for his call, she had wished he'd cough or clear his throat.

"Mom's gone."

Nel had listened, dumbstruck, as he explained what had happened ...

"She went to bed as usual last night ...

"Didn't complain of feeling ill at all ...

"Doctor gave her a clean bill of health a couple of weeks ago. Tweaked her blood-pressure medication, sure, but nothing more than that ...

"No signs she wouldn't wake up this morning …

"Mattie is helping with the details …

"Mom had her wishes written up and taped to the inside front cover of her Bible. Hymns picked out and everything. Already paid for a plot for both of us in the cemetery …"

The man in the seat next to her stirred. He'd taken full advantage of the hospitality kit the airline provided, removing his shiny loafers and tucking them neatly under the seat in front of him, pulling the nonskid footies over his gold-toed black socks—the same sort Dad wore—crossing his arms as if he wished there were something, or someone, between them, and pulling the cobalt sleep mask over his eyes soon after the wheels of the plane left the tarmac. She noticed the thick gold band on the ring finger of his left hand and found herself wondering what his life was like. Did he have children? He was certainly middle-aged, the gray around his own temples giving that much away, but he was trim, lacking the paunch of extra weight common on so many of her peers. Had his wife aged along with him, or did she have to work hard now to keep the flesh beneath her skin taut and smooth? Was he a hard and detached businessman like many of her parents' friends, or had being born in the middle decades of the century softened and aroused him as it had her, growing up serenaded by the music of Buffalo Springfield and Arlo Guthrie, Bob Marley and Joni Mitchell and the like?

Nel thought of Dr. Sam Tucker, with whom she enjoyed her most recent and ongoing affair, though currently things were getting rocky between them. Sam hadn't been able to get off work to come to the funeral, and if she were honest, she was relieved. He was a doctor—an anesthesiologist—and quite good at it if one judged by his fancy car, designer clothes, and condominium overlooking one of Santa Fe's most beautiful vistas. She had been careful to avoid dating someone like him, cultured by most standards but essentially arrogant and materialistic. Up until she'd met Sam, she'd been content to enjoy informal but sensuous relationships with other artists like herself, affairs that almost seemed to be set to music, with Cat Stevens's songs and long monologues of Wallace Stegner and Walt Whitman playing in the background. She and her lovers would lie back on woolen Pueblo blankets under the golden canopy of autumn aspens of the Sangre de Cristo Mountains until the stars appeared, and then make love beneath the vast expanse of the Milky Way. She loved being surrounded by artists of all kinds, reveling in the undulation of a potter's wheel, the back-and-forth strokes of a paintbrush, like Georgia O'Keeffe's, bringing life to the deep, inner folds of desert flowers, or, as in Nel's case, the wrapping and stringing of beads, the rounding and polishing of stones, and the forming and hammering of metal.

Sam had been a major donor to Nel's artist colony, and as such, the guest of honor at a gala celebrating local folk artists at the New Mexico Museum of Art that spring. He'd caught her off guard as she stood, merlot in her plastic cup, swaying as she studied the way Cézanne had sketched the hard rock of the mountains along the horizon in his work *Les Baigneurs*. Cézanne's work so closely resembled the Rio Chama near Abiquiú that Nel wondered if the painter had actually been to New Mexico—though she didn't think so.

When Sam came over and introduced himself, she'd felt her cheeks redden—had it been from Sam or from the wine? Had he left her so immediately undone? Or was it the fact that they met near

Les Baigneurs featuring six unclad men, while over her shoulder was the gesso-on-wood of Juan Amadeo Sanchez's *Christ on the Cross*— Jesus's downturned head, His simple expression, the horizontal lines of defeat.

Nel smiled to herself as she peered unseeing into the steaming cup of airline coffee she held with both hands. She remembered how Sam had placed his hand so gently on the small of her back that night at the museum, allowing his fingers to travel up her back and down again. As they walked to his car well before the gala ended, the summer wind had lifted her floor-length muslin skirt, causing it to billow behind her. It reminded her of the way Sanchez had painted Jesus's loincloth, as though the rags wafted against the Golgotha winds. Sam hadn't seemed to think anything odd of the fact that she was forty-three and had never married. No, Sam hadn't thought of her as an old maid at all. Quite the contrary, as he enjoyed every part of her that night and countless nights since then.

But those had been their best days. Until recently, through summer and into the fall, he'd been content to play by her rules: no commitment, no questions, no problem. The night before, they'd had another of the major fights occurring more and more often, but she was too worn out from the sudden news of her mom's death to make amends before she left town for the funeral.

Her ears popped, and she finished the last swig of coffee as the Fasten Seat Belts light illuminated and Nel prepared, along with everyone else, for landing.

CHAPTER 2

"How is he really?" Nel said over her shoulder as she reached for a suitcase that was about to pass by on the silver treads of the airport conveyor belt.

Jakob and Catherine's longtime next-door neighbor, Matilda—or Mattie, as she preferred to be called—had offered to pick up Nel in Grand Rapids that morning. Though she'd seen Mattie less than two years prior when she'd come home for Christmas, Nel was surprised by the way their old family friend had aged, deep new lines on her face, the way her lipstick—which she never went without—ran into the fine creases around her lips. Nel began to worry about how her father would look, and her mother, for that matter, in the casket the next morning. Nel recognized how absurd it was for her to have assumed time never advanced, that life and nature and thoughts and feelings in her hometown, no matter how long she'd lived away, somehow stayed unmoving and unchanged like a Polaroid photo.

"He's not well, Eleanor," Mattie replied.

Eleanor.

The last time she'd heard someone call her by her full name, she'd been talking to her mom on Tuesday. She imagined Catherine then, standing in the kitchen, perhaps leaning against the aluminum-trimmed Formica counters, the red phone they'd purchased in the seventies and never replaced held against her ear, which most certainly smelled of White Shoulders cologne or Mary Kay cold cream, or both. Her toes might've been wiggling at the ends of the pair of fuzzy pink slippers Nel had sent her for her birthday earlier that summer. Catherine had been asking her to come home for Thanksgiving. Or Christmas. Or both.

"Come home, Eleanor Louise. I want to *see* you."

Nel had felt the words sting. At the time she'd supposed the feeling had been regret. But in hindsight she realized it was more than that. It was grief, a premourning of all she'd lose when her mother passed, of all the things they'd never do—like sit on the porch swing and knit, have lunch or tea in town, spend a Saturday together watching old movies, and whatever daughters and mothers did when they lived close. Her mom had been right. Visiting once every year or two wasn't enough, and Nel deserved whatever guilt consumed her because she'd simply been too independent to come back to live in South Haven. If there was one thing she couldn't stand, it was disappointment in her parents' eyes, and she'd felt that when they'd spoken on Tuesday, even across a long-distance phone line.

Nel had tried to offer her mom an alternative. "I'll fly you and Dad out here in the spring, when the weather breaks up there. We'll visit the museums. You can see the O'Keeffes and the Beauregards, the—"

"Pshaw. I don't care about those right now. And I don't want to wait for spring. Besides, your father and I are getting too old to sit on an airplane for that long. Why, it'll take half a dozen stewardesses and wheelchairs to get us on and off the darn thing. Just come *here*, Nel-Belle."

"I'll think about it," she'd said.

The next morning, her dad had called to say her mom was gone.

Nel piled her two suitcases and two carry-ons into the trunk of the white Mercedes as Mattie fiddled with the heater controls on the shiny wooden dashboard. Mattie dressed as stunning as ever, wearing a black felt hat trimmed with purple feathers pulled quaint and snug over her head, a neat bob of gray curls resting precisely at the top of her thin shoulders, her protruding bones visible even beneath her mink coat.

"Brrrrr," Nel said, plopping into the front passenger seat. The bing cherry–color leather matched the rest of the car's interior. She pulled off her fogged-up glasses and wiped them with the bottom edge of her T-shirt sticking out from beneath her surplus jacket.

"I'll say. Winter's coming early around here. Most of the leaves are already gone. The maples and ash finished turning last week." Mattie turned up the defrost on the fogging front windshield. "Would you like to stop for a bite to eat, dear?"

"No—but, thanks. I'm not hungry."

"You sure? I don't mind stopping."

"I'm sure."

As Mattie pulled away from the curb, Nel watched through the sliding-glass doors of the airport as the middle-aged man who'd sat next to her on the plane squatted and received two children— a school-age boy and a toddler girl—into his outstretched arms. A woman approached them, but she wasn't the toned, coiffed person Nel had imagined. Nor was she a dowdy, disheveled housewife. She was somewhere between those presumptions. Someone who looked real. Nel turned back toward Mattie, who had pulled off her hat and glanced in the rearview mirror to smooth her hair.

"So. About Dad."

"He's a mess. Your mom's been worried about his mind for a while now."

"His mind? She never mentioned anything to me about Dad's mind."

"Little things, forgetting where he put something, the usual sort of fogginess, I think, for someone his age." Mattie cast a glance at Nel, who was staring at her intently. "I'm sure if it was something to be concerned about, she would've told you."

"I hope she would have. He didn't seem out of the ordinary when I was home Christmas before last ..." Nel fished for details or assurance. The thought of Dad losing his mind was more than she could stand to think about in that moment.

"It's probably nothing more than his age, then."

Nel would take Mattie's word for it. Besides, she'd see for herself soon enough how he was.

"Anyway," Mattie offered, "losing someone after fifty-some years together, well, you can imagine it's taking a toll."

Nel shook her head and tugged at a loose string unraveling from the bandage the flight attendant had given her. She couldn't imagine loving someone intimately for as long as her mother and father had.

"Yeah ..." Her exhaled response created a circle of fog in the center of the passenger-side window.

Mattie reached over with a leather-gloved hand and patted Nel's knee as she had so many times when Nel was a young girl. "Tell me about you, Nel. What's new with you and all those exciting things you must be doing with your jewelry out in Santa Fe?"

Nel's weighted thoughts about her father lifted some with Mattie's gracious change of subject. "It's good. Really good. I design pieces for three national catalogs now, and I've been so busy with commissions I had to hire out a couple of apprentices to do my rock hunting and buying for me. It's nice having them around. They do some of the reproduction and prototype work too."

One of her best apprentices, a young man named Matthew, had studied and even taught for a while at the William Holland School of Lapidary Arts in Georgia. He had helped her with the most recent design she was especially proud of, a ring formed from a thick and weighty band of silver hammered and then etched with the shapes of a tree, tiny birds in flight, and a small round sun. The design had gone to auction, several companies wanting exclusive rights and asking for similar pieces to match—bracelets, pendants, a wedding set. The ring would have to do for now, and she trusted that Matthew and the other freelance artisans whom the companies hired to make a large supply of copies would have enough work to keep them busy with this new piece, in addition to her other designs that were still in demand, and increasingly so as the holidays approached.

Her father was her biggest fan, and she'd grown up learning much of what she knew about gemstones, minerals, rocks, and the basics of jewelry design from him. Even though he was a hobbyist, his passion for lapidary far exceeded Nel's, and she imagined him as she'd watched him so many times, sitting at his table, open-bulbed lamps positioned around his faceting equipment just so, adjusting his

magnification headband goggles over his eyes to amplify the angles
and imperfections, the measurements and positions of the stones he
carved, dismissing everything around him as he worked. Her earliest
memories were of herself sitting on a high stool next to him watching
his every move, every tool he used to cut and smooth cabochons,
tumble and shine raw stones, and facet precious gems. As she grew
up, she began to realize he was a bit different from other fathers, but
she never minded. In fact, she admired the way he could hyperfocus
on his hobby, a skill she also learned, which helped her achieve a
great amount of recognition and high-quality work compared with
her peers. She'd followed hard in his footsteps, sometimes literally
stumbling behind him when she'd begged him to take her along to
local rock shows, and when they had traipsed as a family down barren paths in the deserts of Arizona and New Mexico, where rusty
dust swirled around their ankles and the earth's hills rose in waves as
if straining to meet the sky above.

Traveling to rock and mineral shows with Jakob and observing
his dogged pursuit of the perfect stone (or stones) were some of Nel's
favorite memories. The shows were hosted mostly in fairground pole
barns, flea market–style, with booth after booth and glass case after
glass case of rocks and stones, raw and faceted, creating an endless
maze of treasures and new things to discover. She remembered one
man in particular who had a long white beard and wore overalls. At
first glance, the stock he pitched and peddled at his tables appeared
to consist of tree stumps and severed branches. Closer observation,
however, revealed the specimens were pieces of petrified wood, aged
circles of pulp hardened and solidified into rock-hard rings of rust
and amber.

"Here, touch it. It's all right," the man had offered, his beard rising and falling with each syllable. Her fingertips grazed the cold, inner concentric surface of the once-living piece of wood.

Nel and Jakob had continued to browse past massive hunks of the sharp-edged pink crystals of rhodochrosite; bright-orange carnelian; layered slices of chatoyant quartz (tigereye), agate, and jasper; emerald malachite as bright as the grass of their backyard when the sun hit it full on after an autumn rainstorm; fist-sized lime-green clusters of pyromorphite; deep-blue star sapphires streaked with white, which reminded her of the star of Bethlehem when finished into cabochons; fossils embedded with replicas of dragonflies, scorpions, and centipedes so perfect that Nel had wondered how they held so still for whatever massive event paralyzed them and then ended their fragile lives. Beyond the display cases and tables, rack after rack bent under the weight of strung beads in skeins that created a rainbow of colors before her—azure lapis lazuli, burning red hematite, sunny orange amber, and every shade in between; and an entire section of buckets overflowed with turquoise, her favorite then and now.

This is where they'd lost each other one particular day. She wasn't paying attention when Jakob stopped with a growing crowd of other rock hounds (as they called themselves) at a booth where a man who reminded her of a sideshow attendant dressed in a striped vest and bow tie demonstrated the newest Facetron laps—round stones about the size of a 45 vinyl record and used on the cutting machine for faceting. Rows of turquoise vendors were on one side of the main aisle, and the Facetron representative was on the other. Nel walked between the tables, stopping every so often to poke around in the heaping piles of nuggets, and by the time she realized her father had moved on, he was well out of sight, engulfed by a show hall now crowded shoulder to shoulder with people. She'd become so afraid, she didn't realize she'd stuffed into her dress pocket a pebble-sized piece of turquoise she'd been admiring when she'd sighted a security guard and pushed her way through the leggy crowd toward him.

It hadn't taken long for the guard to reunite Nel with her father. The guard had asked her for her father's name, and since her father was well known in the gem and mineral community, someone—an attendee? a salesperson? she couldn't remember—knew right away who and where he was.

"Daddy!" she'd cried, hot tears still moist on her flushed cheeks, knee bleeding through her white tights from when she'd tripped on a piece of carpeting bubbled up from electrical cords as she'd run toward the guard.

"There you are, my sweet baby bird!" He scooped her up and enveloped her with his great, solid arms. He cupped her face with his giant hand, wiping the tears from beneath her eyes with his calloused thumb. "I thought I'd lost you forever."

That was the first time Nel had ever seen him so afraid, and the first time she knew a grown man's eyes could make tears.

She realized suddenly how much she'd missed him, too, living away for so long. Of course there was the everyday sort of missing him, like when she needed something fixed in her house, advice on turning a particularly difficult piece of stone, or the reassurance of his burly shoulder after a tough breakup. But this was more than that. It was, as with her mother, regret that she'd moved away at all. She'd chosen to live in Santa Fe on purpose when she left South Haven, because the town had been a favorite place for the three of them to travel when she was growing up. Part of those memories lingered there in her father's beloved Southwest, where rocks and gems could be plucked and found, as plentiful as blueberries at roadside stands in Michigan. But now, facing the loss of her mother, whatever original reason that drew her there—independence? the gathering of other artists?—dimmed in comparison to how badly she wanted to feel his hand upon her head again, to see the gleam of pride in his eyes that no other man had been able to replace. Not even the award-winning status she'd unintentionally garnered as a jewelry designer equaled how much her father's approval meant to her.

"Is he home?" Nel asked as they passed dried-up fields of corn, and others with the skeletons of sunflower stalks, their brown faces hanging lank. As they approached South Haven, Nel noticed how many storefronts had changed hands, new strip malls had been built, and everything felt bigger and yet smaller than she had remembered. She pushed her glasses up on her nose to get a better look as Mattie drove past the homes of her high school friends and others she'd hoped never to see again. Strange cars were parked in the driveways of old friends' homes. Young mothers stood talking on front-porch stoops where older mothers used to, and watched as toddlers pedaled trikes and Big Wheels and pink motorized miniature cars.

"Billy Esposito offered to drive him to the funeral home for an appointment around noon to finalize service plans. You remember Billy; his father, Frank, worked for your father for years at the plant. You should have the house to yourself for an hour or two."

Mattie steered the car east past Huron Street and Clementine's restaurant on the corner, over the Dyckman Bridge, which crossed the Black River, and on until the road through town came to a head

at North Shore; then she turned the car north toward Nel's childhood home. A single row of houses rested between the road and
the lake to the west now, and Nel strained to glimpse the steely gray
water beyond the neatly trimmed grass and shrubs between them.
On the east side of the street, abbreviated side roads passed and eventually turned from paved to gravel, until finally Mattie flicked on the
turn signal, slowed the car, and turned left into her driveway. The
drive, with a lawn mower's width of grass along the outside border,
ran parallel to the one leading to Jakob and Catherine's home. Nel's
childhood home. There'd been no need for the two families to build
a fence between their properties, even though the rest of the people
who lived on the street had, especially since many of the original
owners had sold to people who bought for summer and vacation
rental homes. The Stewarts had never quarreled with Mattie, or her
husband when he was still around, as far as Nel was aware, and they
had even shared the costs of building and maintaining a seawall and
the steep set of stairs leading to the beach.

"I should warn you," Mattie said. "The house, when you see it
… well, I don't think either one of your parents were up to realizing
how much work it was beginning to need."

The gravel driveway crunched beneath the tires, and Nel noticed
a man balancing on a ladder set precariously against a high eave of
Mattie's house. "What's going on at your place?"

"Gutter cleaning. He's replacing some rotten trim and painting
some too."

Nel squinted to get a better view of the man and felt her face
redden as she gasped, "Is that David Butler? I thought he'd moved
to Florida."

Mattie studied Nel for a moment. "Ohhhh, yes. He was your date to the senior prom, wasn't he?"

Nel whipped her head toward Mattic. "How'd you remember that?"

"Who could forget? All the hullabaloo about pictures, the bonfire your parents set up on the beach for you all afterward. That was quite an evening, as I recall."

"And I recall him driving home with someone else."

"You're not still holding a grudge now, are you?"

"No …" Nel looked at David again. "No, of course not."

"Good. Because he'll be spending plenty of time here the next week or two. Maybe you can both come for dinner one night before you leave. For old times' sake."

"Don't be trying to fix me up already, Mattie."

"Wouldn't think of it." She winked, then put the car in park and pulled Nel toward her in an embrace. "Your mother wouldn't have thought of it either."

Nel allowed herself to relax into the fur collar of Mattie's mink, to inhale the scent of perfume lingering on the sagging skin of her neck. Mattie and Mom had been trying together unsuccessfully to marry her off for nearly two decades now. She couldn't blame Mattie for still trying.

"Thanks, Mattie, for picking me up. It's good to see you. Good to be home."

"Of course." Mattie patted Nel's knee. "The house is unlocked. Like always."

Nel pulled her bags from the trunk and made her way toward the front door. The glossy black paint gleamed against the slant of the early afternoon sun. At a glance, the house was beautiful in an all-American, lakeside sort of way, like the houses featured in the background of magazine ads. An exquisite original slate roof topped off the white clapboard siding and sixteen-paned, double-hung windows framed by black shutters and spaced evenly across the second story. A set of the same windows flanked both sides of the ebony door, and a matching set of bay windows flanked those. But as she neared the threshold, Nel began to notice flaking paint, and the gray stains under the windows indicated mold, perhaps even rot. Moss and clover, oxalis and chickweed crept over the edges of the brick sidewalk, and ivy grew over the sides of the front steps. The yard was overgrown with the broad leaves of dandelions and clover, and enormous thistles grew up through the center of untrimmed yews and boxwood.

Tears threatened to form as Nel recalled Mom and Dad giving her a set of her very own gardening gloves, and the three of them spending hours trimming and pulling weeds, identifying and planting new perennials, and collecting various species of daylilies and hostas, astilbe and sedum to plant. Where there hadn't been flower beds they made new ones, and their yard had been featured in many town garden tours over the years. Few of the plantings, besides weeds, remained, but of course it was October, Nel reminded herself, and many of them would not be adequately visible until spring.

The bronze door latch stuck a bit so that she had to pull the door toward her and shake it slightly before it opened. As it did, the smell of oil soap and aged wood caused another pang of regret in Nel's heart. Of course she had wept at the news of her mother's passing. But now, with the smells and the sights—needlepoint pillows Catherine had labored over tossed on couches, her handmade afghans draped over the arms of chairs, collections of baskets and old buoys and sea glass—everywhere she looked, she saw her mother, and it was almost too much for her to bear.

She set her bags down and made her way to the straight wooden staircase, flanked on one side by the living room and on the other by the library. Tears fell freely now, settling on the lenses of her glasses. She rubbed her hands up and down the nearly threadbare knees of her jeans, as if trying to console herself in the foyer where her mother had sent her to school, on dates, to work and had welcomed her home again with a hug and the smell of pot roast or fried perch or snickerdoodles.

"I'm so sorry, Mom." The sound of her audible apology startled her as it echoed across the emptiness of the house. She pulled off her glasses and wiped her face with the arm of her olive-green army-sur-plus jacket, then hauled her belongings upstairs to her old bedroom, which, except for the few things she'd added or moved when she'd been home for holidays, remained exactly as she had left it back in 1975.

CHAPTER 3

I should've treated her to a new one for her birthday, Jakob thought, his head bent as if in prayer, and his great weathered hands resting on the faded-purple, vinyl makeup bag centered on his lap. The undertaker, Mike Wisowaty, had asked him to bring a nice outfit— something Catherine might wear to church, he'd suggested—and her favorite makeup to prepare her body for the viewing the next day. He'd left Mike with the makeup—a shimmery pink lipstick (he figured this was the one she used most often, since it was much more worn than the others), rosy-red rouge, brown liquid eyeliner, and black mascara—and he kept the blush and powder brushes and sponge applicators from the compacts for himself. Along with dozens of others like them in old coffee cans, cigar boxes, and cottage-cheese containers back in his lapidary workroom, they would come in handy for brushing the dust off rocks and minerals as he polished and shaped them into gemstones.

He'd asked Wisowaty for Catherine's wedding band too. The hospital had removed one ring and the gold cross necklace that rested daily in the soft place between her collarbones, but they'd left the wedding ring on her finger. Mike had placed the band gently into Jakob's outstretched palm, and Jakob ran his finger along

the thin edge of gold before pressing it into the inner crease of a
gray velvet ring box, shutting the lid, and tucking the box between
a half-empty bottle of Catherine's prescription blood-pressure pills
and an unused tube of travel toothpaste in the bottom of the purple
makeup bag.

"You all right, Mr. Stewart?" Billy Esposito's voice reminded
Jakob so much of Billy's father, Frank, that the similarity caused
Jakob to shiver. He glanced at the middle-aged man beside him
to make sure it was Frank's son driving and not his old friend,
somehow resurrected.

"Fine."

Of course he wasn't fine, losing his wife, his best friend, the
one he counted on to take care of things. He'd been afraid for
a while now that she'd go first, the way her blood pressure had
been so out of control. She'd been having episodes of staring into
space, jumbled words and phrases, and forgetfulness too. *Transient
ischemic attacks*, Dr. Benson had called them. Besides the fact that
she was his better half, the one for whom the phone rang, the one
to whom the longhand, slanted script of personal envelopes was
addressed, the one to whom neighbors brought meals when joints
were replaced, she was also the one who baked for new neighbors
when he'd preferred to watch the tube or fiddle with his rocks, the
one who volunteered at the food pantry when he preferred to hoard
cans of Spam and tuna "just in case," the first to pray when he'd
preferred to gripe, the one for whom life was the book of Psalms
when all of his was Lamentations. These were the characteristics
that had first attracted them to each other, but as with most mar-
riages, they were also the characteristics that pushed them apart.

They'd spent the past fifty years together, years full of emotional tides roiling and pulling, falling and careening into each other, but neither of them—he was certain of this—would have traded those years for anything, or anyone.

Over the past year or so, it was Catherine who had been covering for him. The lines between past and present, real and not real blurred more and more frequently in his mind. One morning at three o'clock, she'd found him wandering in his boxer shorts in the middle of North Shore Drive. Thank God it was the off-season, and the only evidence of life was the bugs zapping themselves against fluorescent street lamps. Later, once they were home safe, he'd attributed it to sleepwalking, like the other times she'd found him in odd places at odd times. The next day, Catherine begged him to see a neurologist.

"Why? For what? So he can give me a pill and tell me my brain is shrinking?" he'd argued.

"I worry about your safety. He might know something that can help."

He'd tried to brush her off, annoyed that she was right. She was always right. Yet in the end he'd acquiesced and gone to see a doctor, but only because his greatest fear was becoming a burden to her. Dr. Steve Sandler, whom he actually enjoyed talking with, was on staff at a center for memory loss in Grand Rapids. Jakob's memory lapses, occasional falls and bumps on the head, and not knowing where he was had been happening more frequently. Before the incident on North Shore Drive, he'd gotten lost while driving home from the grocery store they'd shopped at twice weekly since it'd opened in 1953. A policeman had pulled him over for a burned-out taillight, and Jakob had been able to reorient himself from the street name the officer had written on the warning ticket. Dr. Sandler suggested a couple of newer medications that might help slow the process, but Jakob adamantly refused pills. Overall, however, he and Catherine both had felt some comfort in the doctor's encouragement about the strength of Jakob's long-term memory and the options available to them if things worsened.

"We're still learning so much about the brain," said Dr. Sandler. "And with age-related dementia, the progress is unpredictable. It can worsen and improve depending on your overall health. Infections, falls, those sorts of things, can wreak havoc and cause acute flare-ups, deliriums that can be frightening both for the patient and family members. But I've seen plenty of folks around your age—some even older—return to a relative baseline of where you are now after those scenarios. We can't say for sure what your prognosis is."

Jakob sighed and tried to straighten his blockish frame in the front seat of Billy's Chrysler LeBaron. Billy's short Italian stature (acquired honestly from his father) required him to move the single bench seat annoyingly close to the dash, forcing Jakob to sit with his knees bent into his chest. Ninety-four years had done little to diminish Jakob's size—six foot four and still over 200 pounds—which, in his youth when he weighed in at nearly 250, had garnered attention from football coaches across the Midwest. He never played, though, after tearing his knee up in one of the last games of his senior year of high school. Instead, he'd found a job at the Brake-All factory near South Haven, where his size had also proved helpful. Brake-All manufactured brake parts for many of the major auto factories and some government accounts, and as a floor supervisor, he was responsible for keeping disgruntled workers in line.

Jakob removed his glasses, then pulled a yellow-edged handkerchief from the inside pocket of his zippered, navy windbreaker, the one with the Brake-All logo embroidered over the heart, and cleaned both lenses.

"Mattie said Nel will be there by the time we get back," Billy said.

Nel.

His baby bird.

He hadn't wanted children, and he'd told Catherine as much when they were dating. And yet, as the years passed, he couldn't help noticing how she couldn't take her eyes off of mothers pushing baby buggies past the house, or children flying kites and skipping beach pebbles across the lake. He eventually realized the hole in the heart of a woman who longs for children is not something he—nor any man—could fill. Besides that, she had given up a lot by choosing to marry him. Her father had been so disappointed in their union since Jakob was not only an older man, but also lacked a genuine pedigree, even though his hard and established work provided her with anything material she wanted. Surely he could set aside his own misgivings to give Catherine that one desire.

It wasn't that he didn't like children. It was more that the world was too wretched a place in which to bring them up. Eleanor Louise had been conceived in 1951, and he had watched soldiers returning from two world wars now as half men, physically or psychologically or both. Details of the Holocaust had only recently been fully realized, and reports and confirmations of Stalin's forced famines during the previous decade—*Holodomor*—were rippling through the Eastern European immigrant communities of Chicago.[1] Reports told of up to eleven million dead from starvation in a land more—or at least as—fertile than America. Of course, the Soviets had denied it all, as they had everything else, and anyone else who dared speak of Holodomor specifically suffered severe, if not deadly, persecution.

But as bad a place as the world was to bring up a child then, the real reason Jakob didn't want children was because of the shame he carried with him, an accusing shadow in his heart reminding him of events far worse than wars and starvation for him personally—events that if discovered would reveal the worst truth of all: that Jakob should never again be trusted with caring for a human being, especially one so fragile as an infant. And yet one look at Eleanor as the nurse lay her in his arms for the first time, and Jakob had pushed the shame and fear deep inside him. Her tiny mouth shaped like a rosebud and pink like rhodochrosite, or maybe a shade lighter, like rose quartz. Jakob was immediately smitten, and yet the coos and aahs that came so naturally for other fathers lodged in his throat. His eyes had stung with tears and his chest had swelled with the ferocious certainty that he would do whatever was necessary to care for his baby girl, to make sure she was safe and loved. If God gave second chances, Jakob knew Eleanor was that for him, and he would not, could not, fail again.

"It was my fault," he mumbled as Billy Esposito's car whirred past the homes and businesses of South Haven.

Billy reached over and squeezed Jakob's shoulder. "It couldn't have been helped, a stroke that massive. You can't blame yourself."

Jakob didn't bother to tell Billy that he wasn't talking about Catherine. Or Nel, for that matter.

The fault he felt ran too deep for words, and only one other person in the world had ever known his secret.

1904–1906

_____

Rotterdam, Netherlands – New York City – Chicago

CHAPTER 4

The *Statendam* chugged so slowly out of the harbor in Rotterdam that the only way Jakob knew it was even moving was because he stood at the stern and could see the milky trail of bubbles from the giant engines rumbling under the deck beneath his feet. He lifted his head and watched as the busy port grew smaller and eventually faded into the fog, along with the rest of the Netherlands and everything he and Peter had ever known.

Jakob felt the outline of the large aquamarine in his coat against his chest as he braced himself against the harsh sea air. The stone was one of the few objects that had calmed the trembling within him ever since Peter had—against Tato's instructions—returned to Chudniv. Peter had found Jakob, and only Jakob, left alive. Their journey since then, from that place of nightmare to the sea, had been miraculous, or so Peter said.

"Everything that's happened to us since Chudniv has been by the hand of Yahweh, by the grace of Yeshua."

Jakob felt a growing desire to cover his ears when Peter went on about divine interventions. Galya's strength, the generosity of strangers, and Peter's wit had gotten them this far. The hard work and talent of Tato cutting the stones they sold—not miracles or grace—had fetched them steerage tickets aboard the *Statendam*. And it would be luck that got them to America in the huge hunk of floating steel. As grand as she was in size, her great steam tower and twin masts had grown ugly from frequent trips back and forth across the Atlantic bringing cargo after cargo of immigrants to America. Besides that, steerage practically guaranteed the boys would come down with some sort of illness; the air was thick with wet coughs, vomit from passengers suffering motion sickness, and other unsanitary filth. The two of them clambered up to the deck as often as possible for fresh air, but these opportunities were few and clogged with first- and second-class passengers.

On the whole, the journey across the Atlantic was a blur for Jakob, whose eyes only reached the level of the filthy skirts of women and the threadbare, reeking pants of men. So many people were stuffed in with them, they could hardly move. Being stuck in one place caused Jakob's head to fill with images of making himself as small as possible in the kitchen cupboard back home in Chudniv, but the priority of survival eventually and thankfully forced that memory from his mind. Still, he jumped at every creak and jerk of the ship, and though Peter assured him they were safe, he kept himself close against his brother, never daring to leave him. Peter never dared to leave Jakob either, even when they had to relieve themselves.

After thirteen days on the ship, Jakob supposed he should have been happy and singing a Psalm with Peter when they steamed into New York Harbor, the enormous Lady Liberty greeting them with her torch held high and spikes upon her head. But he was not happy. His head itched, and he couldn't help scratching until it bled, along with most of the other passengers similarly infected with lice. So many were terribly sick from the journey, coughing and aching from the cramped quarters, and pale from the horrid smells and lack of fresh food. Worse, Jakob had heard Peter talking to other passengers who were all certain the immigration authorities would find reasons to send them back to Europe. Diseased eyes, a crooked gait, whatever the reason, Jakob knew he couldn't rest until they'd been cleared at the immigration station.

The boys were stripped of any dignity or hope left in them before they stepped off the *Statendam,* as their heads were shaved and they waited naked in examination lines. Doctors probed and prodded them for eye diseases and other maladies. When they were allowed to dress again, the doctors' assistant used a piece of chalk to write "SC" and "P" on both of their backs, the first indicating their obvious scalp infections, and the latter indicating they needed to be quarantined for possible lung infections before being granted permission to enter the streets of the city and begin the arduous search for work and a place to stay. But their sentence to two weeks in a quarantine house turned out not to be a detriment. As Peter would later say, it was the moment they met their fortune. Less than seventy-two hours before they would've been released and shooed into the streets of New York City, they were adopted.

"Come with me," the head caretaker in quarantine, Mrs. McGafney, said to them one day. She was a fat woman, and Jakob had been intrigued with her from the start, wondering how much a person had to eat to become that fleshy. After all, he hadn't ever seen a fat woman, since half of Europe and all of the immigrants on the *Statendam* were starving. Mrs. McGafney was a redhead, and she had the patience of one, too, as she yanked Peter and Jakob from their cots by their shirt collars. Jakob had grown weak, feverish, and even more scrawny than he had been when they left Europe. He could not move as fast as Peter, nor could he help but yelp as Mrs. McGafney pulled him by the ear to get him going.

They were escorted to the foyer, where a man stood dressed in the finest suit of clothes either boy had ever seen. A woman stood next to him, holding on to his elbow. She was wrapped in beautiful gray fur, which accentuated the brilliant emeralds and diamonds hanging from her earlobes. Peter and Jakob didn't know much English yet, but they understood completely what the exchange of money looked like, as the dapper man handed a large roll of bills to Mrs. McGafney. She escorted the couple to the reception desk, where he and the woman signed a few papers. At the same time, she eyeballed Peter and Jakob with a look that said, "You'd better behave."

"There, you're all set now," Mrs. McGafney said as the man shook hands with the official at the desk, and the couple turned toward Peter and Jakob. She pushed the boys toward the couple, her voice pointed and cold with thinly veiled relief.

The woman with the diamonds and emeralds in her ears came toward Jakob and placed a white-velvet-gloved hand gently on his shoulder. She knelt in front of him, not bothering to fix her skirts so they wouldn't be soiled by the damp, muddy floor of the Ellis Island dormitory. She pointed to herself and said, "Mama." Then she pointed to Jakob.

"Vin ne hovoryt',"[†] said Peter, pressing the finger of his right hand—the only finger left on that hand besides his thumb—to his

---

† He does not speak.

lips in Jakob's defense. He couldn't blame Jakob for not wanting to speak to anyone since they left the Netherlands.

The gentleman raised an eyebrow, looking to Mrs. McGafney to see if she understood.

"The young boy, we think he is mute. Hasn't spoken since he got here. His brother always speaks for him. None of the orphans arrive whole, after all."

"Do we know why the older one—"

"Name's Peter." Mrs. McGafney interrupted the man.

"Peter. Yes, of course. Do we know why Peter is missing his fingers?"

The caretaker shook her head and shrugged her shoulders.

"No telling what they've been through," said the woman, clicking her tongue against her teeth with pity. "I might not speak either if I were him. But he will most surely in time."

Their names were John and Harriet Stewart, a wealthy couple from Chicago involved in the shipbuilding business, who'd been unable to have children of their own. As such, they'd felt compelled to do what they could to help ease the growing problem of orphans clogging East Coast orphanages, and they hadn't minded at all the possibility of adopting older children. Harriet Stewart held cool cloths to Jakob's head as he fevered the whole way to Chicago on the train. The autumn trees and rolling hills of the East turned to patchwork fields of crops in the Midwest, reminiscent of the land surrounding Chudniv. John and Peter tried as best they could to communicate through their language barrier, using hand gestures and drawing on scraps of newspapers until they were clutching their stomachs with laughter—something

Jakob hadn't heard from his brother since long before their journey began.

Once they arrived in Chicago, Jakob's fever broke, as did everything he knew about life before then. The Stewarts' home in Wicker Park was the most magnificent structure the boys had ever seen, scalloped shingles on the gabled roof with finials on every peak. Windows made of stained glass and framed with wrought-iron guards and transoms. A front porch that wrapped around the entire first level, trimmed in fretwork and spindles. The inside was no less grand, with rugs, plush sofas, velvet drapes, intricate paintings taller than Jakob, shiny woodwork, and fireplaces everywhere—even in their own bedrooms.

On sunny days, streets were filled with children, boys dressed like sailors or Little Lord Fauntleroy in knee pants and knickers and hats with streamers, and girls in white dresses with eyelet and organdy, pin tucks and lace, pinnies, hair bows bigger than their heads, and shoes always shining, always neat and new.

The Stewarts provided Jakob and Peter with nannies to clean and dress them, and tutors who quickly taught them English. Jakob discovered books—free books!—from the library, along with boxes full of books bought new just for them.

One night after the boys had been there for several weeks, they sat down to dinner with the Stewarts. Candlelight flickered from chandelier candles and illuminated the room, which was dressed in the finest wallpaper available. The beef roast, carrots, and potatoes were cooked to perfection, and plenty of other sides and bread filled the center of the table. For the first time since their arrival in America, Jakob spoke.

"Please pass the potatoes."

Mama Stewart gasped into a napkin she held to her lips.

After an uncomfortable silence, Papa Stewart grinned. "Well, Peter, pass your brother the potatoes."

"Yes, sir," Peter said, grinning too.

Unbeknownst to them, Jakob had been practicing, whispering English words under the bedcovers after the lights were turned down in the evenings.

Mama Stewart came around the table, the royal-blue taffeta of her dress rustling like a flock of doves. She knelt next to Jakob, who despite his newfound voice maintained the constancy of his stoic and somber expression. Harriet held his face in her hands as she had on the steps in New York City. Tears fell from her eyes. "Praise God! He has heard my prayers. He will redeem the years the locusts have eaten, dear Jakob. He is redeeming them even now."

"Yes, Mama Stewart." Jakob allowed her to hold him, unwilling to squelch her joy. It was not her affection he shrank from, after all. It was that she gave credit to God, whom he knew had nothing to do with his newfound voice. Jakob had merely listened to his tutors and practiced.

1994

South Haven, Michigan

CHAPTER 5

The back of Catherine and Jakob Stewart's home faced Lake Michigan, and Nel stood on the back deck soaking in the mid-afternoon sun. After the stale air of the plane ride and the emotion of the last couple of days, she looked forward to the sunset that evening, which was sure to calm her nerves. She'd learned to love Santa Fe sunsets, too, the jutting, rolling angles of the Sangre de Cristo Mountains browning, then blushing pink before the sun fell behind them, followed by a blazing display of fire-orange against the advancing cobalt sky. And yet as beautiful as those sunsets were, Nel never felt they compared to the gentle eventides on Lake Michigan, breezes rustling through branches of white oaks and black oaks, hickories and sugar maples, and the occasional beech. All the trees around the house that had seemed so small in her youth stretched tall and arched over her as if welcoming her home. Her favorite was the oak growing right outside her old bedroom, where she'd sat for hours on the window seat, curled in her pajamas as she watched the birds flit back and forth, bringing sticks and stiff pieces of dead beach grasses, kite strings, and hair ribbons and weaving nests in the crooks of the branches. Eggs had appeared almost magically, and then even more magically, baby birds from within them. She remembered the patchy spots of fuzz on their translucent skin, their shaking, open mouths stretched wide, their papery-thin gullets straining toward the sky, and their mother's return with food.

Well after Nel moved to Santa Fe, Catherine had gone back to school and achieved a Master Gardener certificate. The combination of all the species of trees on the Stewarts' property demonstrated her gift for landscape and gardening as they created a spectacular display of variegated colors every fall. No wonder so many artists paint autumn at the lakeside, Nel thought as she pulled her sweater tighter. Northeastern gusts whipped around her. She shivered and wondered for a fleeting moment what Sam was doing in Santa Fe. Probably enjoying a round of golf or tennis at the club, although they'd had a few cold spells there as well.

Catherine was going to play tennis with a group of ladies from the church on the spring day in 1975 when Nel announced her plans to leave South Haven. Nel remembered the day as if it were a deckle-edged photo, yellowed and cracked in the center. She remembered her mother's dress—white and sleeveless, cut short above the knees, ruffled hems adorned with navy-blue rickrack—and her navy sweater, arms tied in a graceful knot around her neck. She remembered her own extrawide bell-bottom jeans and a loose shirt embroidered by a local Potawatomi woman. Her VW Bug was parked in front of the house with her belongings stuffed into the trunk and filling up the back. The front seat was reserved for her last suitcase and collection of music tapes.

"You're up early, Nel-Belle," Catherine had said, raising an eyebrow at her then twenty-three-year-old daughter eating Cheerios at the kitchen table.

"Hoped to catch you before you left."

"Oh?"

Nel had understood her mother's surprise at a request for conversation, something that had been strained and lacking among the three of them—Nel, Catherine, and Jakob—ever since she'd returned from her hospitalization a few weeks earlier. It was bad enough that she lived at home. Her other friends had found apartments when they'd come back from college, or homes if they, as most of them (and their parents) planned, had found spouses in college. She had neither a spouse nor an apartment, the first of which had eluded her as she spent weekend after weekend of her college years with different guys, rarely hooking up with any of them—even the ones she liked—for more than a couple of consecutive weekends.

She'd been a combined art history and business major at DePauw University, a small liberal-arts school in Indiana. The degree, she knew, was pretty impractical for a woman in the 1970s. She was supposed to have been a teacher or a nurse, something that would've allowed her to follow the traditional path of marriage, then children, then growing old with a successful husband. Thanks to a professor who'd shared her affection for stones and jewelry, she'd found a spot of unused space in the art building where she could spend as many hours as she wished learning to solder and bend, shape and cut, and pound age into shiny new metals to create rings and pendants, settings and wraps. Friends and neighbors back in South Haven raised their eyebrows when she explained she wanted to be a jewelry artist, but her parents had thankfully encouraged her to follow her passion. To the chagrin of the skeptics, after graduation she had found a job teaching art appreciation and art history at a nearby private high school. But to her disappointment, the pay wasn't enough for her to live on her own. Even so, living at home wasn't so bad. The lake inspired her art. And if she were honest, she'd enjoyed the time with her parents.

Tom Parrish, a theater teacher at the high school where she worked, broke her long streak of uncommitted relationships. As she prepared for the start of the first semester, he'd helped her carry boxes of old art-history books, framed poster prints of Cézanne, Matisse, and Grant Wood's *American Gothic*, and other teaching accoutrements up three flights to her non-air-conditioned classroom. A native of Long Island complete with the big-city accent and in his midthirties, Tom seemed like everything the guys—boys, really— she'd known in college were not: sophisticated, established, and focused on the deeper meaning of life. David Mamet, Dostoyevsky, Antonin Artaud, and Shakespeare lined his classroom bookshelves, and he'd brought along a copy of Emerson's *Self-Reliance* on their first date, a picnic lunch on the beach of Van Buren State Park, sand dunes on one side of them and the setting sun on the other as he read to her and they contemplated why, indeed, it's so bad to be misunderstood, and how, in Emerson's words, "nothing can bring you peace but yourself."

The teenage girls in the halls had gawked and giggled at Tom, blushing if he smiled back at them, and the ones in his classes wrangled

over front-row seats. Nel's physical attraction to him had been imme-
diate, as had his to her. He'd taken her to his apartment—a studio
above a local diner called the Onion, the smell of which lived up to
its name. Inside the apartment, walls covered in tie-dyed tapestries,
Tom lit some incense and a joint, and they took turns smoking and
making out while Jim Croce and Bob Dylan crooned on his stereo in
the background. They slept together every chance they had after that,
and for the most part that autumn, Nel was careful to make sure
either she or he, or both, took precautions. But nothing was fail-safe,
and by November her period was late enough she'd begun to worry.
The positive pregnancy test had resulted in Tom hightailing it out of
Nel's life—he moved back to the East Coast; Nel didn't know where.
And everything that happened after that, including the ultimate loss
of the baby and hospitalization, resulted in Nel deciding to leave
South Haven.

Jakob had left much earlier that spring morning for the Brake-
All factory. Nel had waited for him to leave to announce her plans
to Catherine. If there was anything she couldn't handle, it was disap-
pointing her father more than she already had with the news of the
pregnancy and late miscarriage.

"I'm leaving. After I finish packing the car." She'd dabbed at milk
left on the corner of her mouth by the last spoonful of cereal.

Had her mother dropped her racquet? She couldn't remember.
She did know Catherine's response was sudden and devastating,
and she recalled her mother running toward her, eyes full of tears,
embracing her, rocking her as she had when she was a little girl.

"Oh, my baby," she'd gasped into Nel's long hair, straight and
near waist length at the time, and as dark as a raven's wing. Then

she'd pulled back, wiped her eyes, and grasped Nel by the shoulders. "But I suppose I knew weeks ago that you would."

Tears had filled Nel's own eyes. She thought she'd feel relief when she told her mother, but instead she had felt more afraid and uncertain than ever.

"Where are you going to go? Chicago?" Her mother sat beside her at the table, and Nel noticed her hands shaking slightly as she toyed with the edge of an orange linen napkin, hand embroidered with an owl on one corner.

Nel hesitated. Chicago might've been the logical choice, with the Art Institute and plenty of friends from both college and high school there. "No … Santa Fe. There's an artist colony there—several, in fact."

"Santa Fe? So far? You don't know a soul out there. And when will you come back? It's not like you can just come home whenever you feel like it for a weekend."

"Mom." Nel grasped her mother's hands. "I can't heal here" was all she'd said, unable to put into words her shame of losing the baby, the shame of ever getting pregnant in the first place, and especially the shame of losing her chance to ever have children of her own again because of it. She pushed her chair away from the table, pausing to look out at the lake, gray clouds hovering low above the water, choppy and dotted with whitecaps. "I have to go finish packing."

"If I can't stop you, let me help you, at least," Catherine had offered.

"Okay." Nel wrapped her arms around her mother, the one to whom she'd confessed most of her secrets—her first kiss, her first breakup—although she'd spared Mama the news of her first sexual encounter with the neighbor boy, Walter Prescott, a triple-varsity-lettered, hairy kid who lived down the street. And other than her best friend, Lori, she'd told her mom before anyone else about the unexpected pregnancy with Tom. Nel knew she and Catherine shared a unique mother-daughter relationship and that many would call her crazy to leave—maybe she was. But she was determined to find a place where she could start new.

They wiped their tears, and Catherine had called her tennis partner to cancel their match. Upstairs, Nel explained to Catherine more about the artist colonies and what she hoped to do in Santa Fe, which was to apprentice with someone and then start selling her own jewelry designs. She told her mother about her love for the flowers of Georgia O'Keeffe; the landscapes of Peter Hurd; the oils of Oscar Berninghaus; and the cowboys, Indians, and cavalry of Frederic Remington. How surely breathing the same air and walking the same paths of such great artists would inspire her art to new levels unattainable—lost, even—if she stayed in the tiny tourist town of South Haven.

"Those aren't *jewelry* artists," Catherine had pointed out, tugging a large, sparkling amethyst back and forth along the silver chain around her neck. Jakob had faceted and set the brilliant pale-purple stone for her most recent birthday.

Nel had grinned a little, trying to lighten the mood. "I know, but there are so many kinds of artists out there—all kinds. Art feeds art. I'll find my way." She folded a corduroy blazer and added it to the contents of the suitcase, which was almost full. "Maybe God's in the desert. He was there with Moses. Maybe He'll be there. In the sunrise and the sunset."

"He's here, too, you know."

She looked at her mother apologetically, Catherine's pointed response reminding Nel to avoid the topic of faith, about the only topic in their relationship that caused any major disagreements between them. It wasn't that Nel didn't believe—she did. It wasn't that she hadn't accepted Christ as her Savior—she had, the first time as a small girl in white tights and a pale-peach, lace Easter dress. Kneeling on a dusty tile floor before Warner Sallman's *Head of Christ* in a Sunday school room at the Presbyterian church her parents attended, she'd asked the gentle-eyed man in the frame to come into her heart. His skin, pale and smooth like velvet, and His golden hair, edged with supernatural light, were forever etched into her memory.

The second time, she'd thought of the serene man in the painting and asked Him to please come into her heart again. She was sure Jesus had left her after she got caught making out with Brad Stanislawski under the bleachers at the high school football stadium. The dean of students, Mrs. Edwards, spent an entire hour lecturing her about the dangers and abomination of teenage sex, then called Jakob and Catherine into the office and lectured her some more.

The third time Nel had asked Jesus into her heart was while sitting around a bonfire at Young Life Frontier Ranch camp in the summer of 1969. At the time, Jesus looked more like one of the camp counselors she had a crush on than Warner Sallman's portrait. Over and over and over again, she'd asked Jesus into her heart, though she supposed she knew she only had to accept Him once. But mistakes and regrets and certainty followed by the fumbling darkness of uncertainty had caused her to come to God again, begging for pardon, for acceptance, for some kind of sign or indication that what she was asking of Him—or surrendering to Him—was real.

No, the conflicts between Nel, her mom, and religion arose because Nel hadn't been as outwardly devout or involved with faith as Catherine had hoped. Nel knew it was difficult enough for her mom that Jakob didn't say or do much of anything where church was concerned. If Nel attended, it had been because of Catherine getting her there. Sometimes Jakob joined them, sometimes he didn't. And if pressed, he'd often say, "My faith is personal. I do it in my own way."

As she stuffed the rest of her favorite possessions into a suitcase alongside her mother, she supposed she was more like Jakob than Catherine in regard to her faith. Words from verses swam through her mind out of order, no longer strung together on plastic bracelets from Vacation Bible School or underlined with fluorescent high-lighter in *The Way*, the old Bible her Young Life leader had given her. Like she'd told Catherine, maybe she'd find more of God and find more meaning to her faith in the desert, surrounded by mountains and open sky.

Nel set her last suitcase on the floor of the foyer. The old, flower-power design had seen her through many junior high and high school slumber parties. She and her mother embraced, and in the end it was Nel's arms that slackened first, Nel's legs that stepped toward the threshold.

Catherine had reached out and straightened Nel's glasses, then patted her cheeks.

"Tell Dad I'll be back."

"He'll be upset you didn't say good-bye in person."

"I won't be able to leave if I do."

Catherine held the end of one of her tennis-sweater sleeves to her trembling mouth and leaned against the front door as if trying to steady herself as she watched Nel stuff the suitcase in the car.

And so, without saying good-bye to Jakob, Nel drove south along the lake that chilly spring day, with the top of her red VW Beetle down and the heat on full blast. She drove past blueberry fields, some of them smoking and blackened from controlled burns that would help them produce bigger yields. Miles of road later, as she approached the Indiana border, she began to sing along with the radio to "I Will Follow Him" by Little Peggy March. Then she pushed an eight-track tape into the console and sang every Peter, Paul, and Mary song ever made. Gusts of wind beat her long black hair against her face. Part of her wished she could go back to days when the lake house had seemed like a mansion, when warm summer winds had caressed her arms like a cashmere sweater, and homemade sundresses Mama made out of seersucker had hung just above her knees, when she hadn't minded the tickle of grass in her ears as she lay flat, limbs spread wide in the thick of the yard, and stared at clouds floating past. Happiness had lingered in those days before shame had swallowed her up.

CHAPTER 6

Billy Esposito tried, still, to make small talk as they rattled their way through first a storm door and then the sticky side door of Jakob's house, his voice too loud against the hushed hollowness inside.

The kid must hate silence, Jakob thought as a pang of uneasiness filled him.

Catherine would know what to say to Nel.

He almost turned his head to look for a reassuring phantom of his wife, the pain of her absence jolting him again. This must be what an amputee feels. Jakob recalled stories he'd heard from veteran friends, then later, friends who'd lost limbs due to diabetes, who described how they could still feel a foot or a leg, a hand or an arm even after it had been severed. That the nonexistent appendage itched and burned and ached as if it were still there. Worse, sometimes, than if it were still there. After all, an itch on something that didn't exist couldn't be scratched.

He'd been beyond lucky to marry Catherine, and his thoughts drifted to her and their earlier years together. Had there not been a war going on, and most of the respectable men her age fighting in the Pacific or on some godforsaken front in Europe, Jakob knew he and Catherine would never have had a chance. In fact, Catherine had been engaged before, but her fiancé, the son of a Chicago hotel tycoon, had died a hero on a navy destroyer lost in the Battle of Guadalcanal.

"November 13, 1942. Days before he would've been on leave … for the holidays," Catherine had explained about her fiancé's demise. A tear had rolled down her face and landed on her wrist, next to her triple-stranded pearl bracelet. She and Jakob sat on a scrolled, mahogany-trimmed, velvet settee in the lobby of the Palmer House hotel in Chicago. It was the weekend before Christmas Eve 1943, and the two of them were at a party, complete with Santa, who had arrived and begun giving presents to all the children in attendance. She was there because her father, chairman of the board of a steel company, was hosting the event. Jakob was there because Mr. Grünfelder, the jeweler he and his brother Peter had worked for, had invited him knowing he was alone, as he had been since Mrs. Stewart died from influenza in 1935, and Mr. Stewart died in 1941 from what appeared to have been a heart attack. Jakob had agreed to come to the party out of respect more than loneliness.

The lights of the Christmas party, the strolling strings, the ballroom pounding with the newest sounds of Big Band and jazz, the corks popping and the ice tinkling against the sides of long-stemmed glasses had overwhelmed him. Preferring to keep to himself, he'd been warming one side of the settee for some time when Catherine, breathless from dancing and dressed in a silver, floor-length, single-sleeved sheath, plopped down next to him, at first barely seeming to notice he was there. Her dark-brown hair, pulled up with a glinting, jeweled hairpin into a smooth chignon, gleamed. He had tried not to let his eyes linger on her bare left shoulder, which reminded him of marble; it was, he thought, so exquisitely statuesque.

She spoke, and he listened, as her dance-floor giddiness fell away to slower, more serious conversation. Perhaps the rum caused Catherine to lean toward him, to find comfort in the gray edges of his sideburns and his middle-aged shoulders, broad from lifting presses and running machines at the Brake-All factory every day. Or perhaps it was a subliminal aura of neediness he gave off unintentionally, his singleness exposed in a crowd of couples, that evoked within her a sympathy, initially, before striking an eventual mutual flame of physical attraction that had them both reeling, drunk from their infatuation with each other by Valentine's Day, and married by June.

She had terrified him at first. Catherine, her lithe frame, the way her hips swayed when she walked, teasing him like a puppy to follow her down Michigan Avenue as they'd gone Christmas shopping together the next day, the bottom edge of her wool gabardine dress flipping to and fro, skimming along the rounded edges of her perfect—so perfect—calves. Until Catherine, he'd never noticed the thinness of a woman's fingers, the delicate way they lifted a champagne glass, or a cup of coffee, for that matter, and then the way their soft, cool ends pressed against the nape of his neck as he, trembling, had pressed his lips against hers for the first time. Loving Catherine had shaped him. Broken him, yes, but in ways that helped him live again. She had become, in fact, the religion he had lost long ago.

"Eleanor?"

Jakob's attention returned to Billy, who'd been calling and checking all the rooms for Nel. Jakob saw her first, chin in her hands, elbows resting on the edge of the deck railing. He nodded toward the deck. "There she is."

Billy followed Jakob's gaze to where Nel stood.

"I'll take it from here, son. Thank you for your help today." Jakob reached out to shake Billy's hand, and Billy grabbed him by the elbow as Jakob lurched toward him on his increasingly bad hip.

"Okay, Mr. Stewart. See you tomorrow."

Jakob patted him on the shoulder as he moved past in a heavy hobble. He tugged on the back door that stuck a little before opening to the deck, then the yard, then the sharp drop-off to the lake, dappled at that hour with diamonds of afternoon sunlight. He hadn't intended to startle his daughter, but the sudden release of the decrepit door made her jump as she turned to him. She had aged beautifully like her mother. The resemblance caught his breath.

"Hi, Dad."

He watched the wind blow her hair around her face, how she brushed it away from her small nose—Catherine's nose—and her brown eyes.

"Eleanor." He coughed slightly, then swallowed against the dryness of his throat. "Welcome home."

"Thanks." She leaned back against the railing and pushed her glasses up on her nose.

Jakob noticed her face was wet with tears.

"So," she said with a sniff. "What are we gonna do now?"

CHAPTER 7

Nel and Jakob embraced. As Nel put her arms around her father, the broad shoulders and most of his height remained as she remembered, but the weightiness, the sturdiness of what were once robust muscles felt doughy and lank, even though it'd been only two Christmases ago that she'd seen him. She backed away, keeping a hand on his upper arm.

"How are you, Dad?"

The diminishment of his frame caught her off guard. His eyes, hazel, rheumy, and droopy, like a surprised basset hound, softened before he looked away from her toward the lake.

"I'm okay." He sighed and shook his head, his gaze settling on his loafers. "I didn't think … I thought she'd always be here."

"Let's get out of this wind," Nel suggested, reaching for the door. She held it open and frowned as she watched him totter in. He favored his left hip, and Nel recalled how her mother had said something recently about how he needed to have the right one replaced, but that no surgeon would operate on him because of his advanced age. He'd had the left hip done when he was eighty-six, and she'd stayed with them for a nearly a month then. He'd had both knees done when he was younger, shortly after she'd left for Santa Fe. He looked every bit of ninety-four as Nel watched him lean into the aluminum cane he must've found at a fishing show, if she'd had to guess. Where else could someone find a cane with digital pictures of walleye swimming up and down the shaft?

"Three o'clock already." Jakob raised his eyebrows, long untended and bushy, to glance at the cuckoo clock squawking on top of the mantle. He let his body fall heavily into one of the paired wingback chairs closest to him.

"How did things go at the funeral home? What can I do—"

"It's taken care of," he interrupted. "All planned. She wrote it all out, had it taped to the inside front cover of her Bible."

He'd told Nel this before on the phone, but she didn't want to make him feel bad by reminding him. She wondered if forgetfulness like this was what Mattie had been referring to. She decided to dismiss it, considering much worse stories she'd heard about people with dementia.

"Are there friends I can call? Neighbors? People who might not read the paper?"

"No, no one."

"Mattie said she'll bring us dinner around five."

"I'll never starve if she has anything to do with it."

Nel was glad to see him chuckle at that. "Mattie hasn't changed much."

"No, she hasn't. Same good girl she's always been."

Now that Jakob was home, she could at least try to relax and settle in. "You know, I probably ought to call Sam," she said reluctantly.

"Sam? Have you married that poor guy yet?"

Nel laughed and kissed Jakob on the top of his head. "Not yet, Dad."

She used the phone upstairs in her old bedroom, and when Sam didn't answer, she left a message to tell him she'd arrived safely. Then she sat on top of her old bedspread and noticed a faint smell of fabric softener on the faded-yellow Raggedy Ann pillowcase. She was sure Catherine had washed them regularly, even though they were never used, except for when she was in town. The way her mom took great care to remake the bed exactly as she had when Nel was growing up made her smile. She pulled a red-and-blue afghan over her shoulders and watched the tree limbs outside her window move against the wind, and she drifted off to the distant sound of a woodpecker pelting the side of a tree and the chatter of chickadees and nuthatches.

The doorbell startled her awake, and after reorienting herself to where she was, she ran downstairs to answer the door. "Don't worry, Dad. Don't get up. I'll get it."

"I made you beef brisket." Mattie gleamed as she walked through the front door and headed toward the kitchen. "Been cooking in the Crock-Pot all day, so it'll fall apart just like you like."

After setting the load on the counter, Mattie pulled a Tupperware container of mashed potatoes and two french baguettes out of a basket, followed by a blueberry pie and a carton of whipped cream. She turned to Nel. "Did you get a chance to rest?"

"A little. Thanks so much for this—for everything. Will you eat with us?"

Mattie said yes, of course she'd love to join them for dinner, and together they sat in the dimming evening light and reminisced about Catherine. Nel soaked in memories—many new to her—of church gatherings, July Fourth celebrations with the South Haven Senior Women's Club, road trips to little towns where Mattie and Catherine perused antique stores while Jakob attended gem-and-mineral club meetings. Mattie filled Nel in on who had passed since she'd been home last—Clara Lieberman (cancer), Harriet and Mortie Czylek (six weeks apart; she from a heart attack, and he from a stroke), Gertrude Downing (in her sleep). They discussed the chronic sad state of Ed and Mary Jane Grabowski, who hadn't been well since their only son, James, a high school classmate of Nel's, drowned in a rip current near the lighthouse right after graduation. Sally Medendorp (also from Nel's class) had twins recently—that spring—her first babies at age forty-three. And the new senior pastor at South Haven Presbyterian Church had arrived that summer.

"Catherine adored him," Mattie said. "You'll get to meet him tomorrow, since he'll be officiating."

The next morning, Nel found Jakob standing at the stove making eggs, already dressed in his suit and tie. She leaned against the counter next to him.

"Scrambled?" He winked.

"Yep."

He poured a little water in them. "Makes them fluffier. Just a little smidgen of water."

"I remember." She watched the eggs firm up as he stirred and scraped them around the skillet. "You look good, Dad."

"No one looks good when they're my age," he said, chuckling.

"No, really. That's a nice suit. Mom would say you're handsome."

Jakob frowned and stirred. "Yes ... I suppose she would."

"Did you get your paper yet?" Nel scanned the counters for the *Herald-Palladium* but didn't see a copy. "I'll go get it."

The sun shone bright that autumn morning, already melting the light frost on the east side of the house facing the street. She stretched and inhaled, the cool air taking the edge off the awkwardness of her mom's absence back in the kitchen. She'd been hypervigilant since she'd been home, watching for signs of forgetfulness in her dad, and felt some relief when she'd seen how appropriate he'd been so far. She was a little ashamed he'd gotten dressed and started breakfast before she'd even woken up. Stiff from the plane ride, she bent to touch her toes and saw a brown envelope in the mulch of the flower bed alongside the steps. She hopped off the stoop and pulled it from under the overgrown yew, where it must've blown in the last day or two, judging from the dew stains.

Addressed to Catherine, the postmark read New York City, and it was dated Tuesday, just before Mom died. Nel brushed off the envelope and pulled it open as she walked toward the end of the driveway to get the paper. Inside, she found a note on US Citizenship and Immigration Services letterhead explaining that therein was the information Catherine had requested from them. Behind that was a photocopy of a document titled "List of Manifest of Alien Passengers for the US Immigration Officer at Port of Arrival. Holland America Line." The rest of the paper was filled with a list of names scrawled in barely legible handwriting. Columns next to the names requested information about every immigrant, including age; sex; occupation; whether they were able to read or write; nationality, race, or people; last residence (province, city, or town); final destination; whether they were polygamists or anarchists; how much money they had with them, if any; whether their passage was paid for and by whom; whether they were meeting anyone in the States; and various other details related to these questions.

Paper-clipped to the manifest was an old photo of two boys, one quite young, barely five, perhaps, and another who appeared to be a teenager. Both of them held fur hats, the sort that have flaps that cover the ears, and wore multiple layers of woolens and jackets. Neither boy smiled.

Interesting, Nel thought. Mom must've taken up genealogy recently. A lot of older people did. Curious she hadn't mentioned anything to Nel about it.

Nel set the papers aside to look into later. Perhaps she'd ask Mattie about it. For now she had to focus on getting Jakob and herself through the funeral.

The Reverend Adam Winslow and his wife, Sarah, waited at the threshold of the white-trimmed and pillared red-brick Presbyterian church for Jakob and Nel when they arrived. Mortified she had squealed the tires of her father's behemoth white Ford Crown

Victoria when they'd pulled into the parking lot, Nel sheepishly reached toward Sarah's outstretched hand.

"You must be Nel." A strand of faintly pink pearls peeked from beneath the collar of Sarah's thick, ground-length, navy wool overcoat. She ran the church music ministry, which both Catherine and Mattie had participated in. "Your mother spoke of you often. I can hardly believe we've never met."

Reverend Winslow stepped toward Jakob, who was breathing loudly through pursed lips after trekking up the steps. "How are you holding up, Jake?"

"Fine, fine," Jakob puffed, waving his cane-free hand in the air as if to dismiss the reverend's obvious concern.

Inside the sanctuary, Nel and Jakob took their seats in the front pew next to the reverend and Sarah. Mike Wisowaty, two years Nel's senior, straightened a wreath of flowers over the top of the casket. Catherine and Beth Wisowaty—Mike's mother—had tried to matchmake Mike and Nel for years. She felt relieved that hadn't worked out. His face had rounded out considerably, as had his middle. If Nel had to guess, she'd say he had high blood pressure from the look of his blotchy, reddened cheeks and neck. He glanced her way, nodding with sympathy, and she smiled politely.

She looked around the sanctuary as it filled, recognizing faces, forgetting some names, remembering others. Old teachers, shop owners, neighbors, parents of her schoolmates, couples, widows and widowers of Jakob's coworkers from Brake-All—each person reflected how Catherine spent her life devoted to raising Nel and loving Jakob. The number of attendees was not overwhelming, and in other settings some might have been disappointed in the turnout.

But Nel thought it was all perfect. The people who'd come mattered to Mom, and Nel knew Mom mattered to them.

Then she saw David Butler. She hadn't noticed him arrive, but he sat in the back pew, adjusting his tie in a way that made it obvious he wasn't used to wearing one. His face was ruddier than when they'd been in high school. He'd aged well, the years adding definition and a sort of wisdom to his once-boyish features. His hair was dark, nearly black like hers, except for around the temples. She hadn't realized she'd been staring at him until he nodded at her and grinned. She raised her hand and waved—Waved? How old was she, sixteen?—then snapped back around in her seat, annoyed at herself for blushing and acting like a teenager. The over twenty years that had passed since their senior year had done little to dampen her infatuation with him.

Mike approached Nel and Jakob. "Excuse me a moment, Reverend. Jakob. Nel. Does anyone need more time before we make the final preparations before the service?"

Nel shook her head, lowering her eyes to the handkerchief she'd brought, one she'd found in her mother's vanity, hand embroidered with the letters CBS, Catherine Bessinger Stewart.

"I said my good-byes to her every evening, and the other night was no exception," Jakob said, looking wistful. His damp eyes regarded the casket. Then he turned to Nel. "You know, she had all the verses, the order of the service, "How Great Thou Art" for the hymn—everything picked out—and the instructions taped to the inside of her Bible?"

CHAPTER 8

Praise God from whom all blessings flow,
Praise Him all creatures here below,
Praise Him above, ye heavenly host,
Praise Father, Son, and Holy Ghost.

The pipes of the old organ belted out the familiar refrain, but Jakob did not sing along. He knew why Catherine had chosen this hymn to conclude her funeral, and he did not wish to comply with her reasoning.

"Praise Him even when you don't feel like it. Always, always praise," she'd said.

He figured she'd chuckle at his stubbornness, which transcended the fact that she'd passed. He was tired. Tired of funerals. Tired of watching everyone he knew and loved be buried while waiting for his own burial, which ever eluded him. Tired of the realization he'd had for some time now that life really was meaningless, as Solomon wrote in Ecclesiastes. God seemed to be everywhere around the dead, but Jakob had yet to find much evidence of Him around the living, besides on the countenance of his wife and a few other exceptions like Mattie. More than that, why sing if you don't feel like it?

He felt like hollering this question out loud, jolting Reverend Winslow and the rest of the mournful assemblage, disrupting the plangent vibratos of Catherine's octogenarian friends singing in the pew behind him.

When he got home, he'd put a note on the inside flap of his Bible telling people to read Ecclesiastes, the entire first chapter, at his funeral, about how none of the laboring, the sunrises and sunsets, mattered. How the generations are forgotten. How living long and getting old doesn't mean a hill of beans. And how faith, once you've seen folks slaughtered because of it, becomes something you lock tight deep inside.

As Reverend Winslow began the eulogy, Jakob flipped the pew Bible open to the eighteenth verse of the first chapter of Ecclesiastes. *For with much wisdom comes much sorrow; the more knowledge, the more grief,*[1] he read in silence.

And with age, much pain. He couldn't understand why everyone in America was so fixated on living as long as possible. His body reminded him of an old car, three out of his four major leg joints replaced, three heart catheterizations to keep his blood flowing, uric acid collecting in his gouty feet like oil sludge. He'd consider himself lucky if his alternator went ahead and gave out.

More grief, Solomon had written.

Indeed.

He rubbed a large age spot on his hand, which trembled as he shoved the pew Bible back under the seat and grasped the handle of his cane.

1908

Chicago, Illinois

CHAPTER 9

When Peter and Jakob had learned English as well as could be expected, the Stewarts enrolled them in Saint Stanislaus Catholic School with many other lost and language-challenged children from the neighboring Eastern European immigrant sections of Chicago. Many of the children were from the Ukrainian Village neighborhood bordering Wicker Park, as well as from the surrounding Polish neighborhoods. This thrilled Peter and Jakob and all the children because they could talk in their native languages at recess, in the halls, and whenever a teacher wasn't around to demand they use their English. No one cared whether they were Jewish or Orthodox or a combination either. Everyone honored whatever bits and pieces of faith—if any—had survived their journeys to the States.

Jakob was in the second grade and Peter in high school, a couple of years older than many of his classmates so he could catch up with the language. On a Friday evening as the sun was setting, Jakob walked into Peter's room to find him kneeling, holding the one frayed tassel from Papa's *tzitzit*[1] in his hands.

"Do you remember when Papa made this and the others he wore on the four corners of his garment?" Peter asked.

Jakob nodded. He remembered. Papa wound the strings, teaching them both in what seemed a lifetime ago, what the pattern represented.

"Do you remember what the first seven windings are for?"

"Creation," Jakob said without hesitation.

"Yes. And the second eight?"

Jakob shook his head. He couldn't recall.

"That one is harder," Peter reassured him. "Eight is the number of days from when the Israelites left Egypt to when they sang their song of deliverance when they reached the Red Sea. And the reason for the four tassels?"

Jakob did remember this, but he wouldn't say.

"You don't remember?"

Jakob shook his head, unwilling rather than lying.

"Then I'll tell you."

Jakob wished he wouldn't.

"We're supposed to look for Yahweh, to remember He is with us, on all sides of us. Helping us. Guiding us. Jehovah-Shammah."

Jakob frowned.

"You don't think so?"

Jakob hesitated, then shook his head again. Where was Yahweh on the ship? Where was Yahweh in the woods? Where was he with the girl they'd found in the barn? And most of all, where was Yahweh in the horror that occurred in Chudniv? Yahweh had done nothing but abandon them.

"Papa believed it. He said El Shaddai is always watching over us."

Jakob felt the sickness that always came deep from inside his belly whenever he remembered Papa. What he would give to see him again, to sink into his thick arms, to hear his laughter, his singing, his prayers. Yes, Papa had believed it. But if Papa had known everything that would happen to them, would he still have believed?

"You are mighty forever, my L-rd; You resurrect the dead; You are powerful to save ...," Peter recited from the Amidah.

Jakob's sick feeling turned to anger. "Go on and believe the Amidah, the Shema, and all that old nonsense if you want to. But that's all it is. Nonsense."

"Jakob—"

"God may be real, but He doesn't keep His promises. At least not to us."

"You don't think there's a reason we made it here and have been blessed with a new family who loves us? Abraham had to leave his land, his people, too, and he became the father of our faith. You don't think perhaps Yahweh, even Yeshua, had reasons for delivering us?"

"No." Jakob nearly spat his answer into Peter's face. "I wish Yahweh and Yeshua had delivered the rest of our family instead of me."

Peter, exasperated with what had become nearly constant sulking from his little brother, shoved Jakob onto the bed.

"What's that for?" Jakob held his shoulder.

"Someone needs to put some sense into you. Do you think any of this has been easy for me? Don't you think I wish it were them instead of me too? But I can't. If I think that more than a second, I die inside. But I have to keep going. For you. And for them. They would want us to keep going too."

Jakob pounced at his brother, but Peter pushed him onto the bed again, this time climbing on top of him, straddling him, pinning his arms against his sides. Jakob's chest felt as if it would explode.

"Get … off … me!"

"No. Not until you listen."

"You can talk all you want, but I won't hear a thing," Jakob gasped.

"Listen anyway," Peter growled. "Don't you remember what Mama taught us about giving thanks, always giving thanks? Do you think I want to? No! But I do anyway. It's only because I say the prayers every morning and every night, whether I feel like it or not, that my heart has not hardened like granite."

He crawled off Jakob and sat on the bed, and some of the patience that always comforted Jakob returned to his voice. "Don't you think Mama and Papa would be happy we are alive? It wasn't chance that made me turn around and come back the day after the raid. It wasn't chance that I found you in the cupboard. It wasn't chance that we made it through the mountains so many perish in before they ever reach the sea—"

"Why *did* you come back? Sometimes I wish you'd never found me." Jakob pulled his knees up tight against his chest.

Peter fell silent. The only sounds for a long while were those of a mouse scuttling beneath the floorboards and of embers cracking and popping in the fireplace. When at last he spoke, he whispered. "I think about it sometimes too. About how much simpler it would've been if we could've either all died or all lived. But I can't let myself stay in those thoughts or I'd go mad." He put his arm around Jakob and pulled him close. "You and I have the job now of making the most of this freedom. We have to live and live well. We have to keep seeking God's will, and somehow, in the midst of that, we have to keep thanking and praising Him. If we don't, we die along with them, and they along with us."

Jakob knew Mama and Papa would be happy, yes, but he didn't wish to acknowledge this. Shame and anger overwhelmed him.

And grief.

He missed them all so much.

And for the first time since Chudniv, emotion overwhelmed him. Maybe he finally felt safe enough in the Stewarts' home, where they were surrounded by down comforters and glowing fires. Maybe he was old enough to finally understand what he felt. Maybe there was no reason at all except that it was time for him to cry. Whatever the reason, before he could stop himself, he was weeping. He wept until nothing was left inside him except for the one thing he thought he could never confess. And finally, the confession emptied itself too. "She would've lived if I'd stopped them."

"What are you talking about?" Peter said as he scooted back on the bed to look at Jakob square on.

Jakob hesitated. "Faigy."

Peter grasped his shoulders and looked into his eyes. "Faigy? What about her?"

"Faigy and Papa's second stone, the one he'd saved for their passage. They're gone because of me."

"That's crazy talk. You couldn't have stopped the *pogromshchik*. No one could have."

"It was only one."

"One man couldn't have done all I saw—"

"No. Later. After the many left, one came back. And Faigy was alive," Jakob interrupted. He hadn't wanted to tell Peter, but since he'd started, he couldn't stop.

"Alive? What do you mean?"

Jakob began to cry again. He explained how after the group of maniacs left the house, after they'd killed everyone, he heard Faigy. He'd thought she was dead too, but they must've just knocked her out, because he found her standing next to Zahava, trying to get Zahava to wake up, but of course she wouldn't. Zahava would never wake up. "I found her doll and gave it to her, and it helped a little. She stopped crying. But there was nothing to give her to eat. The milk was spilled, the maniacs took all the food except a couple of potatoes. We both ate a little raw potato, but that's when I heard the sound of horses."

"They came back?"

"I thought it was all of them coming back. I tried to get Faigy to come hide in the cupboard with me, but she wouldn't come. She was afraid of the dark, and she was afraid to move. She wouldn't hide." He buried his face in his hands.

"Then what happened?"

"I hid anyway. I couldn't help it. I hid. And I saw the man through a crack in the cupboard door." Jakob choked back tears. "I watched him ... He grabbed Faigy and ransacked the cupboards and found Papa's stones, the rest of the scraps, and the other aquamarine Papa had hidden in the back of the cupboard ... and ... I ... I could have screamed. If I'd screamed ... then she wouldn't have been taken ... or they would've taken me too ... and at least she wouldn't have died alone."

Peter sat back, face ashen, and studied his little brother.

Jakob was sure Peter would hate him.

"You were only four," Peter said finally.

"But nearly five." Jakob wiped his nose and face on the sleeve of his arm.

"Still, you were a baby too." Peter pulled him close. "You did only what you knew to do. And if you hadn't—"

Jakob pushed away from him. "If I hadn't hidden, Faigy wouldn't have died."

"If you hadn't hidden, you *both* would've died."

Jakob was silent for a moment, considering this. "But I could've at least thought to grab Papa's stone before they came back."

Peter stood and paced, exasperated. "So what if you had?"

"Then we'd have two."

"Okay. Then we'd have two. But who cares about two stones? We have one, and we have each other. And that is enough."

"It will never be enough," Jakob said. Tears continued to run down his face, but he had stopped sobbing. He curled himself into a ball and lay down on Peter's bed facing the window, the darkening sky outside the leaded glass a blur to his stinging, weep-worn eyes.

Jakob recalled the day they'd buried their grandfather Dedus shortly before Easter the spring before they left Chudniv. That same evening, candlelight had flickered across the room as his sisters Zahava, Ilana, and Tova hunched over fragile eggs and used *kystkas*[2] to drip melted beeswax onto the shells. He remembered the way the kitchen smelled as if he were there, honey from the wax, boiled bark and berries, sunflower-seed husks, cochineal, and elderberry, all used to make the dye for the *pysanky*.[3]

Jakob had been sitting on his mama's lap watching. "Why do you make pysanky? We just buried Dedus."

"We don't have to honor the shivah anymore, Jakob, not since we became Christian, right, Mama?" Ilana vaunted, then turned back to her egg, upon which she carefully dripped wax along predrawn lines curled into the shape of a flower.

"No, Ilana. That's not right. Not exactly." Mama raised an eyebrow, a warning against Ilana's prideful tone. "We believe Yeshua is Messiah, yes, but we honor God the Father as we always have." Mama nodded to the Bible Sasha the priest had given Papa at Christmas, in its place on the fireplace mantel. She and Papa had been requiring the children to read aloud from it as often as they could, especially the New Testament. Papa had been adamant that they all—even his daughters—know it as well as they knew the Torah. Sasha the priest came often to visit their shtetl. Father always invited him in, and Mama prepared and gave him the best of their food and drink. The tall, round, black hat he wore made his graying beard more prominent, especially against the rest of his dark clothing. Sasha and Papa and sometimes Peter, too, sat at the table in the kitchen talking about the Talmud and the Torah, arguing and laughing and arguing again, their conversations stretching deep into the night as they burned many candles to their nubs.

"Mama, are you sad Dedus is gone?" Jakob had whispered into her ear to avoid the teasing of his sisters.

"Yes, I am, very much. He was my Tato. And he loved to tickle me as I like to tickle you, my sweet boy."

Jakob giggled as Mama's fingers played against his ribs, her whisper back to him tickling his ear too. When she stopped, he wrapped his small arms around her neck.

"Time for you to go to bed." Mama hoisted Jakob until his head rested cozily on her shoulder, and she carried him to his bed. His was a small cot next to where Peter lay reading by candlelight. Her breath had always felt warm and soft against Jakob's ear. "Do you remember the Kaddish the rabbi said today at Dedus's funeral?"

"Mmm-hmm."

"My brothers, my sisters, and I must say it every day now for eleven months, and also a year from now, on the day Dedus died."

"Why?"

"It's easy when something bad happens, especially when someone you love very much dies, to become bitter and angry at God. The rabbis believe saying the Kaddish can help us remember that God is good, that He is just and righteous, even when bad things happen. Because God does not cause the bad. Man causes the bad. God is always good. And so we are always to praise Him."

"Do I have to say it every day too?"

"You don't have to since you are so young. But it would be good if you can."

"But you will be here to remind me God is good. Why must I say it?"

"Because I will not always be around. And so you must be able to know these things for yourself."

"But you *will* always be here, Mama."

Eliana bowed her head.

Peter put his book down. "Do people who believe in Messiah Yeshua say it too?"

Eliana turned her head toward her eldest child. "I don't think so. But we can."

"Say it now, Mama," Jakob had said.

"Why don't we say it together? Come, hold my hand, Peter."

Then the three of them, candlelight flickering against their hopeful faces, had recited the Kaddish for the second time that day, as they did every day after that.

"I'm sorry," Peter whispered, firelight reflecting off his face as he approached Jakob where he lay on the bed.

"So am I."

Peter grasped Jakob's hand with the remaining thumb and forefinger on his right hand. "*Hakarat hatov.*† It is our duty to praise."

Jakob watched a star flicker and another shoot across the sky outside the window. "Yes," he replied, watching more stars come out as Peter recited the traditional evening prayers as Mama and Papa had done what seemed like ages ago.

---

† Recognizing the good.

1994

—————————————

South Haven, Michigan

CHAPTER 10

After the funeral, Nel considered how little the church she'd grown up in had changed, except for new carpeting in the sanctuary, donated by the Pershing family. Mr. Pershing served as vice president of one of the big auto manufacturers, and the brass, inlaid floor plate with the Pershings' name on it, centered in the aisle, ensured no one forgot their generosity. The rest of the church floor consisted of cold, square industrial tiles, from the narthex to the teen room in the basement. Parishioners—at least the ones who'd come to pay their respects to her mother—hadn't changed either, except for more gray hair and a heavier scent of night cream, Ben-Gay, and pipe tobacco. Nel had a feeling that younger families in town, if they attended, came either because they'd grown up there or married into a family that grew up there, or were new in town and chose the church because they grew up Presbyterian. After all, if there was one thing you could count on in a new town, it was the consistency of the Presbyterian church. A curmudgeonly old man Nel recognized as Mr. Wiley, of Wiley and Sons Lumber Company, stood smiling on one side of the doors leading out of the church as Nel prepared to help her father navigate the concrete steps.

"Mr. Stewart?"

Jakob was more intent òn brushing away Nel's attempts to hold him by the elbow than paying attention to yet another elderly man approaching him on the sidewalk.

"Dad." Nel nudged him, tilting her head toward the man when Jakob looked at her questioningly.

Judging from his walker and tentative gait, the man wasn't in any better shape than Jakob. "I'm so sorry, Mr. Stewart. Catherine was a true lady."

"Lev?"

"Yep. It's been a while, I know. How are you, boss?"

"Well, well, well. Lev Herzog. It sure is good to see you." Jakob shifted his cane to his left hand and extended his right to Lev. "I'd be running races in the parking lot here if my daughter would let go of my elbow."

"Okay, Dad." She rolled her eyes and grinned. She extended her hand to Lev. "Nel Stewart. Thank you for coming, Mr. Herzog."

"Call me Lev. Please, young lady." He shook his head and his eyes widened, looking amazed. "Last time I saw you, you couldn't have been more than knee high."

He turned to Jakob. "Say, boss, do you remember when Dave Carter took over the press room?"

Jakob erupted with deep laughter, and the two began carrying on about their years together on and off the factory floor, Lev leaning on his walker, and Jakob leaning on his cane.

Nel was grateful when she spotted her friend Lori. "Lori! Hi!"

"Nel, I'm so sorry. How are you, friend?"

Throughout school, Nel and Lori had been inseparable. Despite her excellent grades, Nel was always on the verge of trouble, and somehow Lori reeled her in or smoothed everything out. Some incidents were relatively minor, like the junior prom when Nel was so busy swooning over her prom date, she hadn't noticed the salad stuck on her front tooth. Lori yanked her into the bathroom, nearly breaking the stiletto off one of Nel's dyed-to-match high heels, and plucked it out before he'd noticed. Other times were more serious, like the time when Nel snuck out of the house to meet a bunch of boys on the beach for a bonfire. When Jakob and Catherine found Nel's empty bed, they called Lori, who covered for her by making up a sleepover story on the spot, then risked getting in trouble herself by going out to find Nel at the bonfire and bringing her back home.

The most significant save came after college, though, when Nel lost her baby in 1975. Lori was the first person Nel had called as she lay weepy and muzzy-headed from morphine in a hospital delivery room.

"The baby came early," Nel had sobbed into the phone. "And there was a lot of bleeding. Too much bleeding. The blood was everywhere."

"Are you all right?"

"The bleeding stopped. But the baby … He was so small … so beautiful … He was perfect. I felt his heart beating. I felt it, Lori. Until it stopped."

"Oh, Nel, I'm so sorry. I'm on my way over there. I'm so sorry."

When Lori, in medical school at the time, arrived at the hospital, she'd found Nel on the floor of the bathroom in a growing puddle of blood. She'd passed out and hit her head, and if Lori hadn't been in the room with her, the doctors said she would've bled to death before the nurse had found her on rounds. The fall wasn't the worst of it, although that in itself required several stitches above her eye. The majority of the blood came from her uterus, and they'd had to rush her back to surgery. The doctors worked on her for two hours, transfusing her with unit after unit of blood, until finally they'd had no choice but to give her an emergency hysterectomy. She'd never have children of her own.

"It's so good to see you too." Nel embraced her friend, their affection for each other resurrecting itself the way it always did when they hadn't seen each other in months—as if they'd never been apart. "Thank you so much for coming."

Lori stepped back and flipped a long blonde braid over her shoulder as she lifted her toddler daughter, Hadley, onto her hip. Lori was one of the few people Nel knew who could look fabulous wearing overalls with dress flats and cute cardigan sweaters, all after birthing five children, including Hadley, her fifth. "Sorry about bringing this little squirt, and for the jeans … Trey's working, and my sitter canceled last minute. I decided to run over here while I had the chance, before the others get off the school bus."

Nel stuffed back a fleeting sense of envy over her friend's perfectly balanced life as a wife, mother, and part-time pediatrician. "It's totally fine—I'm just so glad you're here."

"You look fabulous … and I love the dreads." Lori reached out and curled one of the thick strands around her finger playfully.

"Really? Thank you. I saw a few raised eyebrows in the church."

"They were probably just wondering how you are. Dreads aren't exactly a new thing." Lori laughed. "You staying in town long?"

Nel watched Lori tug Hadley's hat down tighter over her curly, bright-blonde hair and tiny ears. The air was chillier than it had been the day before. Hadley pressed her head into Lori's shoulder.

"I'm not sure. Dad … well, he's weak. I'm not sure he can be left alone. Mom must've been doing most everything for him. But I've got deadlines, and holiday orders are coming in like crazy already. I need to get back."

Lori nodded empathetically, then followed Nel's gaze to Jakob, who'd finished talking to Lev and now swayed precariously toward the Crown Victoria, each of his lurching steps a totter away from a snapped hip, a twisted knee, a hard and possibly mortal fall. He struggled to pull the giant passenger-side door open, and before Nel could run over to help, Billy Esposito, who'd been talking to a younger group of Brake-All guys, helped him. "They don't have much reserve at that age, that's for sure. What is he, eighty-something?"

"Ninety-four."

"Wow." Lori shook her head, looking amazed.

"The house is falling apart. *He's* falling apart. I'm not sure what I'm going to do." Nel looked up at the sky, the gray billows of clouds rolling in from the lake threatening freezing rain or perhaps snow.

Hadley fussed, the freezing air pinking her plump cheeks. Lori shushed her, then turned to Nel. "We can talk more, maybe grab coffee before you leave or something. I know of some great assisted-living places and home health agencies recommended by colleagues who work with adults, if it comes down to him needing help."

"Thanks, but I'm not sure he'd ever go for that. Losing Mom, then losing their home … I'm not sure he'd survive. Too many memories there. And he'd cringe over help coming in. He's so stubborn."

"Yeah … it's a tough spot to be in. For both of you." Lori leaned in closer to her. "Don't look now, but here comes David Butler."

Nel turned despite Lori's warning and nearly fell into him. He was standing right behind her.

"Sorry to surprise you like that." He grinned and extended his hand. "David Butler, by the way. I'm not sure if you remember me."

"I remember," Nel said, composing herself and shaking his hand.

"I'm truly sorry about your mom. She was a fine lady."

"She was."

"I'll let you two catch up," Lori said, Hadley squirming in her arms. "I gotta get Hadley home before the school bus brings the others. Don't you leave town without calling me, 'kay?"

"'Kay. Thanks so much for coming, really." Nel turned back to David, who was straightening his tie. "I saw you at Mattie's when I arrived yesterday. I thought you'd moved to Florida a while back."

"I did. Didn't work out." He glanced around the parking lot, looking uneasy with her question.

"Oh—I'm sorry to hear that." She decided not to press him for details. "So you're fixing houses?"

"I've got my own handyman service. Started it a couple years back. More and more people buying up and building vacation homes here, so I keep pretty busy."

"I bet. How long have you been working on Mattie's?"

"A couple weeks. I'm just about finished."

"Mom and Dad's place is looking pretty bad."

"I kinda noticed that." The wind blew his hair across his greenish-gray eyes.

"Might need you to take a look at it one day when you're at Mattie's."

"I'd be happy to. Give me a holler if you're home and I'm out there."

"Will do." She struggled to look him in the eye, determined not to reveal the resurgence of her old feelings of high school infatuation. And at her mom's funeral, of all places. Then again, her mom might've encouraged her. "Thanks again for coming. It's nice to see you again."

"Nice to see you too, Nel. And like I said, I'm real sorry about your mom."

She watched him walk across the parking lot to his truck.

"What was that all about?"

Nel startled, not hearing Mattie come alongside her.

"Sheesh, I'm jumpy today. It was nothing … I mean, he was just paying his respects."

"Mmm-hmm."

"Oh, stop," Nel said, giving Mattie a playful nudge on the arm. At the same time, if she were honest, she couldn't help wondering what David was all about either. Could he seriously be toying with the same emotions she was? He was the one who'd dumped her that night. She hadn't forgotten that. Still, she noticed his phone number on the side of his truck.

Yes. She would need to get an estimate from him. Mom and Dad's house was going to need a few repairs.

CHAPTER 11

The following week, Jakob sat near the picture window overlooking the lake and watched through the nearly naked tree limbs as the colors of the dusk sky blended and mingled like the variegated colors of tourmaline. Nel had made a fire in the fireplace, but it did nothing to chase the chill out of his legs, which had felt perpetually numb since the frigid burial service at the cemetery. From this spot in his favorite chair, he could hear Nel washing and clanging around glass pans and other remnants from the dozen or so casseroles Mattie and Catherine's friends from choir had been bringing by. The clamor was a welcome noise. The house was way too quiet without the buzz of Catherine and her activities and housekeeping. The woman had rarely, if ever, sat down.

The day before, Mattie came over, and he'd listened as she and Nel wept and laughed for hours while they cleaned out Catherine's side of the closet, choosing which items to donate and which were too threadbare to keep, and packing away most of the rest. Jakob was grateful for their help. Not only had the initial thought of poking through Catherine's belongings bothered him, he just didn't have the strength or inclination to do any of that himself. His mind had fallen into a sort of haze he struggled to wade through during the days, the creaks of floorboards and the wind against the eaves sounding like Catherine's voice to his waning hearing.

Noises weren't the only thing that vexed him. He saw things too, darting shadows he mistook for Catherine that ended up being the dappled penumbrae of light against walls and doorframes. On the night of the funeral, he'd awakened to pitch-blackness and the sound of a toilet flushing.

"Catherine?" he'd cried out.

When Nel ran into the room, the shadowy outline of her frame was so much like Catherine's, he'd reached for her. Only when Nel backed away from his hand—something Catherine would never have done—had the mirage faded. He'd been glad the darkness hid his embarrassment and hoped it had veiled his confusion too.

He heard Nel shut off the water in the kitchen and pick up the phone receiver. Soon someone greeted her on the other end of the line.

"I have some things to finish up here," Nel explained. "Decisions to make ... I understand, yes, by November tenth. Yes, but I can't get back until the fifth at the earliest ..."

One of her jewelry buyers, Jakob figured, as Nel bantered away. He knew she had work to do back in Santa Fe, but he suspected from the way she fussed over him, she didn't want to leave him. He didn't want to be a burden.

"Maybe ...," Nel rambled on. "I might be able to have someone send some of my stuff out here. There's also the possibility of having Matthew and a couple of other artists I know finish the jobs for the *Frontiers* catalog ... Right ... Yes, I know ... Sure ... I'll make some calls and get back to you as soon as I can ... Sure. Thanks, Sandra."

She set the phone in the receiver harder than she needed to, Jakob thought. If he kept his eyes closed, maybe she'd think he was asleep.

"Dad?"

Jakob opened one eye.

"Dad, we need to talk."

He closed it again.

Nel sighed. "I know you're exhausted. But there are decisions we need to make, and I've only got a short amount of time before I have to head back."

Jakob opened both eyes. "Decisions?" He coughed the word out.

Nel stood at the picture window, her back toward him, and stared out at the lake.

"The house needs repairs. Updates." She turned to face him. "You can't take all these stairs on your own. And as for meals, Mattie's great, but we can't expect—"

"I'm fine. I'll be fine. I made you breakfast, didn't I? I can cook what I need to. Get back to your work. They need you out there."

"Work can wait, for a little while anyway. And I don't know … I was thinking maybe I could work out here until we get you some help. Sam or Matthew can send some of my things, and you have most of the tools here already that I'd need."

"I don't want help." He'd been enough of a burden on Catherine. He didn't want to be a burden on his daughter too.

He couldn't help notice her exasperation with him as she ran both hands through the length of her hair and pushed the dreadlocks off her forehead. She came to where he sat and knelt on the floor in front of him, taking his hands in hers. "Look, Dad. Neither one of us is any good at this asking-for-help business. But we're stuck. And we've gotta figure out where to go from here."

"I have friends. Mattie. Billy. Others who check on me. People from the church."

"That's not enough. The repairs ... they're necessary. You'll need a contractor and someone to supervise the work. And someone to check on you every day. There are home health services; Lori mentioned she might know about some good ones."

"You go home. Take care of your jewelry and Sam. I'll be fine. I'll figure it out." He hadn't meant to be harsh.

"Fine," she said as she stomped toward the stairs. "You figure it out, then. Figure it all out yourself."

Jakob cringed when the door to Nel's bedroom slammed, reminding him of the times she slammed it growing up. He didn't blame her for being upset. He was upset too. Without Catherine, he was a mess. Everything was a mess.

He fell asleep in his recliner by the fire, as he often did, which had frustrated Catherine to no end. When he awoke, it was morning. He knew this not because of daylight—there was no daylight yet. He knew it from the songs of the birds. They cut through the memory of the argument he and Nel had the night before, and his mind began to turn with the advancing realization that Nel was right. Still, he didn't want her help. More than that, he didn't want to be a burden. Hadn't he been burden enough to Catherine? Incontinence plagued him more and more often. The tremors in his hands caused him to drop and break more dishes than he could wash, so that Catherine had long been doing the dishes and most other chores herself. He could barely keep his lapidary equipment dusted, let alone use it to cut even a simple cabochon. And then there were the nightmares that Nel didn't know about yet. He hoped she wouldn't find out.

On the other hand, Nel could use his lapidary equipment. It was older than she was used to, but she could use it. He'd seen her designs, gorgeous tumbled stones, fine metalwork. And he'd love to watch how she worked. He'd brush off his equipment and straighten his workroom a bit for her this morning and offer it to her, at least until he could convince her it was okay for her to leave.

He pulled his cane out from where he'd tucked it into the seat cushion beside him, leaned against it with one hand, and pushed up from the chair with the other. His bladder was so full, he wasn't sure he could hold it. His thighs and tailbone burned from the effort of the long shuffle to the bathroom. He hoped he could make it in time, the stinging pressure of urine threatening to escape.

As he tried to shuffle faster, he heard a loud snap, and a black curtain of pain overwhelmed him as he thudded to the floor, the warmth of urine flooding over his groin.

CHAPTER 12

"He's suffered a pretty bad break in that right hip," the orthopedic surgeon explained. A tall, burly fellow with kind eyes, Dr. Weiss had found Nel sitting in a corner of the lounge outside the recovery room at Battle Creek Memorial Hospital. The surgery to repair the hip had lasted nearly three hours. "His bones are brittle. Normally I wouldn't have done surgery at all on someone his age, but as vibrant as you indicated he was before, it's worth a shot."

"My mom said he's been needing to have that hip replaced."

"She was right."

"When can I see him?"

"Let the nurses get him settled. I'm going to keep him in the progressive care unit for a day or two for closer monitoring before I send him to the ward. After that, he'll start rehabilitation here at the hospital. And depending on how that goes—"

"He won't want to live in a nursing home."

Dr. Weiss sat back and exhaled. "You need to prepare yourself for that. And him. Recovery from a surgery like this takes a lot out of a sixty- or seventy-year-old. Given his age ... well ... folks that old don't have much reserve to pull from. There could be confusion, too, acute delusions and, or, a worsening of his dementia."

"Dementia?"

"You weren't aware of his dementia?"

"I suppose I wasn't. I mean, I've been living in New Mexico for twenty years. I talk to him on the phone pretty regularly and visit during holidays, but I hadn't noticed … Mom never said he had an official diagnosis." Nel thought about how Catherine had refused her offer to organize a fiftieth wedding anniversary party for them. She'd said they preferred a quiet celebration, just the two of them. But now Nel wondered—had Mom been protecting her from Jakob's decline?

Dr. Weiss opened Jakob's chart and flipped through several pages. "Looks like he's been seeing a doctor over at the Center for Aging here since last fall. They've got a great program. But honestly, it wouldn't be unusual for you not to have noticed. The short-term memory goes first. A lot of times these patients can carry on a conversation and remember things from decades ago with great detail."

Nel tried to recall patterns or anything off about their phone conversations over the past several months. He'd told a lot of the same stories over and over, but otherwise he seemed to be the same dad as always.

"So what should I expect?" Nel didn't know if she could deal with losing both her parents within a couple of weeks of each other.

"Expect to take things day by day." He stood, tucking Jakob's chart under his arm, and put a hand on Nel's shoulder. "Some of these folks surprise us."

If the first few days of Jakob's hospitalization were any indication of how things would go, Nel was terrified. When she saw him for the first time in the progressive care unit, he had no idea who she was. The nurses had placed giant, mitten-like restraints on his hands and tied down his arms.

"He's yanked his IV out three times already. The restraints are there to protect him more than anything," one of the nurses explained.

One morning, Nel was visiting when a physical therapist carrying a walker came into the room for the first time. "It's time for you to get up, Mr. Stewart."

Jakob's eyes widened. "And just who do you think you are?"

"My name's Tom, and I'm here to get you moving. Can't stay in bed, or else you'll get too weak, your bowels will stop up, you'll get pneumonia—"

"Where's Peter?" Jakob asked him.

"We don't have a therapist named Peter. I'm Tom."

"But where is Peter? I need to talk to him about all this," Jakob insisted, fidgeting with the blankets tangled around his waist from his restlessness.

"Dad, it's okay. Tom just wants to help you get up."

The troubled lines on Jakob's forehead softened when he turned toward Nel. "Why, Catherine, you look beautiful today. Tell this man to quit bothering me, will you?"

Any hesitation she'd had about correcting him in the past vanished with her frustration with the whole situation. "Dad. It's me. Nel."

"Nel?" He looked at her quizzically. "Oh, Nel! Yes, of course! I'm sorry." He shook his head and turned back to Tom. "What are we doing here? What do you want?"

Tom explained again that he was there to help Jakob get up from bed, but despite Tom's patient coaxing and help from Nel, Jakob barely had the wits or the strength to stand at the side of the bed. He nearly fell as they tried to ease him back down, his feet flying up in the air and knocking the walker over as he plopped precariously onto the mattress.

"We'll try again this afternoon," Tom said, breathless.

That afternoon and the seventy-two hours that followed were a disaster. The nurses gave Jakob pain medicine to help him get up, but the medicine only made him more confused. Even when Nel was there visiting—which was most of the time, since she hadn't wanted to leave him alone—the staff insisted on tying him up. He'd become delirious, fighting the staff when they tried to move him, slugging poor Tom in the gut at one point.

"Don't let them take my fingers! Don't let them take my fingers!" Jakob cried over and over one evening as two nurses struggled to put the mitten restraints on his hands.

Nel backed out of the room as she watched them tie the restraints onto the bedframe. She was beside herself with emotion and exhausted from all the time she'd been there. She couldn't remember the last time she had taken a shower. When the nurses came back into the hallway, she told them she was going home. "Please call me if he gets worse."

"We will," they assured her. "Get some rest. That'll make you feel better."

She doubted that but went home anyway, grateful to find that someone had dropped off another casserole—something Italian, which was a nice change from tuna and chicken. A hot shower had never felt as good as the one she had after she ate. And the nurses were right about getting some rest. She slept for sixteen hours that night, and if the phone had rung, she hadn't heard it.

In the morning, she padded to the kitchen and made herself some scrambled eggs, adding a bit of water to fluff them up. Then she called the hospital.

"He did okay last night. Less combative—we didn't have to put him in the mitt restraints. But he keeps talking about a man coming to take his baby." The nurse chuckled.

Nel didn't get what was funny.

"Never know what these patients are going to come up with when they're confused. Said something about a missing gem too. As though he were reliving that old movie—what was it? … *Romancing the Stone* with Michael Douglas, right? I wish I could go live with them in their make-believe worlds sometimes."

Nel set the phone down and heard the sound of a nail gun coming from the direction of Mattie's house. She stepped out onto the back deck and saw David up on the ladder, working his way around to the back eaves of the house. He must've been there early, judging by all the old wood torn off and strewn around the yard below him. He reached around to his belt for a new strip of nails, and Nel jumped back so he wouldn't see her in her saggy old pajama pants and matted hair. Maybe she'd say hello to him, but she at least wanted to have a bra on and her teeth brushed.

Inside, she sat at the round oak dining table and halfheartedly sifted through a growing stack of mail Mattie'd been bringing in for them. Most of it was junk mail and catalogs addressed to her mom, social security checks she'd deposit on the way back to the hospital, and utility bills. Underneath was the envelope from immigration she'd found the day of the funeral. She opened it again and looked more closely at the ship manifest for clues as to what her mom had been searching for. The information fascinated Nel as she read through the list: Stanislaw Zolinsky, a laborer from Russia, Hebrew. Maryanne Bujeloska, a laborer from Lithuania. Gossel Kalmonowik, a tailor, and his wife, Judes, and children, Abraham and Sarah, listed as Russian and Hebrew. Rudolph Lipelk, a locksmith from Russia, Hebrew. Adam Greschenko, a twenty-one-year-old Russian egg packer.

Nel stopped when she came to a line that read "Peter Maevski, 14," and below it, "Jakob Maevski, 5. Place of residence: Chudniv, Russia. Race or people group: Hebrew."

She studied the photograph of the two boys. They looked sad, but maybe it was because they weren't smiling. Everyone in old photos had sad, stoic expressions whether it was a wedding day or a funeral. She'd never seen any childhood pictures of her father, so she couldn't say if the boys resembled anyone for certain. And the last name didn't make sense, unless … unless they'd been adopted. And if they were brothers who had come from Russia, what kind of life would they have come from? What happened to their mother and father? Why hadn't they come with the boys to America? She didn't know much about that period in Russian history, except that large numbers had emigrated from Eastern Europe in the early 1900s. And the only thing she knew about what life was like there was from *Fiddler on the Roof*, one of her favorite musicals. She and her mom had seen it more than once in Chicago, but her dad never wanted to come. He said he didn't like plays. He was glad his girls enjoyed shows, but the theater was not for him.

And why had her mom grown interested in researching this after so many years of marriage?

EARLY 1904

Eastern Ukraine, Russian Empire

CHAPTER 13

Jakob jammed himself against the wall of the barn and pressed his hands over his ears, but nothing could dampen the sound of Peter screaming. He kept his eyes squeezed shut except to open them momentarily to see if the girl was still there, sitting across from him, her eyes wide open, her face pale, and her expression as vacant as it had been from the first moment they saw her.

He wished Peter had never found the place, but they'd been desperate for shelter. Galya could barely lift his legs to plod through the snowdrifts, and the blizzard itself was so blinding, for all they knew they could've been traveling in circles, or worse, back toward Chudniv. So when they'd seen the large barn, which had appeared vacant at first, they didn't worry about what or who was inside. They were only glad to have a place to stay.

At first inspection, they thought they were alone. The main barn was high and open, and empty stalls lined each side wall. They shook the snow off themselves and brushed off Galya before Peter began a more thorough inspection of the building. At the back of the barn, a corridor led to a smaller, low-ceilinged building. There, the stalls were lined with fresh straw—too fresh. In the far corner, a potbellied stove glowed from a waning fire. Next to it were baskets of beets, potatoes, and jerky.

"Hello?" Peter called. "Anyone here?"

Peter hadn't needed to call out and ask. Jakob had already found the girl, who appeared about as old as their middle sister, Tova. She cowered under a table near the stove and reminded Jakob of the feral cats, timid and wide-eyed with fear, that hid under their front porch at home. She wore only a *vyshyvanka,*[1] sized for a large woman, which fell to her knees. The garment must've been white at some point but was now yellowed with age and dirt. Jakob and the girl stared at each other, silent, until Peter noticed them.

Peter got down on his haunches and smiled at the girl. "Come on out now. It's all right. We won't hurt you."

She only continued to stare past him at nothing, until she glanced toward the one window in the room for a moment before staring back at nothing again.

"What is it? Someone here with you?"

Peter's answer came only too soon, as a man burst through the door, cursing and coughing until he nearly ran into them.

"What's this?" the man said, brushing the snow off his coat and tossing a rabbit carcass onto the pile of straw nearby before taking a gulp from a filthy, tarnished flask. "If I'd known we'd have company, I'd have tried to catch another. Then again, the trap's only big enough to catch one."

Peter scooted closer to Jakob, who was glad to feel his brother's arm around his shoulders.

The man came toward them, and as he bent near, the boys could smell the thick scent of alcohol on his breath. "I was getting tired of only one around here." He nodded toward the girl and laughed in a way that caused Jakob to shiver. The man paused for a moment, as if in thought, rubbing his chin with his gloved fingers. "You can stay, I suppose, but there'll be chores as long as you're here. For starters, skin that rabbit."

Peter nodded. "Do you have a knife, sir?"

"Right here." He pulled a blade from beneath his pants leg, and the metal gleamed against the glow of the coals in the stove. Just as it looked like he was going to hand it to Peter, the metal flashed, and the man had the tip of the knife pointed against the side of Peter's neck.

Peter stiffened, not daring to move.

"Don't be getting any ideas, little Jew. This is my barn, and I decide who goes and who stays. For the time being, you two are staying."

"Yes, sir," Peter said.

Galya whinnied from the stalls in the large section of the barn.

"Ah, so you have a horse. We'll make good use of him too."

The man pulled the knife away from Peter's neck and handed it to him. Peter skinned and cooked the rabbit, and the three of them ate in silence while the girl still hid under the table. The man offered some rabbit to her, but her countenance did not change, nor did she move. He threw a chunk of meat at her. "Have it your way, little miss. I don't care much now if *you* starve, seeing as how we've got company. Worthless little Jew whore."

Eventually the man drank until he passed out, and Peter and Jakob made a warm nest for themselves in the straw. "Do as he says for now, Jakob. We'll leave as soon as the storm stops," Peter whispered as he held Jakob close.

Peter began to recite the evening Shema, and Jakob tried to listen, to find comfort in the words, but he was unable to keep his eyes open. It was the first time he'd been warm in days.

What seemed like minutes later, he awoke to the sound of the girl whimpering. Jakob sat up to see what was the matter, but Peter pushed him down into the straw. "Stay there. Close your eyes and don't get up again. Don't *move*."

Peter inched in the direction of the sound, and Jakob couldn't help but look and see what was the matter, though he soon wished he never had. The man was on top of the girl, still under the table, her bony leg pushed to one side at an impossible angle, and he thrust against her in a way that made bits of the rabbit supper come up into the back of Jakob's throat. Jakob saw Peter grab a shovel and continue to move toward the man, who was working too hard at whatever awful thing he was doing to her to notice.

"Stop now, or this goes into your skull!" Peter yelled.

The man rose so quickly, apparently forgetting he was under a table, that he hit his head and cursed.

Peter brought the shovel down hard in the direction of the man's head, somehow missing entirely and slamming the shovel onto the floor. The man began to laugh, a sick, throaty laugh. Peter grew all the more angry, until the man turned over and pointed a gun at his head.

"You're no match for lead, boy." He cocked the trigger.

Peter backed up a step and dropped the shovel.

The man stood, pulling up his pants with his free hand.

The girl pulled her shirt over her knees and scurried back farther under the table, so far the darkness caused her to disappear from Jakob's sight.

"Over there." The man nodded toward a post at the corner of the empty calf stalls.

Peter obeyed, and the man grabbed a rope and ordered the girl out from under the table to help him tie Peter to the post. The girl's black hair fell in strings around her face, and though her face showed no emotion, new tears had washed the dirt away, leaving trails of clean skin in their path. She tied Peter's hands, then his ankles as the man continued to bark instructions at her and hold the gun to the side of Peter's head. She stayed close as the man walked across the room to get the knife Peter had used to skin and clean the rabbit, and before he returned, Jakob saw her whisper in Peter's ear, then kiss him, her thin lips like the wings of a butterfly against his face. Then she hurried back to her spot underneath the table.

"I should kill you, but you could come in useful. Instead, I will teach you the place of a Jew." He moved behind Peter with the knife, and spread the fingers of Peter's hand flat against the post. "I was thinking one finger, but there are three of you here. I will take one for each of you, so you will know what will happen to them, too, the next time you try to protect one of them."

That was when Peter's screaming began, as the man sliced through Peter's fifth finger. If it hadn't been for the snow, the screams would've awakened anyone within three kilometers of the barn, for certain. When the man started on Peter's fourth finger, Jakob clambered through the straw across the room and under the table to where the girl cowered.

All Jakob could do was close his eyes and cover his ears as the man sliced and laughed like a madman, moving on to the third finger. The knife, though shiny, was quite dull, and he hacked more forcefully. Peter screamed on and on, Jakob curled into himself as he had in the cupboard in Chudniv.

The girl nudged Jakob with her foot, startling him. She said nothing, only nodded toward Jakob's right, where the shovel Peter had intended to use lay half hidden under the straw. She nudged him again and nodded; then Jakob grabbed the shovel as the man focused on riving and holding down Peter's struggling arm. She took the shovel slowly from Jakob so as not to create a sudden movement the man might see. Surely she wasn't thinking of using it, Jakob thought. He'd never seen anyone with arms and legs so thin and pale. But she was on her feet before he could take another breath, tiptoeing behind the man, who was still laughing like a lunatic.

Jakob squeezed himself tight against the wall beneath the table as the girl raised the shovel without a sound. She lowered it as hard as her small arms could toward the man's head. As she did, the man turned. The sharp edge of the shovel embedded itself in the man's temple, and he crumpled to the ground.

She dropped the shovel and stared at the unmoving man. For what seemed like forever, Jakob watched as she stood and the man lay still in a heap at her feet.

"He's dead," Peter gasped.

Jakob knew this already, too familiar with the unmistakable slump of flesh in the absence of a soul. But it did not make him brave enough to come out from under the table. Once again he'd hidden and done nothing while someone else he loved was hurt. He thought of Faigy and how she'd whimpered so, her cries for Mama choked by the darkness closing in around her when the man in the black robes stuffed her under his cloak. Jakob had done nothing then, and he'd done nothing to help Peter either.

Peter sagged against the post, sweat and splatters of blood and tears of his own running together down his neck, blood pooling on the floor under his hand. He struggled to lift his head and look at the girl. "You saved our lives."

The girl moved toward Peter, grabbed the knife, and began cutting the ropes on Peter's wrists and ankles. Only then did Jakob run to Peter and cling to him.

"My name is Raisa," she finally spoke as she wrapped Peter's hand.

"Thank you, Raisa."

"I'm the one who should thank you." A flush of color rose to her cheeks, the only sign of emotion she'd shown besides silent tears since they found her. She continued bandaging Peter's hand with scraps of the dead man's shirt. "When the bleeding slows, I know how to sew up and clean a wound."

Peter's pain didn't keep him from helping Raisa pull the dead man from the barn. The snow still fell in a near-whiteout torrent, so Jakob held a lantern at the barn door to make sure they found their way back from the edge of the woods where they dragged him. Later, by the warmth of the potbellied stove, Raisa made strips of bandages and boiled them in lye and water. She sewed the gaping holes over Peter's knuckles as gently as she could and spread a poultice made of dried yarrow over the sutured wounds, then wrapped it all with the clean cloths.

"How do you know how to do this?" Peter asked.

"My mother was a medicine woman in our village." She nodded in the direction of where they'd dragged the man's corpse. "He kept me from running, but he didn't pay attention to anything else I did. I collected herbs in the fall when I had the chance."

"Where is your family?"

She stopped wrapping and met Peter's eyes. "I am the only one who survived."

Raisa went on to explain how she ran when the raid began, as far and as fast as she could, and how she'd watched from a distance as the whole village burned. She had nothing, of course, and this man had found her and seemed kind at first when she came upon him and the barn. He'd provided her with food and basic clothing. But when the winter set in, he began to rape her, and it became obvious she couldn't leave unless she wished to die either from him or from exposure, since she had no horse or warm clothes or shoes (he'd made sure of that, burning them in the fire one night when she'd tried).

"Come with us, Raisa," Peter said. "We can at least take you to the next town, somewhere with a safe family."

She agreed, and the three of them stayed in the barn until the snowstorm broke, eating all they could, mending themselves and their tattered clothes, altering shoes and *valenki*[2] for Raisa. Even Galya eventually appeared rested, happy to munch on the straw and a couple of stray bags of oats the pogromshchik left behind.

The snow stopped and the sky turned blue again, and though it was cold, the world appeared clean and new.

1994

South Haven, Michigan

CHAPTER 14

"Coming!" Nel hollered at the ringing phone, sure she'd hear the sound of the nurse or Jakob's physician on the other end of the line.

"How are you, Nel?"

"Oh, Sam. Hi." She tried to catch her breath.

"Were you out running?" he asked.

"No, no, just running to get to the phone. I thought it might be the hospital. I talked to the nurse earlier, but I thought you might be the doctor. Dad's not doing well at all." Did he sound annoyed with her? They'd only spoken a couple of times between the funeral and the day Jakob fell, but that couldn't be helped. She tried to ignore the hurt in his voice. "I'm so glad you called. I was wondering if you might help Matthew send some of my supplies out here."

"So you need your *supplies* but not me?" His emphasis of the word hurt. He knew about her deadlines. More than that, he knew all she'd lost, and now with her dad in such bad shape … was he really that self-centered? Or had she simply not realized that about him before?

He had actually offered to come out there and be with her the day Jakob fell, to find a partner to cover his cases for a few days, but she'd refused, telling him she was too stressed and needed to handle it on her own. She was glad now that she'd declined. She didn't have the energy or patience to assuage whatever insecurities or needs he had at the moment.

She paused, trying to maintain her composure. "Never mind about the supplies. I'll have Matthew send them. It's just that Sandra's on my back about these deadlines, and the doctor said yesterday that Dad has a long road of recovery ahead of him. I don't even know if he'll make it out of the hospital at this point. But I've got to at least finish the bracelets for Anna Wilds and get those necklace prototypes to Sandra before the end of the week."

Sandra was Nel's tireless but demanding agent. And Anna Wilds was a Hollywood producer who'd paid a hefty advance for Nel to make a set of six matching bracelets personalized with inlaid birth-stones and unique engravings representing each of the six members of her family.

Sam sighed on the other end of the line. "So you don't know when you're coming back?"

A part of Nel wondered if she would be coming back, but she didn't dare tell him that. "No. I'm sorry—I just don't know. Dr. Weiss said recovery could take a long time. Regardless, I can't wait to work on my orders."

Sam was silent.

Nel couldn't contain her impatience. "What is it, Sam? Just tell me. Just say it." She knew he was still frustrated with what she'd said during the argument they'd had the night before she left for South Haven. That night she'd thought perhaps she could calm herself down by meeting Sam for a couple of drinks before having to face the reality of flying home the next day for her mom's funeral.

"The usual?" Sam had asked Nel when the waiter came to the table.

"Yes, the usual, thanks."

"I'll have the same. Thanks, Stu." Sam, on a first-name basis with the staff, unfolded his napkin with a flip of his wrist and laid it on his lap. On the Half Shell was the nicest seafood restaurant in Santa Fe and had been the site of their first date. Sam's cordial pleasantry faded, and he had looked at Nel in a hard way that caught her breath. "This might not be the best time to bring this up, but I need to talk to you."

Stu set a plate of raw oysters, condiments, and two martinis on the table.

Sam poured a generous amount of Tabasco on one of the jiggly creatures and let it slide off the shell onto his tongue before he swallowed, then followed it with a soda cracker. "It feels like you run from me every time I try to get close, Nel. And you're running more and more. Now you're going home for the first time in how long? Two years? And I guess before you leave, I feel like I need to be sure of you."

"Sure of me, how? You have me most every night, Sam." She unfolded her napkin, spread it over her knees, and smoothed it down.

"In case you haven't noticed, I care about you."

She nodded, sipping her martini.

"I don't know if I can do this whole 'without strings' thing any-more. We're not getting any younger."

"What am I not giving you? What's not enough?"

He leaned toward her, reaching under the table to grab one of her hands. "A lifetime."

Nel sat back and crossed her arms. "That's not something I feel like I can give."

"Why? What's really keeping you from diving in?"

"Sam, as much as I enjoy our time together, you'll get tired of me and you know it. If you're asking me for honesty, at least be honest with yourself." He'd had as many, or more, short-term relationships as she had over the years, his reputation for wooing nurses widely known, even outside the hospital community.

"My point exactly." He sat back, crossed his arms as well, and smiled provocatively at her.

"Exactly what?"

"Your sass. You're making me fall in love with you."

Nel, incredulous, studied him. His perfectly shaved face. His strong, handsome features. His forehead, wrinkled with sincerity. "Did you say what I think you said?"

"And what would that be?" He reached across the table and offered her his hand. But she stayed where she was.

"Love. You said love."

"I did. And?"

Nel was speechless. Disappointed, more than anything. She cared about him, yes, but she didn't want to marry him.

He sat back, looking resigned. "I'm sorry, Nel. Really. This was too much to put on you, especially with your mom's funeral. I'll get the tab and we can go."

Frustrated, Nel didn't argue. She pushed the chair away from the table and headed out to the restaurant's patio, which backed up to the black desert, the mountains barely visible as looming shadows in the moonless, starless night. She felt Sam behind her and turned.

"Go take care of things with the funeral and with your dad. We can figure this out later." Sam leaned in to kiss her forehead.

Nel stepped past him and headed toward her car in the parking lot.

"Good night, Sam," she called over her shoulder. Her breath turned to mist in the air that had chilled considerably.

Now, on the phone hundreds of miles away, Sam's voice held an air of entitlement. "I've thought a lot since you left. About me. About you. About us. About the best decision of my life."

"Which is?" Nel was glad he couldn't see her cringe on the other end of the line.

"Deciding I want to marry you."

The phone line crackled faintly as Nel twisted and twirled the cord around her fingers.

"Don't you get tired of it, Nel? The one-night stands? The loneliness? The thought of never having children or a legacy to leave behind? Life's got to be more than that."

"Yes. I mean, no, I'm not tired of it. I don't think about it. I haven't had time. Why are you pushing for this so much right now? I can't even think straight with everything that's happened in the past month—" She stopped, the realization hitting her like a ton of bricks. "Who is she, Sam?"

"What?" He sounded incredulous.

"You're giving me an ultimatum because you want out. There's someone else, and you want out, right?"

He was silent for a moment too long. "Look, Nel, it's not that simple."

Unbelievable. "Sure it is. You knew I would say no, and you need out, but you don't want to be the bad guy."

"Come back to Santa Fe, Nel. There's nursing homes and home health services in South Haven, people you can hire out there to take care of your dad. Just come back and let me love you."

"You essentially admit to me there's another woman, and in the same breath you tell me to come back? When Dad's near death in the hospital? Not to mention Mom dying?" Outside the window above the kitchen sink, she watched David as he stood alongside a couple of sawhorses he'd fashioned into a workbench in Mattie's side yard. He sliced through a long piece of trim.

"I didn't admit anything. When you get back, we'll start new from where we left off. It's like I said before you left. I need to be sure of you," Sam said, his voice rough and sensuous. For a fleeting moment, the anger left her gut, until she looked back out the window at David.

"I don't believe you." She hesitated. "Besides, something new has started, Sam. Just not something with you."

CHAPTER 15

The plastic mattress of the bed in his new room at Lakeview Meadows Nursing Home did nothing to cushion the metal frame beneath it, but Jakob had to admit it was better than the hospital bed, which had felt like lying on a medieval rack. Neither bed did anything to ease Jakob's muscle and hip pain, which were so intense he needed help turning from side to side. Throughout the night Jakob's aides would turn him over every couple of hours and replace his urine-soaked pads at the same time.

"Hurry up, now. Don't you know I have to get back to the office?" Jakob blurted, then grimaced in pain.

"You're in the nursing home. Been here nearly a week already, don't you know that? Ain't no office for you to go to anymore," the nursing aide huffed as she rolled him on his side toward the window.

Jakob watched a crease of yellow stretch wider at the horizon, the cockcrow ushering in a shade of blue—the "welkin blush," as Shakespeare had called it—that reminded him of the blue of the lost stone, of Catherine's eyes.

"Catherine?"

"I'm Joan," the aide barked. "Ain't no Catherine here." Joan was rougher than some of the staff. She didn't speak a word—neither a kind nor a rude one—as she used the sheets to turn Jakob like a drenched log floating in a river. His eyes watered from the smell of her drugstore perfume, which was nothing like the gentle scent of White Shoulders he used to buy for Catherine.

"Don't be so rough," he pleaded.

One of her fingernails, painted bright red and embedded with cheap, fake rhinestones on the squared-off tips, scratched at the skin around his privates as she cleaned him with cold baby wipes. She rolled her eyes and mumbled something about drinking wine when she got home, and never mind that it was morning; it was five o'clock somewhere.

Jakob remembered little from his three-week stay at the hospital, except that the doctor—Weiss, he thought his name was—said he couldn't tell which came first, the fall or the fracture. When he was lucid, Jakob tried to explain he heard his hip *pop* before he fell. But like so many others lately, Dr. Weiss had nodded his head but essentially dismissed what Jakob had been trying to say. A ninety-four-year-old man can't be playing with a full deck after all, especially a man who recently lost his wife and required rehabilitation, occupational therapists, speech therapists, and physical therapists pushing him with exercise and recovery techniques just to get him to function.

"The old elevator's skipped a few floors," he'd heard staff cackling outside his door. Jakob wanted to yell at them, but he didn't have the energy. And for all he knew, they were right. Scenes from his past got all mixed up in his head. Sometimes he realized this. And events of the past few weeks were entirely blank. But memories he hadn't thought of in decades resurfaced, terrifying him and reigniting a shame he'd stuffed away for years. He remembered burying

Catherine one moment, and the next, he expected her to walk into the room, which on occasion looked an awful lot like his bedroom until one of the nurses or aides came in and turned him again. When he was aware, he felt like he might as well be dead, the way staff talked about him as if he weren't in the room. Nursing aides laughed and sniggered about their sex lives like he couldn't hear them while they changed his soiled briefs. They wiped his hind end with the door wide open as if he didn't care about his privacy anymore. He wished he had the wherewithal to tell them how well he and Catherine had put his parts to good use back in the day.

"Time for your meds, Mr. Jake." Nyesha, one of the day aides who doubled as the medication nurse, set a pleated paper medicine cup full of pills on the table beside his bed as the night aide left the room.

"Are you wantin' to eat in here this morning, or can I take you to the dining room?"

"Catherine will be here soon. I'll eat with her."

Nyesha cocked her head to the side and forced a grin. "Now Mr. Jake, do you know where you are?"

He looked around the room. "Home."

She frowned.

He looked around the room again, his brow furrowing as he frowned.

"You're at Lakeview. And it's a Tuesday morning. It's November already. Thanksgiving'll be here before we know it."

"Morning?" Jakob could've sworn by *The Andy Griffith Show* on the TV that he'd just had dinner. He rubbed the stubble on the jowly skin around his chin.

"Yes, sir, it's morning. So would you like me to get you cleaned up a bit and take you to the dining room for breakfast?"

"Nah."

"You sure? Old Ms. Biernacki'll miss you at her table out there." Nyesha winked. "Besides, do you good to wake up a bit, socialize. Nel's coming before lunch, remember?"

"Nel?"

"Yes, your daughter. You love when she comes and reads to you."

A bit of the fog lifted from his head then as he thought about Nel. "That's right. I'll eat and clean up in here if it's all the same."

"Sounds good." Nyesha smiled.

Jakob admired the small gap between her two front teeth. The shapely girl couldn't have been more than twenty, but he was no good at estimating a person's age anymore. Everybody looks like a baby when you're ninety-four years old. Her skin was the shade of milk chocolate. She wore her hair cropped, which showed off the curvy features of her face. Jakob caught himself wishing he could reach out and run his fingers along the smoothness of her cheek, even her hand. But he was an old man. He might have to be reminded of the day and where he was, but he knew better than to have the nursing-home staff think he was a pervert.

Nyesha pulled the rolling table over the top of his bed, then set a washbasin of soapy warm water and a stack of white washcloths on it. To this she added a cup of cold water, his toothbrush, dentures, and a plastic spit pan. She plugged in his electric razor and set it on the nightstand next to him so he could reach it. "Did I forget anything, young man?"

"Pshaw."

"If you're sure, then." She turned the channel to a morning news program then turned back to face Jakob. "Wash your face and get your teeth in as best you can. I'll come back before your breakfast arrives to help you get at the rest of your body and set you up in a chair. We'll get you looking all spiffed up for your daughter." The silver cross around her neck glinted against the first rays of sunlight coming through the window.

EARLY 1904

Eastern Ukraine, Russian Empire

CHAPTER 16

"Scho vy tut robyte, dity?"[†]

Peter, Jakob, and Raisa, traveling together, jumped at the voice and then exhaled relief as an elderly woman, her bent form wrapped in layers and her head covered in a floral, hand-embroidered scarf, stepped into the kitchen.

Raisa had seen the little house they stood in before either of the boys. She had been in charge of Galya's reins on account of Peter's severed fingers, and Jakob had been pressing his cold-numb face tight against Peter's back. When he'd finally lifted his head, he, too, glimpsed the little wooden home with whitewashed window frames and a bright-blue door in the valley below them. They had been riding up and down the foothills of the Carpathian Mountains for a couple of days by then, afraid to get too near villages but desperate yet again for food and warmth. All three of them figured the little home in the valley would be emptied and looted like the rest they'd found, or worse, with a murdered family decaying inside. But regardless, none of them cared anymore about the dead bodies. They'd be grateful to put anything in their growling bellies with or without

---

† What are you children doing here?

corpses staring at them. And if someone was there who would kill them, at least they'd have eaten something before they died.

As they rode closer to the cottage, their assumptions that it was abandoned appeared accurate. The turquoise front door creaked as the wind pushed it back and forth. From the smashed objects and furniture strewn across the front yard, it was clear that the home had already been ransacked and cleared of most anything of value.

Peter ran his hands above the coals in the fireplace. "They're still warm. But barely. The pogromshchik must've been here recently. They probably won't return anytime soon."

Jakob stood by the fireplace next to Peter, and he tried to glean whatever warmth he could from the coals while Peter and Raisa began rummaging through cupboards to grab whatever they could find, a morsel of food, anything that might help them on their journey.

That's when the old woman scared them as she shuffled out from the shadows of the back bedroom.

"My name is Luda," she offered, her face reminding Jakob of a dried apple with all the wrinkles and framed by her bright-red head scarf. Her left eye was nearly swollen shut and severely bruised.

Peter explained, "We don't intend to harm you, *baba*. We are only injured and hungry children."

The saggy folds of her cheeks curved into a grin when she saw Jakob. She ran to him, scooped him up, and held him, rocking him close like Mama had. Jakob shrank back from her affection.

Soon the old woman began to weep, then wail, as she told the boys how the pogromshchik came in the early morning hours a few days earlier, raping her and leaving her for dead, then taking her family, her son and daughter-in-law and their four children, to the woods nearby, where they shot them. Her youngest grandson had been about Jakob's age. She'd give anything to hold him again.

Luda's lack of teeth made her appear chinless, Jakob thought as she held his face in her hands. Her knuckles were fat and crooked. And her swollen eye only added to her harsh appearance. Even so, Luda's pale-blue eyes felt like a lake of sympathy washing over him. "Do not let the evil harden your heart, my son. You must believe God is bigger than all this."

Later, over the weak borscht Luda made with Raisa's help from the few beets and onions she'd hidden under the floorboards, she told the boys they were not far from Hungary. She sketched out a map for them detailing how to reach the border. She told them about the location of a village of Christians who would help them. She said many Christians all over Austria-Hungary and Germany were trying to help the Jews escape, and that with the stones Papa had given Peter, they should be able to buy a train ticket to Rotterdam and then the ship passage to America. She knew this from many others who had passed by her house, tens if not hundreds like them. That is why the pogromshchik had raided her home—they learned that Luda and her son were helping Jews escape.

"Stay as long as you like here to rest and heal," Luda offered.

Jakob and Peter, and Raisa especially, hesitated. Surely the home would be raided again.

"They have no more use for an old woman. They finished what they came to do here," Luda assured them, as if sensing the reason for their hesitation.

Once again desperate for warmth and exhausted from running, the boys stayed, the longest they stayed anywhere on their journey.

They were careful to blow out the candles at night and search the hills for invaders before they went out to check the traps they'd set for rabbit or squirrel during the day. Luda helped Raisa nurse Peter's severed hand until the gray and yellow oozing stopped and new, pink skin began to grow around the edges. Luda had stockpiled dried yarrow, too, and together, she and Raisa made more poultices.

When it was time to leave, the trio offered—Peter nearly begged—for Luda to come with them, and she finally, tearfully agreed, collecting what was left of family photographs and mementos. She covered Jakob and Raisa in extra shawls and woolens. She gave Peter what was left of her son's clothing too. Peter walked while Luda, Raisa, and Jakob rode on the back of Galya. In the end, Luda would only go as far as the next shtetl, to the home of one of the Christian families she'd told them about.

Their names were Russie and Chaim, and the couple and their three children—one daughter close to Raisa's age—recognized Luda. Despite their polite protests, Jakob, Peter, Raisa, and Luda were presented with dish after dish of soups and sausages and desserts, the best of what they had, which wasn't much, judging from their dirt floors and leaky roof. But still the family insisted on lavishing the four tattered guests with hospitality, as Luda had with her meager borscht, and just as Mama and Papa always had for visitors too. Russie and Chaim tucked them into their warm beds, while they slept on the floor. Chaim even fed and watered Galya and gave him a spot in one of their barns for the night while one of their horses stayed outside.

Jakob lay on the straw mattress, the first mattress he'd slept on since home, and he listened to Raisa giggle for the first time as she snuggled in with the other children on the other side of the room. On the wall next to his bed hung an icon of a kind-looking man with a beard whom he recognized as Messiah Yeshua from the icons and books Sasha the priest brought to their home in Chudniv. Blue-and-red robes fell gently around the icon Yeshua's shoulders. In the painting, His eyes were dark and gentle like a doe. A circle of light rimmed in gold surrounded His soft, brown hair, and His right hand raised in a way that reminded Jakob of his mama's as she had reached toward his forehead on dank days when she worried he might have a fever. To the right of that image hung a large cross, like the kind Sasha the priest had worn around his neck, with Yeshua hanging there, dead. Lifeless. Unable to help them or deliver them or save them from the long and ever-cruel nights and days.

Which image of Yeshua was real?

Or were either of them?

Hear, O Israel, the Lord is One …

Jakob heard Peter faithfully whispering the evening Shema, and he wanted to believe the words.

Jehovah-Shammah.

He wanted to believe they weren't alone.

"Be brave," Raisa whispered as she held Jakob tight and kissed him good-bye on the cheek the next morning.

"Keep your heart soft, little one," Luda whispered next.

Chaim lifted Jakob onto Galya behind Peter and pulled the buckles and ties of supplies tight on the saddle, then gave Galya a cheery smack on the hindquarters to start them off.

As they rode away, Jakob turned and kept his eye on Luda and the family waving until they rode over the hillside. It was the only time besides the day they first left home that he looked behind, and when he did, he saw a silver cross around Luda's neck gleaming in the sun.

"Our help doesn't come from the hills, Jakob," Peter said over his shoulder. "Our help comes from Yahweh. Psalm 121. Do you know what that song was written for?"

Jakob shook his head.

"For pilgrims. Pilgrims headed to the Promised Land."

1994

———————————————

South Haven, Michigan

CHAPTER 17

A teenager in an overtrimmed Camaro threw his arm in the air, middle digit raised, and laid on his horn as Nel struggled to steer and ended up curbing the right wheel of Jakob's Crown Victoria as she pulled into the parking lot of Lakeview Meadows Nursing Home. She shrank down in the cream leather seat and felt heat rise to her face. She'd been driving the behemoth ever since she'd arrived in Michigan, but still she hadn't gotten used to the difference between the enormous size of it compared to her little Volkswagen Jetta back in Santa Fe. She'd never told her dad about the Jetta. He'd throw a fit if he knew she'd never bought an American-made car since she'd bought her first VW Bug all those years ago.

As she walked toward the entrance, she waved at the usual half dozen hunched and graying residents staring at her from behind the panorama windows, where nurses parked them in their wheelchairs after lunch. She considered the stretched-out, single-story nursing home, yellow brick from the seventies adding to the morose facade of the building, and guilt squeezed at her heart for the hundredth time since Jakob had fallen and she found him on the floor. If only she'd heard him get up that morning. If only she'd found him sooner. If only he hadn't gotten an infection that kept him in the hospital three weeks instead of one. If only he hadn't had to go to Lakeview for rehabilitation. If only she'd brought him straight home.

Now she felt guilty for not arriving before lunchtime to visit him, but she'd been sidetracked. Matthew had been kind enough to pack up and send her four boxes of her jewelry supplies so she could stay on deadline as best she could. Catalogs and their customers couldn't have cared less about the woes of her nonagenarian father. She'd unpacked the supplies and taken over Jakob's lapidary room and was relieved to find that she remembered, with only a few initial glitches, how to carve cabochons with his outdated equipment. She was especially grateful that Jakob's old rock tumbler still worked since her own would have been way too large to ship. She used a tumbler more than anything with her designs, which were much more rustic than Jakob's precise work. Matthew could work on the replicable designs sold in the catalogs. He really didn't need to be apprenticed—he had taught Nel many new techniques. He'd be more than capable of taking her prototypes and expanding on them once they were approved by Sandra and the catalog buyers.

But many orders she had to create herself—commissioned orders from wealthy customers who paid for her signature, personalized line, and the trademark scripted "Nel" she discreetly engraved on those items alone. She'd been putting the finishing touches on a turquoise cabochon for one of those commissions when she'd realized the time and remembered her lunch date with her dad.

Lakeview's revolving door pushed her from the cold December air into the moist warmth of the front lobby, where the smell of disinfectants and fresh greenery greeted her, reconfirming her decision to bring Jakob here instead of the other nursing homes she'd visited in the brief time she'd had to choose one. She'd had an aversion to any facility, but if he had to go to one, Lakeview's attention to detail, the decor and holiday celebrations, and the administration's conscientious efforts to personalize care took the edge off the inevitable decision. She'd heard horror stories from friends and the news about patients lying for hours on urine-soaked pads, bedsores festering deeper as they lay neglected for hours while aides sat around laughing, thumbing through catalogs, and stuffing snacks in their mouths. Lakeview seemed to offer the best geriatric specialty care and amenities available. Art therapy. Music. Exercise classes. Pet visits. Games. She'd felt certain this was the best place for Jakob. And so far, the kind staff helped affirm the choice whenever she visited. Between Mattie and Nel, Jakob was rarely without a visitor for more than a day. Not even Mattie, who was more particular than Nel, had found anything concerning when she came to visit Jakob.

Nel found her dad sitting in a chair by the window in his room. He wore his old gray wool cardigan pulled loosely over the top of a blue oxford shirt. The sweater was buttoned up crooked, the left side hanging lower, which matched the lopsided droop of his saggy neck. He lifted his bloodshot eyes to her, the weakened eyelids too loose for their bony sockets. There again was the look of an old basset hound behind the thick bifocals.

Nel leaned toward him and grasped his hands. "Hey, Dad."

"Well, well, well. Look who's here." Long wrinkles on his jowly cheeks stretched into a smile, and his eyebrows lifted in a moment of acknowledgment before he looked back out at the snow collecting on the arms of the evergreens dotting the rolling hills of the pasture and golf course beyond.

Nel sat in a chair next to him, and she fought the temptation to get weepy, as much from the drastic, rapid wasting that had occurred since his fall as from feeling so overwhelmed by this disaster happening so close to her mother's death. She knew from friends and stories in the news how people married so long often die within a short time of each other. Living away from Mom and Dad had done more harm than good by isolating her from the more gradual ebb of life others who lived close to family experienced with their aging parents.

She picked up one of his favorite books, *Reflections from the North Country* by Sigurd F. Olson, which sat next to his empty denture cup on the nightstand, beside a framed picture of him and Mom. He'd grown quiet—the doctors had said depression was common in elderly patients who fall—and she'd discovered reading helped ease the sometimes awkward silence of their visits.

"Now where'd we leave off? Here we go. The chapter on 'Flashes of Insight.'" Jake's countenance relaxed as Nel read. When she finished the paragraph, the room stilled, and both of them stared out at the snow. Eventually Jakob turned toward her when he realized she had quit reading, and she looked deep into his hazel eyes that were flecked with all the colors of a fall hillside. How fast the seasons had changed.

"I gotta talk to you about something," she finally said.

His eyes widened and wrinkled, his mouth flattening with concern. "What is it, Catherine? What is wrong?"

Catherine. His lapses in lucidity, compounded with the severity of his episodes of delirium in the hospital, broke Nel's heart. For a while she wondered if she should correct him, but that only agitated him. So as much as she could, she went along with his confusion until he slipped back into reality and remembered who she was. His short-term memory was the worst. Most days he was quick to talk about stories from when she was growing up, from when he and Catherine dated, and about the trips they'd taken. But then he couldn't recall if he'd eaten breakfast or where to find or how to use the nurse call light, which he'd been taught to do tens of times. She wondered more and more about dementia, his family history, and the mystery of his past that Catherine had been researching.

"Nothing's wrong … There's a few things to fix around the house, and I think I'm going to ask David Butler to do that for us, if that's okay."

"Okay."

"And I figured out how to get you some help at home. I'm going to stay here with you for as long as I need to."

He didn't reply.

"Dad? Do you understand what I'm saying? I'm going to be your help."

He turned toward her, and she was surprised to see tears puddling in his eyes. "I never wanted to be a burden to you, Catherine."

She scooted her chair closer to him. "Dad. It's me, Nel."

He studied her face, and she saw recognition flash across his eyes. "Nel. Of course. What did I say?"

"Never mind that. You're not a burden, Dad. I want to do this."

"It's all too much." He turned away.

Nel sat back and studied him, this man who had held her on his shoulders for summer parades, hooked fish for her, carried her into the house and lifted her into bed on moonlit summer nights after she had fallen asleep on burlap-covered cushions under the stars. He'd always been the strongest, kindest man in her life, and she wasn't going to risk going back to Santa Fe and leaving him to die without her mom. "I don't want to waste whatever time we have left."

With as much lucidity as he'd had since his fall, he searched her eyes, and the tears that had been gathering in his fell. "Neither do I."

"Okay, then. It's settled. I'm staying."

Nyesha nearly tumbled into the room before he could argue. Her arms were loaded with a stack of linens and waterproof bed pads. "I brought your linens since you're up, Mr. Jake." She set them down and nodded toward Nel as she began stripping the bed. "Meant to get this done before you came to visit."

"Thanks, Nyesha."

"You're welcome." She smiled and gave Jakob a quick hug, then she tucked in the sheets and spread out the clean pads.

Nel took a deep breath, considering whether or not she should broach the other thing she wanted to talk about with him. She didn't want to upset him. But at the same time, she didn't know how many more times she'd have to talk to him about her mom's research. And what if it was information she and her dad both needed to know?

"There's one more thing I wanted to talk to you about, Dad."

Nyesha wrapped up the dirty linens and stuffed them into the hamper as she left the room.

Nel pulled the envelope out of her bag and showed him the picture of the two boys.

"Dad … who's Peter?"

Jakob's eyes widened as he took the photo from her, then squinted as he strained to see the image clearly.

"Where did you get this?" His voice held an urgency Nel hadn't heard before.

"Mom had been working on some genealogy before she died. An envelope came from New York, immigration services, and this picture was in it. I don't recognize the name Maevski. I thought Mom's family came from Pennsylvania. Who would we know from Russia?"

"Ukraine," he corrected her.

"Ukraine? You know about this?"

He continued to stare at the photo. His hands were trembling now.

"When you were in the hospital, you kept mentioning someone named Peter. Is that one of the boys in this picture? Was he a friend of yours?"

"I ... I had a brother."

CHAPTER 18

A brother?

Jakob had never mentioned a brother. Nel couldn't remember a time he'd talked about his parents, for that matter. Catherine never mentioned anyone either, besides Jakob's parents on occasion, and mostly about how they'd built the lake house and passed it down in their will to him. Maybe it had been a generational thing that he had never wanted to talk much about them, or anything, for that matter. But maybe there was more, and that's what Catherine was trying to find out before she died.

How could Nel continue with that research? She hardly knew where to begin besides the envelope with the ship manifest. She couldn't stop thinking about the names.

Peter Maevski, 14.

Jakob Maevski, 5.

The boys in the photo had to be her father and who she now knew was his older brother. It made sense for Peter to have passed away already, but when? And how? How had they come to America? And why had they come alone?

All kinds of scenarios were running through her mind, but she'd have to look into it more later. She would ask Mattie about it all—maybe Catherine had confided in her about what she was looking for. In the meantime, she had to finish her prototypes and that bracelet.

As Nel finished setting up the supplies and equipment Matthew had sent her, she admired how Jakob had arranged his lapidary worktable to catch the daylight as the sun moved from east to west. The long table had a view of several bird feeders hanging from the sycamores and river birch, and the lake beyond that. On one end of the table sat a Facetron machine. Across the back wall, he had placed several multidrawered metal boxes. On the other end sat old coffee cans full of tweezers and dop sticks, wax and needles, and gem-finishing tools of all kinds. Various sizes of plastic containers— former ice cream, cottage cheese, and salt buckets—and stacks of cigar boxes labeled with the names of raw stones rested beneath the table.

Nel picked a chunk of quartz off the windowsill, crystals jutting in different directions. She blew the dust off it. "You and your rocks, Dad." She smiled, thinking of the hundreds of times she sat by his side as he worked the Facetron machine, sketched designs, and examined each rock for the perfect angle of cuts with his loupe on one eye.

She picked up a squared-off, deep-green stone from a coffee tin full of them and studied the lines Jakob had drawn on it with pencil. "Only someone with a heart for the stone can see the best angle to make the first cut. Someone who loves the stone well. Who takes time to get to know it. Who's not afraid to feel the edges and get close to it. Who sees beyond the dirt and finds the precise section that will most reflect and refract light," he'd explained over the years.

Collections of uncut stones called *roughs* peeked from beneath the lids of their overfilled cigar boxes: purple and lavender amethyst; chunks of emerald jade; nuggets of turquoise; slabs of tigereye, glass obsidian, Ceylon sapphire, blue Burma spinel, ruby, and topaz. Under the windowsill, Jakob had set olive jars filled with various types of opal swimming in pools of glycerin to keep them from drying out and cracking. Boxes full of halved geodes and beryl, corundum, and tourmaline rested under the table.

Oversize mayonnaise jugs full of grinding and buffing powders lined an antique oak dressing vanity, and within each drawer were more coffee cans of various tools he used to polish and shape and secure stones as he worked them on the Facetron or by hand. One can held a dozen old brushes from Catherine's blush compacts. Another held toothbrushes, tweezers, hemostats, and chisels. Another drawer held ring boxes and baby-food jars and square-inch boxes lined with aging, yellow-edged foam for storing finished stones. And a bookshelf against the back wall of the room was stuffed full of gem-club and magazine journals, binders straining with faceting designs and techniques, graph papers covered with angle calculations and diagrams. All the years spent measuring and developing mechanical equations at Brake-All had helped Jakob hone his hobby well. He'd even created his own faceting designs, which had won awards at gem shows and had been published in *Lapidary Journal*. The mathematical aspects of those designs alone were a feat few hobbyists were able to perfect, and the sheer volume of all he'd created, museum worthy.

Nel pulled open the tiny drawers of a desktop cabinet where Jakob kept all his metal findings, many similar to the sorts she worked with: silver and gold clasps and holders, rings and pendants—all for securing and displaying finished stones for wear. The settings depended on the type of cut: faceted, like the traditional diamond sorts of cuts, or cabochons, a smooth, usually oval-shaped cut that looked as if they were sliced off the side of an egg and polished to a near mirror-like finish. These fascinated Nel the most because it took the greatest amount of skill and talent to see precisely how to choose and center the section of stone to reveal its prettiest pattern. She'd practiced at shaping stones for nearly a decade before her craftsmanship matched Jakob's. And to think that folks walked by rocks like these along footpaths and hiking trails every day, with no idea what such rocks could become.

A trickle of sweat rolled down the small of Nel's back as she pushed and lifted as best she could the boxes full of unused laps and long-forgotten supplies from under the table and moved them to one side of the room.

She wasn't trying to be nosy when she made the next discovery in a box in the farthest corner under the table. As she had with the other boxes, she lifted the flaps to see what was inside so she could arrange the boxes by their contents, if similar. At first she only noticed more dowel rods, wrapped chunks of dop wax, and a large collection of old tweezers. She was about to set the box aside when a tarnished silver cup, with something wrapped in cheesecloth stuffed inside it, caught her eye. She studied the intricate design of a village etched on the outside of the cup, thatched-roof homes, fences, livestock, and rolling hills scrolling across the cup's surface. The work reminded her of the etchings she used in her silver and rose-gold jewelry.

As she pulled the cheesecloth out of the cup, the doorbell rang, startling her. Something fell to the floor and slid across the wood beneath a pair of old horsehair, swivel chairs.

"Coming!" she called as whoever was at the door followed the ring with knocking.

"You're out of breath."

"David—hi! What are you doing here?" She ran her fingers through her hair, suddenly self-conscious.

"I never did apologize for the prom."

She feigned annoyance and crossed her arms. "As a matter of fact, you never did."

He held up a bag with the Sherman's logo on it. "Thought maybe ice cream would be a start?"

"I was kind of in the middle of something ..."

"It's okay. I know I'm unannounced. I can just leave it and come back another time. But you've been having to handle some rough stuff. And if I remember correctly, mint chocolate chip is your favorite."

When she hesitated, the look on his face reminded Nel of a middle school boy who'd overspent on a Valentine's gift for a crush. "Oh, come in. Maybe you can help me—I lost something. Besides, I've been wanting to talk to you about fixing some things on the house."

He followed her into the kitchen.

"Just set that on the counter and come with me," Nel said over her shoulder as she headed back to Jakob's lapidary room. "Remember how Dad's a rock hound?"

"Yeah, sorta."

"I've been moving stuff around to set up a workspace in here. My agent—Sandra—she's breathing down my neck about finishing a couple of projects that can't wait." She got on her knees and pressed her cheek to the floor to scan and feel around under the chairs. "Anyway, I dropped something just when you rang the doorbell."

Sam crouched down and held something out to her that flashed in the sunlight angling through the window. "Is this it?"

She sat back and gasped. "Yeah … I think it must be." She took the stone from his hand. Nel had never seen a gem faceted so beautifully, round in shape and at least as large as a golf ball. "Aquamarine, maybe. Maybe sapphire. Topaz. But probably aquamarine."

"You've never seen this before?"

"No … it fell out of this cup I found stashed at the bottom of this last box of Dad's things I was moving to make room for my stuff." She nodded toward the cup on the edge of the table. She turned the stone every which way, up against the light of the window, the light of the ceiling lamp, studying every facet. "I think the top facets create a Star of David."

"Yeah?" David, sounding distracted, picked up the silver cup and turned it in his hand. He pulled a couple of folded pieces of paper out of the bottom of it, as well as a tattered object resembling a tassel. "Did you see these, Nel? This one looks like it's written in Slavic or something."

He handed her the two papers. On one, a friable piece of parchment, someone had drawn a faceting diagram with words that did look Slavic, although if Nel's growing hunch was right, they would prove to be Ukrainian. Angles were jotted down the right-hand side and words on the left, with lines and notes pointing to various parts of the shape, which seemed the same as the stone she held in her hand. She'd have to look closer with a loupe to know for sure, but the design did indicate the top of the stone was faceted in the shape of a Star of David.

The second paper wasn't quite as old. It was a death certificate from a place called the Battle Creek Sanitarium in Battle Creek, Michigan. The full name on the certificate was Peter Maevski Stewart, the date of death May 14, 1915. Cause of death: consumption. His birth information was listed as June 12, 1890, Russia. His parents were listed on there too: Josef Maevski, place of birth, Russia; Eliana Maevski, place of birth, Russia.

"What do you think it all means?" David asked.

"I'm not exactly sure," Nel said. "But I'm going to find out."

CHAPTER 19

Jakob did decide to eat his dinner in the dining room eventually, and more often as the days passed. No use sitting in his room letting his joints stiffen further. He'd lived too long, that was the bottom line. People aren't supposed to live into their nineties. If he were dead and in the ground next to Catherine where he should be, the choice about where to eat his meals wouldn't matter.

"Here with the guys, or by the window with the ladies?" Nyesha asked as she wheeled his chair into the dining room, a large, open room with a severely pitched ceiling and exposed rafters. A stone-encased, double-sided fireplace separated this room from the recreation room, which featured plenty of couches and therapeutic, industrial recliners for broken-down residents who wanted to read or knit or sit and watch all their final minutes and hours drift by, each one, if the truth be told, wishing death would hurry and go on and take them.

Jakob considered the two tables. At one sat old Judge Golladay. In his prime he was the county prosecutor most feared by drunks and wife beaters and other good-for-nothin's. Now he sat hunched in his wheelchair, thinning, peppered hair combed back with Vitalis, coffee dribbling down his chin, and a chunk of scrambled egg stuck next to the Izod logo on his green, button-down cardigan. Lloyd Loeffler, whom Jakob had hired to work on the line at Brake-All decades earlier, sat next to him. Back then he'd been a recent high school graduate with barely a whisker on his face and a very pregnant, newly wedded wife to care for. Jakob had hired him against the advice of his supervisor, but he was never sorry about it since Lloyd was such a hard worker. Sidelined by early-onset Parkinson's, Lloyd watched the dining-room aide cutting his pancakes for him and Lloyd struggling to keep each bite from falling out of his mouth as she fed him. His bride from back then visited him nearly every day, and all the lucid residents were a little jealous of that.

Next Jakob considered the table of ladies. Guaranteed their prattle would distract him from feeling sorry for himself, as the four of them barely paused to breathe before they were on to their next woe or fracture or dental crisis. Either that or they argued like a brood of barnyard hens pecking at one another. Rose Habiger, cloud-white hair meticulously coiffed each morning, had been the matriarch of a blueberry farm before a massive heart attack and resultant congestive heart failure created a need for oxygen and care so great her wealthy progeny couldn't deal with it, so they stuffed her away at Lakeside and rarely visited.

Vicky Wilson wasn't much better off, a lifetime of cigarettes and secondhand smoke from spending decades of office hours in the high school teacher's lounge crippling her lungs and oxygen-starved heart. She wore her hair in the same snug bun she had when Nel had been her prize English student. And lipstick. The same red lipstick he remembered her wearing at Nel's "meet-the-teacher" nights. She never left her room without it on.

Helen Tuttle, a former housewife, was in better physical health than the others, but her mind had lost the battle to Alzheimer's a long time ago. Still, she had enough spunk and wherewithal in her to have managed to avoid the locked memory unit. So there she sat each morning wearing an overstretched, overwashed "I left my heart in Daytona" sweatshirt (complete with emblazoned checkered flags and stock cars) and talking to Rose and Vicky as if they were her daughters and—if he chose to sit there—as if Jakob were her son. Everyone played along. Everyone except Mabel, that is. Parkinson's had stolen her voice years ago. She could hardly lift her head, but they wheeled her out to the dining room every morning anyway.

"It'll be good for her," the staff often said.

Somehow Jakob doubted that. He watched as Mabel lifted her head with heroic effort, looked around, and scowled. She didn't want to be around anyone anymore. She'd died inside a long time ago, as others had done. Didn't matter how many times they wheeled her out, she would have none of it.

"The ladies."

"You got it, Mr. Jake." Nyesha wheeled him up to the table and across from Mabel. She wore a cameo brooch he hadn't noticed before. Most folks wore the same thing every day, with an occasional change of top or pants. Residents usually came in with plenty but ended up with only a remnant of their original wardrobes. Staff and visitors stole all the best while the residents slept, then told them they were imagining things when they asked about their stuff gone missing. As if all their brains had quit working. Especially those residents pushing one hundred.

So of course Jakob noticed Mabel's cameo.

EARLY SUMMER 1904

Tokaj, Austria-Hungary

CHAPTER 20

The woman named Zsófia winked as she set the borscht in front of Peter and Jakob.

"*Dyakuyu,*"† Peter said for both of them.

"*Proshu.*"‡ She smiled and tousled Jakob's hair.

The farther they traveled, the better Peter had become at finding warm homes of kindly people who agreed to take them in for a night and a meal, and this woman was no exception. Each town they came to, Jakob pressed against his chest the family *kiddush* cup and the aquamarine wrapped carefully inside. He may have been a coward before, and he may have almost lost it, but he knew if it came down to it, he would forfeit his life before giving that away. Thankfully he hadn't had to worry about that yet. When Galya needed new shoes, Peter found a blacksmith. When they needed new shoes, he found a cobbler. Plump-waisted babushkas tucked worn but quite usable clothes into the boys' sacks as they left a home before dawn. There were still many times they rode for two or three days before finding food and a place to stay. But somehow they always found homes

---

† Thank you.

‡ You're welcome.

where kindhearted babushkas wearing bright scarves like Mama and
Luda took them in and fed them warm stew or porridge, sourdough
bread, and port, on occasion, to warm them and help them sleep.
Many times the people they stayed with insisted Peter and Jakob eat
first, before they and their children did.

Eventually, in early summer, the boys made it across the
Carpathian Mountains to Tokaj on the eastern edge of Austria-
Hungary. The hillsides, emerald with new growth, were covered with
rows of emerging grapevines as Peter and Jakob made their way into
Tokaj, where Zsófia and her husband, Makár, ran a local stable. Peter
had chosen them purposefully, since this is where they would have to
sell Galya to buy their first train tickets.

Luckily, Zsófia, head covered in a lavishly embroidered, floral
print scarf, knew enough Ukrainian for Peter to communicate their
plight to her, and she had enough mercy to feed them. She even
gave them new socks and mended their torn clothing as they slept.
And Makár was merciful enough to give them exactly the amount of
money they needed for Galya, plus a little extra for their train tickets.

The couple escorted them to the train station, where Zsófia gave
both Jakob and Peter a pocket-size, three-bar, Orthodox wooden
cross. Jakob would not forget Zsófia's hazel eyes, rimmed in black,
wrinkled skin downturned with concern, when she placed the piece in
his hands. She searched his eyes for understanding as she explained in
broken Ukrainian that Messiah Yeshua was with them in their journey.

Jehovah-Shammah.

Makár promised Peter the two of them would at least be safer
in Hungary. He said Budapest was full of Jews, many respected
and prosperous, and there they could buy tickets to the Wien

Westbahnhof train stop, which would lead them to Rotterdam and the ships to America.

The planks of the station platform creaked as they walked toward the gigantic engine, which snorted, coughed, and steamed as they boarded. It would have been enough to terrify any young boy, but not Jakob. Men, he knew, could do far more harm to humans than any machine. Besides, the small compartment with the hard, wooden seats was a warm comfort, confining the ache in his heart that felt too wild in the wide, open spaces they'd wandered for weeks. And as the train crawled then pushed full throttle through mountains and hills, farms and fields, villages and larger towns of Austria-Hungary, the blur lulled him into a shalom the likes of which he couldn't remember feeling since before what happened in Chudniv.

When the train stopped in Budapest, Peter and Jakob opted to stay on board even though they could have explored the town for a couple of hours. They'd need to buy another round of tickets, but they didn't have to switch trains. Still exhausted from their weeks of travel, they watched the many new passengers boarding. Their lightness of step and laughter was an awkward contrast to the devastated countenances of Peter and Jakob and most everyone else who'd boarded from the east.

"I'll be right back." Peter tugged his fur hat tighter over his ears, gave Jakob a pat, and set off to speak with the conductor about payment for passage to Wien Westbahnhof. He was gone a long while, and Jakob began to worry as the train filled to near capacity and grew warmer by the minute. He unfastened his coat and took a moment to peek at the aquamarine tucked deep in the inside pocket. The stone glinted, despite the darkness of the pocket.

"Whatcha got there, boy?" A man with a gold front tooth and two rotting teeth on either side of that leaned over the seat from behind him. His rancid breath overwhelmed Jakob, who couldn't help but cough in the man's face.

Jakob did not reply except that he pulled his coat closed tight.

"Sure about that?"

Jakob felt something cold and hard being pressed against the side of his throat, the same place the man in the barn had held a knife against Peter's neck.

"Get off the boy, Gergo," another man said from behind him.

"He's got somethin' in his pocket we might be interested in, this one does," Gergo said, not moving what Jakob figured must be a knife.

"He has nothing, and you'll sit down," a third voice boomed from behind.

As Gergo pulled the knife away, Jakob sighed with relief. He turned to see a second conductor coming down the aisle, a man who had to be a giant, as tall and enormous as he was.

"Now give me that knife," the conductor said to Gergo.

"I told you not to be stupid," Gergo's companion snorted.

Jehovah-Shammah, Jakob thought.

The conductor knelt beside Jakob's seat. "Are you all right, little one?"

Jakob nodded.

"Are you traveling alone?"

Jakob shook his head as Peter returned with their tickets.

"Everything okay here?" Peter asked, his face flushed.

The conductor stood and offered Peter his huge hand. "'Tis now. I made sure of that. See to it that you let me know if these two behind you give you any trouble, hear?"

"Yes, sir. Thank you, sir." Peter handed the conductor their tickets.

Jakob would not remove his hand from over the top of his coat, where the stone lay beneath, warm and safe. He rested his head back against the seat, only to lift it again when Peter explained what took him so long.

"The tickets were very expensive. I had to give him both the ruby and the sapphire." All they had left to sell for food and passage to America were a few smaller sapphires, a small bag of rough amber, and Mama's cameo. That might still not be enough for the tickets, Peter explained.

Like all Papa's work, the cameo was exquisite. The woman, carved into the white layer of agate against a deep-blue background, looked just like Mama—the slope of her nose, the soft curve of her lips, the swirls of hair falling against her neck, and a braid pinned above her ear with a flower. Even the details of a pearl necklace lying against her collarbone were perfectly etched.

Jakob folded his arms tight across his chest and felt his heart beating thin and bird-like against the hard outline of the silver cup and Papa's aquamarine within. As difficult as selling the piece would be, though, the aquamarine was off-limits. Even if they had to stay in the Netherlands he would never give that up. He and Peter would find work there and forget about America. Forget running.

When the boys finally arrived at the shipyards of Rotterdam, though, Jakob reconsidered. The air of urgency among would-be immigrants created a near panic among the crowds. More than once, Jakob saw mothers and fathers trading young daughters for tickets, yelling over the girls' petrified shrieks that it was the only way, and promising them they would send for them once they got to America, though Peter and Jakob both knew their fates would be more like Raisa's—if they were lucky. Jakob's constant fear of being lost or trampled or held at knifepoint again, along with the stench of unbathed, travel-weary bodies, kept him not more than an inch from Peter's leg at all times. Peter pulled the cameo out of his pocket, and Jakob knew that meant he needed to sell it.

Jakob hugged Peter's leg as Peter negotiated for their ship passage. Finally when he set the cameo in the hand of the steamship salesman, Peter received two tickets in return.

"They would've wanted us to sell it," Peter said, resigned, as they turned to push through the crowds again. "Mama and Ilana, Papa and Tova, Zahava and little Faigy—they would've wanted us to get these tickets and start a new life."

Any images of Mama would have to come from memory now.

As Jakob stood on the cold boarding platform in the Netherlands, the Atlantic Ocean felt more like a grave than a way to freedom.

While Peter recited the Shema, all Jakob could do was stare into the salty wind.

EARLY 1995

_____

South Haven, Michigan

CHAPTER 21

Christmas came and went without much celebration, since, without her mom, Nel couldn't bring herself to pull out a lifetime of holiday memories packed in boxes. Besides that, Jakob wasn't able to come home from Lakeview, and Christmas decor can feel desperate, even strangely eerie, without anyone around to enjoy it. So Mattie, David, and Nel had brought Christmas to Jakob as best they could, joining in the celebrations Lakeview offered and bringing Jakob a basket full of home-cooked food, a photo album Nel made of favorite pictures of Catherine over the years, and a new cardigan sweater. Nel had attended church with Mattie and David. She hadn't minded when David had reached over and held her hand during the candlelight singing of "Silent Night." And even though the service at her hometown church had changed little over the years, the predictability of the songs, the liturgy, the message filled her with a sense of grounding, even assurance that though she wandered, she wasn't completely lost.

Nel had rolled the car windows down a smidgen to inhale the scent of spring that sneaks into the air between late-winter snowfalls. She was headed for the local library, where she'd been doing as much research on Ukraine, the Russian Empire, and her father's genealogy as she could between jewelry orders. She played with the cameo around her neck and felt the fine outline of the sparrow beneath her fingers. She'd forgotten about the piece but found it, along with old journals and trinkets from years spent attending and helping with church summer camps, while she was rummaging through an old drawer in her bedroom. Jakob had made the piece for her when she turned sixteen, and she had watched him work on it many times. He'd shown her the raw, uncut piece of blue agate and explained how the layers formed in holes in the earth, how water bubbled through the rock over the ages, depositing silica, which turned into quartz, which hardened into the variegated layers.

"When you etch away the top layer of the stone, you create a raised image called a *relief* that contrasts with the different-colored layer of stone beneath," he'd explained.

Do not fear therefore; you are of more value than many sparrows.[1] She wasn't proud of the fact that she couldn't recall very many scriptures, but because of the necklace, she often remembered that one.

A low-hanging mist hugged the blueberry fields and dips in the landscape on the outskirts of town, and white church steeples rose high above newly barren branches. The last of orange and yellow leaves contrasted with the lustrous sky. In town, storefronts with crisp blue-and-white nautical displays beckoned tourists inside as they made their way toward their obligatory stop at the red lighthouse at the end of the South Haven pier. Bait, tackle, and marine outfitters made it obvious the lake wasn't far. But the displays would be relatively unnoticed, since it was still several weeks before the start of the tourist season. And the beach would be nearly empty, except for perhaps a woman walking a dog or a gaggle of preschoolers with their moms watching them collect stones to skip.

Inside the library, Nel caught the scent of new and old book bindings that reminded her of all the times her mom took her there as a child, even as a teen. Growing up she must've read every book in the youth and young-adult sections, and then some, and her mom must've read every book from the gardening and hobbies collection. Nel took her time wandering up and down the stacks knowing she could search the catalog for what she was looking for but choosing instead to take her time and thumb through titles on her own.

When she reached the 947s section, she pulled out every selection available on Russia and Ukraine. Her pile grew higher when she reached the 973s and pulled out several books on Eastern European immigrants. And when she reached the 739s, she was thrilled to find three books on Russian jewelers and artisans. She'd learned enough about world history to know that the land and people of Ukraine had been in a political tug-of-war for generations, so information about anyone named Maevski could be in nearly any resource that referred to the Russian Empire or Ukraine.

She stacked the references around her at a large study table and dug into the books. She'd had no idea that millions and millions of immigrants, Jewish in particular, had escaped severe persecution and genocide well before World War II, and at precisely the time Peter and Jakob had arrived in New York City. She'd also had no idea what the Pale of Settlement was, and how difficult life had truly been for Jews and non-Jews alike living in shtetls all across the Ukraine region of the Russian Empire. She had to stop reading some accounts of the forms of torture and murder techniques used on innocent women and children, who were hacked open and cut apart and buried alive, and whole villages of people brutalized, then immolated, in endless and unimaginable ways.

As if that wasn't enough, she read about Babi Yar, when tens of thousands of Jews were slaughtered in Kiev and thrown into a ravine; about waves and waves of immigrants who fought and died trying to escape what seemed to be unending uprisings and genocides from the 1600s through World War II; about forced famines in the 1930s; about Stalin and Lenin ... It was too much to take in, the horrors that never seemed to end in that land. If these were some of the things her dad had lived through, particularly the genocide in the Pale of Settlement, then no wonder he didn't want to speak of it.

But not everything she read held such darkness. She learned about missionaries like Stuart Hine from Britain, who in the early 1900s preached the gospel to villages all across the Carpathian Mountains, the beauty of which inspired him to translate and set to music "How Great Thou Art"; about Metropolitan Andrey Sheptytsky, the head of the Ukrainian Greco-Catholic Church, who saved thousands of lives of Jewish refugees during the turn of the century and up until World War II, when he was murdered by the Nazis. And as she flipped through pictorial accounts and glossy travel guides of the region, she had a hard time fathoming how such horrific events took place in such a breathtakingly beautiful land. No wonder missionaries were inspired to write hymns when they were there. No wonder, as many accounts described, the people they ministered to soaked up the gospel so willingly. What else besides faith in Someone bigger, Someone above and beyond all that pain, could have given them hope in the middle of all that death?

Nel pushed the history and geography books aside and turned to the books on jewelers and artisans from the region. Some of the greatest designers and faceters had lived in the Russian Empire as it advanced and ebbed across Eastern Europe over the centuries. One book in particular, *Gemstones of the Tsars*, consumed her. Page after page detailed the stones and faceting designs of artisans who'd worked on the imperial collections creating fabulous and intricate designs for stones inlaid in scepters and orbs, crowns and sabers, and Fabergé eggs. She lingered over pages full of items adorned with tens and hundreds of diamonds and emeralds, tourmalines and sapphires, rubies and pearls, and every precious gem and mineral in between. She was so caught up in the brilliance of all she read that she almost forgot why she'd come to the library … until she got to the appendixes. There, faceting designs and explanations and origins of many of the larger imperial stones were described in detail, including diagrams and measurements—triangles and round cuts, cushion and navette, marquis and recoupe-rose, baguette and heart, star brilliant and briolettes. She stopped when she got to the section featuring aquamarines. She ran her finger across the columns of the names of artisans who'd perfected or contributed to imperial gem designs, and there it was.

Maevski.

Josef Maevski.

From Chudniv, Zhytomyr Oblast.

Could this be a relative? The chances were minuscule, so she couldn't let herself get too worked up about the possibility. Her dad might not be able—or willing—to recall enough of this to confirm or deny anything about this Josef fellow. Although Jakob was getting better, stronger and more lucid each day, she still hesitated to bring up anything that might upset him. Seeing him in a state of acute delirium or worsening dementia was hard enough without drawing attention to something he couldn't remember, or didn't want to remember. But again, she considered that maybe there was a good reason her mom had been doing the research. Catherine loved Jakob, so she wouldn't have started researching and delving into Jakob's ancestry if she hadn't either been really interested in it or onto some bit of history that was important enough to pursue. Anyway, what harm could come from investigating?

The copy machine clicked and whirred into action as she laid the page with the Maevski name on the glass. She tucked the photocopy into the front of one of the dozen or so books she checked out and hurried out to her car. She had told David she'd be at the house that afternoon so he could look at the eaves and roof and other exterior parts of the house to figure out what needed renovations.

Already parked out front, David waved as she pulled into the driveway. She regretted how unaware she'd been of how hard it had become for Mom and Dad to keep up with maintaining the house. Even at her advancing age, Mattie managed to keep her pale-pink stucco home freshly painted and looking alive by comparison. The bird feeders Jakob so loved to keep full dangled crooked and empty, and corncobs sat bare on feeding posts he'd crafted especially for the black squirrels. She made a mental note to fill them later.

Nel pulled into the garage, grateful (again) she hadn't scraped the sides of the giant car on her mom's old bicycle with the basket on the front. She intended to fix it up so she could ride in to town on warmer spring days.

"Thanks for coming, David."

He ambled up the driveway toward her and eyeballed the stack of books she lugged out of the backseat. "You've been busy."

"Yeah. I was there at the library all morning. I had no idea of the horrible history of Eastern Europe."

"Learn somethin' new every day, right?"

She rolled her eyes at him, trying to veil the flush she felt rise to her cheeks every time he came around. "You are still *such* a dork."

"Some things never change."

"And full of clichés, too, I see."

"Here, let me help you." He grinned, then gathered a half-dozen books that had fallen onto the floorboards and carried them into the house behind her.

"Would you like a soda or something? There's a bunch in the fridge by the back door. Take what you'd like." She grabbed one of Catherine's old windbreakers off a hook by the back door and pulled it over the thick, cable-knit, wool fisherman's sweater she wore, which she'd had since high school.

Out front, Nel looked at the black stains along the eaves, the gutters bent and hanging in places from the weight of leaves, and the roof, which sagged where the edges of the gables met. David stuck a finger between a window casing and the siding, and with barely any effort, he displaced a long, rotted piece of wood that tumbled to the ground. His eyes drooped with apology.

"I have a feeling this might end up being a big project." She sighed.

"Nothing I haven't seen before. Doesn't take long for these homes to get worn down. Even if they'd kept it up until a couple years ago, a couple years is all it might take for the lake to get at it."

Did he sense the guilt she felt about not being around? Even if he didn't, she appreciated his reassurance. The lake was hard on homes.

"I can do some things if the weather cooperates," he continued. "Some of the window casings, siding, and such. But the roof … that might have to wait until late spring, once the threat of snow is gone. No telling how much of that needs replaced until we get started, and if there's a lot of problems, snow would make them impossible to get to."

"One thing I know I need are ramps to all the doorways."

"Are you bringing your dad home soon?"

"The doctors say just a few more weeks. He still has times when he's pretty loony, but overall, he's improving."

"Can't be easy for a guy his age."

She thought about the things she'd seen and learned at the library earlier. "I'm beginning to realize life's not easy at any age."

After David left, Nel settled down with the piles of library books and compared the stone specifications in *Gemstones of the Tsars* with the one on the handwritten piece of parchment and was stunned to see they matched exactly. That they were the same could not be a coincidence. She scoured through the books to find as much as she could about the village of Chudniv, the village where Peter and Jakob and the gem artist were from. Details were sketchy, even in the well-researched books, most likely because of the Iron Curtain. Current information about the region was either sketchy or glossy and ad-like because of the decades of Soviet communications lockdown.

One book, however, listed the name of the Orthodox church in the town, and Nel figured that'd be as reliable a place to start as any. She hoped the post office could help her verify an exact mailing address, and she knew what she was going to send. If this Josef Maevski was as well respected as the book indicated, perhaps the town would have some record of him. And if they had some record of him, maybe they'd have some record of Peter and Jakob. She'd send the church a photocopy of the page from *Gemstones of the Tsars*, a photocopy of the diagram and dimensions she and David had found inside the silver cup, a photocopy of the ship manifest and the photograph of the two boys, and a photograph of the aquamarine.

Then she would have to wait.

She might hear nothing, she realized that. But if she heard something, it could prove to be well worth the time.

Nel climbed the creaky, worn, walnut stairs to her room but stopped outside her parents' bedroom. The same queen-size bed with a scrolled, black-iron frame was set against the same wall it'd been on since she was a child, and the sun had faded a permanent outline of the bed's scrollwork onto the wall. Between the two pillows at the head of the bed, Dad had neatly placed a needlepoint throw pillow with fishing bobbers and the phrase "I'm not old, my bobbers just don't float like they used to." On either side of the bed were matching bedside tables and white carnival-glass lamps. Above the bed hung a painting of seagulls flying toward the sun, which hung low in the sky over a grassy beach. It looked like the view of the lake from the house, and she wondered if they'd asked someone to paint it at some point over the years. The same wedding-ring quilt was folded at the end of the bed, neatly made with a candle-wicked bedspread smoothed over the top, neither of which could hide the two parallel sunken spots in the mattress where her parents had lain side by side. She ran her hand across the pieces and threads of the quilt as if to bring back the life that had placed each stitch. Mom had let her help make that quilt and many others on lazy afternoons on the upstairs sleeping porch.

Nel grabbed a quilt from her room and headed to the upstairs sleeping porch, which faced the lake. She sat for as long as she could bear the cold and listened to the soft barks of the black squirrels as they no doubt vied for sections of the new corncobs she'd set out. She thought she'd been so sure of her life in Santa Fe and the life and business she'd established among the other artists. But now that she was home, she wondered if this was where she might need to stay.

CHAPTER 22

The staff always had an activity of some kind lined up for residents to do each day, and those healthy enough were required to attend as part of their rehabilitation program. This morning featured "Rockin' and Rollin' with Debbie," a bubbly instructor who led residents in wheelchair exercises set to either Big Band or early rock-and-roll music, depending on her mood. The exercises weren't so bad, and Jakob knew moving around would help him get out of the place sooner.

Besides, Debbie wasn't so bad to look at either, blessed with bleach-blonde hair and a pretty decent figure. Jakob couldn't figure out if she thought all the old men like him were blind, or if she liked dressing in a way that caused them all to gawk at her. If one of them drooled, she chalked that up to the aftereffects of a stroke or Parkinson's. At any rate, she was awfully cute, dressed in her Jane Fonda, formfitting exercise clothes, which made exercise time a fabulous distraction from the death and dying all around them.

"You all are in for a treat! I brought my collection of best swing music today. Everybody ready?"

It was a rhetorical question.

"Okay, let's go. We're starting with hand swirls."

The jungle-beat drums of Benny Goodman's "Sing, Sing, Sing" rose from the speakers, and Debbie stuck her hands straight out in front of her, making circular motions in opposite directions with her hands. Never mind that none of the residents could move their hips. She moved hers plenty enough for all of them.

After a couple minutes of that, she switched things up. "Okay, everyone, we're reaching to the stars. Reaching. Reaching. Grab those stars!" She raised both her arms, then grabbed at invisible stars somewhere above her stiff blonde hair, one arm at a time, up and down and up and down as the trumpets and trombones of Goodman's band continued to wail from her CD player.

"Let's do 'the drummer,' everyone!"

Jakob's upper arms burned with the acid of inactivity as she pushed the class along in the exercise routine. He lifted his arms and struggled to keep up with the whine of muffled trumpets and the jangle of the tambourine in Irving Berlin's "Steppin' Out with My Baby."

"And let's see everyone's dazzle hands before we slow it down a bit!" Her energy level alone exhausted Jakob, as he brought his hands close to his chest, then stuck them out in front of him, stretching his fingers and waving at the air.

Ridiculous that my life has come down to exercises fit for a bunch of kindergartners, he thought.

"Good job, everyone! Time for 'the simple sway.' It's a slow one, so y'all can catch your breath." The shrill, woody sound of Glenn Miller's clarinets, cornet trumpets, and saxophones playing "Moonlight Serenade" floated through the room, and at once Jakob was back at his wedding reception, his hands cupped against the small of Catherine's back. Her dress, a champagne-colored silk, draped gracefully over her bodice, and whispers of chiffon had played in the wind against her creamy neck and shoulders. It'd been an outdoor wedding, she'd insisted on it, at her parents' stately Chicago waterfront home on Lake Shore Drive. At the time, neither of them cared so much about having a church wedding. Who needed religion when they had each other, a perfect June night, and the moon shining like a spotlight on them alone?

"Mr. Stewart, are you okay?" Debbie had moved closer to him and looked ready to check for a pulse in his neck before he answered her.

"Fine, I'm fine." Jakob craned his neck to see if Nyesha was around. "I'd like to go back to my room, please."

They'd danced on her parents' veranda to the song "Moonlight Serenade." Catherine was everything Jakob wasn't, everything he'd never experienced. Her soft edges consumed his hard ones, and in her eyes Jakob found liberation from the pain that had always enervated him. They'd spent their courtship on back roads sipping bootlegged, homemade strawberry wine and tasting each other. The curve of her neck, tendrils of her hair falling against it in the moonlight, enraptured him, and he couldn't get enough of her. She was educated. Established. High society. She was everything warm and satin, velvet and sweet in his otherwise cold, bitter, and caustic world.

As much as Catherine enamored Jakob, she frustrated him as well, always wanting to know what he was thinking. What was the matter. Why he looked as if he was brooding. What had happened to Peter and him. How they'd come to America. What life was like back in Ukraine. Jakob supposed he was a sort of novelty to her—she knew precisely who she was, after all. Relatives kept precise records of the Bessinger family tree, which traced back to Boston and the American Revolution. She came from old family money made first in the steel mills of Pennsylvania, and then in the newer ones in Chicago. Marrying an immigrant orphan like Jakob was way outside the realm of normal for her family. She couldn't help her curiosity.

One evening shortly after their marriage, they were halfway through dinner when she set the tarnished silver cup on the table. Jakob's head spun from the effects of the Chianti, and he had been hoping for a little living-room dancing, maybe a walk in the moonlight.

"Tell me about it, baby, won't you, please? What happened that's so awful you can't tell me?" She'd stroked Jakob's hand, and for the first time ever, her touch felt like a knife searing his skin. He rose from the table too quickly. Grabbed the cup and threw it. Smashed the dining-room window. Papa's tzitzit, which he'd kept since Peter died, flew into the air along with the aquamarine, which rolled out of the cheesecloth and bounced along the wooden floor with the rest of the shattered glass. A couple of neighborhood dogs barked, and the only other sound was the muffled cry of Catherine.

She retreated to their bedroom and shut the door behind her, and Jakob had obligingly slept on the couch that night, half sickened by his reaction, the other half sickened by memories and the fact that Catherine wouldn't leave his past alone. He drank the rest of the bottle of Chianti and at some point, long after midnight, fell into a cramped and hard slumber. He awoke the next morning to the glass in the dining room all cleaned up, the kitchen sparkling, coffee brewing, and a note that read,

My dearest Jake,

I'm sorry I pushed you to talk about your past. I won't mention it again. I've gone for a walk on the beach.

Yours,
Catherine

For a week or so thereafter, conversations between them felt stilted. Polite. But like many things in marriage, they learned to let things go for the sake of having and holding. Catherine was true to her word, and neither of them talked about that night, or his past, again. Soon, Eleanor was on the way, and they were back to their overall joyful social and work-related routines.

Even so, if someone asked Catherine if that night changed things between the two, she might have said yes. Jakob would have too. Since then, Jakob carried an additional weight of regret, along with all the others, that he did not bare his soul to his one and only love, the one person who could have listened and encouraged and *understood*—not because she had felt the same sorts of pain, but because she loved him that much. Instead, Jakob had carried the weight of what happened in Chudniv for nearly a century.

None of it mattered anymore, as close to the grave as he was.

Solomon was right.

Everything eventually turns to dust.

CHAPTER 23

"I'll be right back with your drinks." The waitress, Julie, smiled.

Nel sat with Mattie in a booth at Clementine's, grateful for a break in her lapidary work and the monotony of driving to and from Lakeview visiting her dad.

"How is he this week?" Mattie asked.

"He's okay. His hip is healing well—the doctors and therapists are really pleased with his progress. But his mind ..."

"I've noticed the same thing during my visits. But I'm not surprised, honey. We've been losing him for a while now."

"How long? I mean, Mom never let on to this when we talked on the phone. And when I was home two Christmases ago, I didn't notice anything other than maybe a little forgetfulness. Certainly nothing that alarmed me."

Mattie thought for a moment. "Probably the spring after you were home last for Christmas ... when was that, two years ago? That's when the noticeable decline began. Like you said, it was subtle at first, losing his keys, not paying the bills. But then he started to forget bigger things, including where he was at times."

The waitress set their drinks on the table. "Have you decided on anything yet?"

"A few more minutes, please." Mattie held up her hand.

"Of course. I'll be back."

"I wish Mom had told me." Nel shook her head as she stirred a packet of sugar into her tea.

"The hardest thing for her were the nightmares … and the time she found him in his skivvies at three in the morning walking down the middle of North Shore Drive."

Nel's jaw dropped. "Are you kidding me?"

"I'm sorry, I shouldn't laugh." Mattie tried to suppress a giggle. "It really was mortifying to her at the time. And for him, once he realized where he was. Blamed it on sleepwalking when she told me about it the next day. But not long after that, Catherine began asking him to see a doctor. He refused for a good while. You know how men can be about seeing doctors."

"Why didn't she take him anyway back then?"

"Honestly? I don't think she wanted to know what they'd say any more than he did. And she felt they were managing."

"Managing?"

"When you've lived that long, been married that long, I think there's a part of you that simply takes each day as it comes. Probably why she didn't mention it to you too. She didn't want to be confronted with the truth of how bad things were getting for the both of them … the possibility of having to sell their home and move to assisted living or someplace they didn't want to be."

"I guess I can see that. I only wish she'd told me so I could've helped. I'd have been happy to help pay for a housekeeper or for home repairs or whatever."

"I'm sure your mother knew that. But I'm also sure she was determined not to be a burden to you."

"It wouldn't have been a burden." Nel sighed. "You mentioned nightmares. Dad was having nightmares?"

"That was the worst part."

"He had nightmares in the hospital, too, delusions that seemed to really scare him."

"He'd been having a lot of those—night terrors, I suppose. Catherine told me he'd wake up drenched with sweat and screaming, but he'd never tell her—or he couldn't remember—exactly what the dreams were about."

The waitress came back and took their orders—they both ordered chicken-salad sandwiches and fries.

"Do you know if that's why Mom was doing research into Dad's past?"

"She never mentioned that to me, but I suppose it could be."

"The day of the funeral, I found an envelope addressed to her from Ellis Island. Inside were papers about immigrants along with this really old photo of two adorable little boys." Nel pulled the photo, the ship manifest, and the tarnished silver cup out of her purse and laid it all on the table in front of Mattie. "I was hoping maybe you could help me make heads or tails out of some of this."

Mattie picked up the cup and traced the outline of the etched bucolic village scene with her fingers.

"I found that cup when I was moving things around in Dad's lapidary room. There was an absolutely brilliant aquamarine inside it too, that I left at home, and a faceting diagram written in Cyrillic. A death certificate, too, for a young man named Peter Maevski

Stewart. And Peter Maevski is the name on the ship manifest, see?"
Nel pointed at the lines where the names of Peter and Jakob were
written. "There. Peter Maevski, fourteen. And Jakob Maevski, five.
It's gotta be connected somehow."

"It would seem so," Mattie said, turning her attention back to the
cup and sighing. "I've seen cups like this, but not for a long time."

"You have?"

"Not since I was a little girl. Not since my last *Shabbat.*"

"*Shabbat?* Sabbath? You're Jewish?"

"I know it probably seems strange. I haven't thought about that
part of my life for a long while. But yes, I'm Jewish."

"But you don't observe your faith anymore."

"My family abandoned their faith when they came to America.
It happened with some immigrants. Times were much too dangerous
for many to take the chance of someone finding out you believed in
God. I was born in Germany, and I haven't practiced the Jewish faith
since I was a small girl there. I became a Presbyterian when I married
my ex-husband. By then it was the fifties and we wanted to raise our
children in the church."

"So your family came to America during the Holocaust?"

"Shortly before the actual Holocaust, yes. Things had been horrid for Jews in Germany for a while, of course, and our experiences
were no exception. We couldn't buy food except at Jewish groceries,
which were always in short supply. I had a friend, Katrina, from a
Christian family who lived down the street. Her mother let Katrina
bring us bread from their grocery every day. But it became more and
more dangerous for Katrina and her family to help us. They risked
their lives; I understand this now."

"How'd you all get out of there?"

"Father explained to us later, when we were older, that he had saved a lot of money in cash. He'd kept it hidden in the walls, under floorboards, in teacups, wherever he could. I was too young to remember that, but I do recall we left in the middle of the night. Left everything behind except for the clothes on our backs. I didn't have a chance to say good-bye to Katrina ..." She paused and toyed with the corner of her napkin. "We took a train to Amsterdam and then boarded a ship to New York."

"Did they make you wear stars?"

Mattie smiled sadly. "They did. My friend Katrina, the one who brought us bread? She wanted to wear a star too. She thought it meant we were special. She didn't understand. Neither did I, until later."

"It must've been terrifying for you."

"Yes and no. It was hard to leave my friends, but I had my family. We all came here together. Only later did I realize what we'd escaped." She picked up the photo of the two boys. "It was horrific for the Jews in Eastern Europe well before the Holocaust. During the pogroms. Judging from the year these two immigrated, they probably escaped something similar."

"The stone I found, the top of it, the crown, has a six-pointed star, like the Star of David."

Mattie raised her eyebrows. "Now that is interesting. Especially with this cup."

"What do you make of it?"

"It's a kiddush cup, usually used on Friday evenings before the Sabbath. The father in the family, the head of the home, fills it with wine when the Sabbath blessing is read." She handed the cup back to Nel. "We may have to talk more about your heritage."

"You think I could be Jewish? That Dad was Jewish? That Mom was researching that?"

"Could be …" Mattie sorted through the papers and looked at the boys in the photograph again. She met Nel's gaze, her countenance appearing suddenly grave. "You know, some things are too painful, too shameful to speak of. The people who emigrated from Eastern Europe around the turn of the century, like this paper is dated … so many were Jews."

1912-1915

Chicago, Illinois

CHAPTER 24

After Peter and Jakob settled into Saint Stanislaus Catholic School, the boys worked in Mr. Grünfelder's jewelry store. Grünfelder and his wife were next-door neighbors of the Stewarts, and he'd noticed both Peter's and Jakob's interest in his work. The boys swept the floors, polished the counters and glass jewelry cases, and helped him lock up so he wasn't alone at closing time in the evenings. Mr. Grünfelder had brought his family's gemstone and lapidary business over from Idar-Oberstein, Germany, around the same time Peter and Jakob had emigrated. Peter, of course, thought it was a sign from Yeshua that they were supposed to work there, since Papa had studied in the same region for a time. Jakob was just glad to have a job to pay for little things at the market so as not to have to ask Papa and Mama Stewart for money—although they insisted the boys didn't need to work.

Happy to oblige their interest in his work, Mr. Grünfelder allowed Peter and Jakob opportunities to cut on leftover agates, quartz, carnelian, and on rare occasions, amethysts. Even with only two fingers on his right hand, Peter was able to handle the cutting and polishing, faceting and setting as well as any man with a whole set of fingers intact. Peter opened up to Mr. Grünfelder about Papa, how he had worked with crude (by comparison) and often handmade lapidary tools to create his designs. In turn, Mr. Grünfelder told them stories of the lapidarists in Idar-Oberstein who had to lie on the floor and use the weight of their whole bodies to turn giant sandstone wheels mounted vertically to polish agate. By the time Peter was in his senior year at Saint Stanislaus, Mr. Grünfelder considered him an official apprenticeship, and Peter decided that gem cutting would be his profession. Some of his faceting designs were so perfect, Mr. Grünfelder placed them in the sale cases alongside his own. Demand for Peter's stones increased, along with his reputation, and at the perfect time too. Mr. Grünfelder had to travel often to obtain diamonds and other precious gems, and he couldn't keep up with the business alone.

One Saturday morning, as they often did, Peter and Jakob roamed through the neighborhood markets, buying fresh produce or bread or whatever Mama Stewart needed. Peter, who'd been losing weight, began to cough. He'd been complaining of a tickle in the back of his throat for weeks and constantly cleared his throat. Occasionally he had fevers, too, which quickly passed, and the family doctor dismissed them as a mild flu. But on this morning, as they passed a booth full of fresh-made sausages, Peter fell into a fit of coughing, and when he pulled his handkerchief away from his mouth, the cloth was covered with blood.

During the initial weeks afterward, Peter received the dreaded diagnosis of consumption, undoubtedly picked up on the ship to America and dormant for years. His future with Mr. Grünfelder was put on hold, and he was sent to live at the Edward Tuberculosis Sanatorium in nearby Naperville, Illinois. The Stewarts had learned that one of the foremost authorities on tuberculosis, Dr. Theodore

Sachs, was in charge of the institution, and that the doctor believed in new and open-air treatments of the disease. Dr. Sachs was enamored with Peter the moment they met, having learned they were both from Ukraine. Dr. Sachs was born in Odessa in 1868 and received his medical training at the university there. But as much as Dr. Sachs doted on Peter, his condition worsened. Sachs recommended that the Stewarts move Peter to the Battle Creek Sanitarium in Michigan, the most respected and high-priced sanitarium in the region. Over the next year as Peter's condition seemed to stabilize there, the Stewarts built the lake house in South Haven so they could spend as much time as possible with him in the summer, and on weekends and holidays as he recovered. But even the cutting-edge breathing therapy and the water and fresh-air treatments could not slow the advance of his disease.

A month before Peter's twenty-fifth birthday, Jakob sat in math class at Saint Stanislaus, struggling to keep his eyes open along with most of the other students in the class that day.

"Jakob Stewart?" The principal's secretary, Mrs. Truszkowski, jolted him out of his daydream. She was a spindly woman with a long neck and a thin nose perfect for looking down upon unruly children. Jakob's teacher, a kind, wrinkled nun named Mother Rose, nodded at him to get his things and go with the secretary.

"Your father is waiting for you in the car out front," Mrs. Truszkowski urged. "Hurry along."

"He is not my father." Jakob didn't say this to be belligerent. He simply stated it as fact.

"I know, Jakob. I'm sorry." Her sudden softness surprised Jakob, since it was so different from her usual stern and dismal countenance.

"Why is he here?"

She looked down at Jakob with eyes full of pity before saying, "It's your brother. He's not well."

Jakob climbed into the backseat of the ruby-red roadster behind Papa Stewart, who steered the car to the train station faster than Jakob had ever known him to drive.

"I thought you might want to bring this to your brother." Mama Stewart sat next to Jakob on the train as the conductors prepared for departure. She handed him the kiddush cup, the stone still wrapped and tucked inside it. Jakob looked at her in disbelief. As much as they were grateful to the Stewarts, he and Peter had always been careful to keep those things hidden, whether under their mattresses, in the corners of closets, or in their shoes. "How did you know … Where did you find it?"

"Never mind how I knew," she said with a look that assured Jakob he was not in trouble for keeping it from her and Papa Stewart. "The important thing is that it brings comfort to your brother. And to you." She turned forward, focusing silently on the buildings, then the factories along the east side of Chicago near the lake, and then farmland of northern Indiana passing outside the window. Occasionally, she wiped a tear off her face.

Jakob knew death was coming. He recognized the shadow of it, which had followed him since Chudniv, and all he could do was wait for it to strike again and again and hope that it would take him, too, someday. Gently, though. Jakob hoped death would take him gently.

Later, Mama Stewart tried to make small talk to break the silence, but the conversation fell flat about school and Mr. Grünfelder, new shows at the theater and the latest books that had arrived at the library. They each could only think of Peter.

Once the trio reached Battle Creek, Papa Stewart paid a driver to take them to the sanitarium, the emerald lawns spreading wide like endless winter wheat fields in Ukraine. Residents in white gowns sat in wheelchairs or hammocks reading, light shining dappled and ethereal upon them through the budding spring trees. On an upstairs terrace, beds were lined up outside like dominos, patients in various states of respite visible in each of them. Mama and Papa Stewart plodded up the concrete steps ahead of Jakob, and the smell of bleach and lard soap greeted the three of them as they walked through the front doors. Papa Stewart talked to staff in white coats while Mama Stewart and Jakob sat on a bench by the front desk, which was manned by a very large woman in a white nurse's cap, a white dress, buttons pulling against the bulge of her bosom, and a navy-blue cape across her shoulders and tied at the neck. Coughs and retching came from every direction as they walked up the stairs and down the long hallway toward the room in which Peter lay. Jakob sat on a bench outside Peter's room while Mama and Papa Stewart visited with him first.

Finally it was time.

"Yakob … ỹdit' … syudy … "† Even from the doorway, Jakob saw Peter's chest heaving with the effort of gasping out each word. The finger of his right hand curled as he motioned to Jakob to come sit beside him. In his left hand, he held Papa's tattered tzitzit.

"He mostly speaks in Ukrainian now," Papa Stewart said over Jakob's shoulder as he passed.

---

† Jakob … come … here …

The starched sheet felt stiff and cold as Jakob sat on it. The thought of Mama splayed out on the hard kitchen table … of Zahava, as white as the sheets, curled up on the hard kitchen floor with a sea of blood beneath her—the memories brought the taste of bile to his throat. He realized then that even on a mattress in a bleached room surrounded by tidy nurses and staff, death would come no more gently for Peter than it had for the rest of their family. The blow of it was different but no less painful. And for certain, no more merciful.

Jakob took hold of Peter's pale hand, feeling the empty spots where fingers should have been. Blue veins showed through his skin, as visible as the blue stripes of the mattress beneath the sheets. As blue as the aquamarine stone in Jakob's pocket. Jakob gently traced the veins under Peter's skin like roads on a map and considered how far they had journeyed together.

"Jakob, listen to me."

Jakob stared into Peter's eyes, still fierce with life.

"What is it?" Jakob was surprised at his own use of Ukrainian. He had not uttered a word of it since they left Chudniv.

"Did you bring the stone?"

"I did." Jakob was immensely grateful to Mama Stewart now, first for respecting the "secret" he and Peter shared, and second for bringing the stone for them. He pulled the cup and the stone from his coat pocket, unwrapped the stone, and placed it in Peter's hand.

Peter barely had strength enough to grasp it, but he managed to hold it in his hand and pull it to rest on the center of his chest. "Say it for me," he gasped.

"What do you want me to say?"

"The Kaddish."[1]

"And promise me"—Peter choked—"that you'll say it when I'm gone."

"But it doesn't mean anything. And besides, you aren't dead yet."

"Say it … Say it always. The words in your head will help the truth return to your heart …"

Jakob shook his head in disagreement.

"Don't argue … Forgive them … Forgive yourself …"

Jakob grasped Peter's hand tighter, reluctant to let death gain the victory over his brother but powerless to fight its advance. There was no cupboard where he could hide, no table he could run beneath. And for once he was sure he wouldn't have, even if there were.

Peter's whole body worked to cough and inhale air, and a trickle of blood ran down the corner of his cracked lips.

Jakob looked away and hoped Peter couldn't see the anger that threatened to overshadow his grief. How could Peter suggest they believe in the God who'd abandoned them, let alone forgive the maniacs? Let alone forgive himself?

"Forgive … and believe. Don't let … hate … win …"

Jakob let go of his brother's hand, stood, and walked toward the window, then looked down at the patients on the lawn basking in the sun, unaware of tragedy in the room above them, aware only of their own promise of recovery as they rested or leaned against a tree, lost in a book, a story, a hope.

"Jakob …" A fit of coughing, more feeble this time, drowned his words. More blood trickled out the side of his mouth and his nose. "Jakob … you must … forgive …"

Peter's life left his body along with those last words, and it was then that Jakob picked up the prayer book on the bedside table and turned to the earmarked page. He grasped his brother's limp hand, the warmth already leaving it. Jakob's whispered words echoed against the walls of the room as Peter's body grew even colder.

Magnified and sanctified be His great name.

In this world which He has created in accordance with His will, may He establish His kingdom during your lifetime, and during the life of all the House of Israel, speedily, and let us say, Amen.

Let His great name be blessed for ever and to all eternity!

Blessed, praised, glorified and exalted; extolled, honored, magnified, and lauded....

He is greater than all blessings, hymns, praises and consolations Which can be uttered in this world; and let us say, Amen.

May abundant peace from heaven descend upon us, And may life be renewed for us and for all Israel; and let us say, Amen.

He who makes peace in the heavens, may He make peace, For us and for all Israel; and let us say, Amen.

Jakob loosened the aquamarine from Peter's lifeless grip, then kissed his brother on the forehead.

As he had kissed Mama.

Zahava.

Ilana.

Tova.

And as he wished he could have kissed Faigy good-bye too.

He found Mama and Papa Stewart in the hallway on the bench. "He is gone."

Mama Stewart burst into tears, trying to stifle her sobs with a lace handkerchief. Papa Stewart pulled her into his arms, and Jakob wandered toward the stairs. He played with the strings on Papa's tzitzit, winding them around the end of his finger and watching the tip turn blue, then releasing the blood to flow through to the end again.

SPRING 1995

South Haven, Michigan

CHAPTER 25

Nel sat on the front steps and watched Mattie working in her front yard, her back hunched as she edged the front flower beds by hand with a spade. Her wide-brimmed straw hat was outlined by a scarf she tied under her chin to keep it in place on the breezy spring afternoon. Tendrils of her gray hair curled against her coat collar.

"One of these days I'm gonna buy you a gas-powered edger, Ms. Mattie," said David, ambling up the driveway.

"Won't ever work as good as my own two hands, and you know it, Mr. Butler," she said over her shoulder. A smile spread across Mattie's face, wrinkles morphing into multiple parentheses highlighting her joy of sinking her fingers into the dirt again after winter.

David extended a steaming cup of coffee toward Nel. "Brought you a little pick-me-up."

"Thank you."

The time they spent together had increased to near daily as winter turned to spring. Sometimes he'd bike into town with her to the library as she continued to check out and special-order books on Ukraine. Sometimes he surprised her with lunch as she worked away, forgetting the time, on her jewelry orders. Sometimes he visited Jakob with her at Lakeview.

"Everything okay?"

"Oh. Yeah. Sorry." Nel ran her fingers through her hair and exhaled audibly. "I can't believe Dad's really coming home tomorrow."

Careful to avoid her coffee, David sat next to her on the step and pulled her close to him. "It'll be fine. I'll help. Mattie will help."

"I know. I'm ready from that perspective. I'm just worried he'll fall again when I'm not around, or something worse ..." Nel sipped the coffee, grateful for the earthy taste and the warmth of David beside her. Her recent, marathon efforts to finish more prototypes and commissions left her feeling dazed and worn out. She wanted to finish as much work as she could before Jakob came home so she could devote the majority of her time to getting him settled.

"I know. But you can't think about that. You've gotta take one day at a time." He grabbed her hand and pulled her toward his truck. "Like today, for instance. Come see what else I brought you."

He pulled out a long, thin bag from the bed of his truck.

"What's that?"

"You'll see. This way."

"David, I don't have time—"

He pressed a finger gently to her lips and led her down the path and the steep stairs to the shore.

The late-afternoon sky shone deep blue, and she was glad she'd grabbed her down parka as the wind pushed against her. Tree limbs edged with the chartreuse of spring buds hugged the shoreline, and waves danced with froth on their tips. The shore was different every day, and it reminded Nel of a poem or a psalm with new meanings every time she read them.

She nodded down the beach toward a small stack of wood and Adirondack chairs tucked into a spot of sand surrounded by tall grass. "Someone has a good idea. It's a great afternoon for a beach fire."

"Glad you think so. It's for us."

She put her hands on her hips and tried to look annoyed with him. "David Butler. I have to finish those orders today."

He ignored her qualms and handed her a roll of string, then pulled a kite out of the bag. "You wanna be the runner or the thrower?"

Nel hadn't flown a kite in years. Perhaps decades. Not since Dad used to build his own and take Nel and her summer friends out to fly them. "I'll run I guess."

"Okay. That makes me the thrower."

She ran hard into the wind, pivoting and running backward, facing him, as the string between them lengthened. "Now! Throw it now!"

He did, and the kite, a diamond of red, orange, and yellow with a tail of bandanna scraps, rose into the air. Back and forth it seized under the pull of crisscrossed currents of air. Diving and jumping and diving again, threatening to crash into the glimmering sunlight on the lake, the kite struggled with the wind. Nel's legs strained to run farther and force it higher where it could rest and float, and when it did, she fell to her knees in the sand and laughed.

"Thank you." Nel smiled at David, who'd joined her.

"You're welcome." They sat on the beach a good while and watched the kite waltz on the currents of air above them.

David broke the silence. "Hungry?"

"Starved."

They reeled the kite in, then trudged up the beach to the campsite where David began to work on starting the fire.

"May I?" Nel nodded toward the picnic basket.

"Yep. Nothin' fancy. Comfort food."

She pulled out a bag of hot dogs; a container of potato salad; a baggie of fat, green grapes; a sack of marshmallows; and oatmeal-chocolate-chip cookies, still warm from being wrapped in foil.

"I made the cookies," he confessed.

"Seriously?"

"I like to bake." He shrugged his shoulders and grinned at her over the smoke rising from the kindling beneath the logs.

"What else do you like—besides baking and kite flying and bringing me food?"

"S'pose you'll have to hang around and find out."

The more time she'd spent with him, the more she realized she'd be happy to do just that. She twisted the top off a thermos and smelled the toasty scent of hot chocolate. The pinking of the sky, the emerging stars, and the rising moon were a perfect backdrop to the evening. She sat on her haunches and roasted a hot dog, spinning it in quarter turns until each side was a perfect brown.

"So, you ever gonna tell me why you moved back from Florida?"

The marshmallow David roasted turned into a blazing torch.

He blew out the flame, and the fingers of the bonfire reflected in his greenish-gray eyes, which Nel felt darken as they fixed on her from across the fire pit.

"Story is, I came back to start my handyman business. Fix places that haven't been tended to."

Nel stirred the fire, and sparks popped and danced on the heat rising up from it. "No one comes back to South Haven. Not if they don't have to."

"Some do. People who have no place else to go. People who realize they never should have left in the first place."

She wanted to press him, but the way he said "no place else" stopped her. There was a sadness to it that felt fragile.

"So what's *your* story?" David said after a few silent moments.

She shrugged. "I don't have one. Unless you count the old saying 'Time flies when you're having fun,' I guess."

"I guess."

Nel grew more uncomfortable as he gazed at her and was glad when he changed the subject. Clearly it wasn't the right time for either of them to divulge details about their pasts, though they'd been dancing around them for months. Mattie's advice came to mind: *You know, some things are too painful, too shameful to speak of …*

"Anything new with the research about your dad?"

"I haven't heard anything from the church in Ukraine, and I've sent over a half dozen letters. For all I know, none of them ever got there. I may try to send another one. Or maybe I should just leave it all alone." She furrowed her brow, discouraged.

"Have you asked your dad about any more of it?"

"I took the photo and ship manifest to Lakeview one day and showed it to him. At first I thought I saw a flash of recognition when he looked at the photo, but then he got agitated. So I haven't brought it up since then."

"Maybe he knows but doesn't want to talk about it."

"Maybe. Part of me wants to let it all rest, but part of me wants to know about where he came from, what he survived. It's his story, I know, but it's mine, too—is that selfish? It'd just be nice to know before it's all gone forever."

"Do you think he'll be more apt to talk about it once he gets home and settled?"

"I don't know," she sighed. "I'm worried the move will make him confused again. But the doctors have said if anything, he might be less confused when he's back around his own things."

"I can see that. Everyone likes to be home." He gazed past her at the churning lake.

"Yeah …"

He stood, brushed the sand off his jeans, and grabbed another roasting stick. "You ready for a s'more?"

"I guess I oughta be, since you've already had two."

Instead of sitting across from her where he had been, he came and crouched next to her in the sand. He balanced the stick so the marshmallows roasted over cooler embers, then leaned toward her, brushing her hair away from her face. "You've gotten prettier after all these years, Nel Stewart."

"Have I?"

"Mmm-hmm. Mind if I give you that after-prom kiss I should have?"

She answered by leaning in and kissing him first, then giggled. "Better check those marshmallows."

"Dang it! I always do that." He grabbed the stick and blew out the flames on the end of it. The marshmallows looked like charcoal. "Sorry about that."

They laughed and abandoned the s'mores in favor of lying back and picking out constellations, which brightened and connected as dusk settled around them.

The next day, Nel tried to rub nervous emotions out of her arms as she sat on the windowsill in Jakob's room at Lakeview. While she was glad to be bringing him home, she knew the risks of him falling again were great. And if he fell and broke the same hip, or something else, she knew he most likely wouldn't recover.

The room already looked sterile with everything all packed away, a blank slate for the next resident to decorate with decades of a life propped up in picture frames, potted in decaying planters, and played out on cards and torn-edged coloring-book pages, scribbles of "Love you, Grandpa" in the unsure strokes of a preschooler.

Jakob struggled with the buttons of his argyle cardigan—the one she'd bought him for Christmas.

"Here, let me help you." Nel pressed the buttons gently through the buttonholes. She bent and pulled his socks up, then let him push his feet into his house shoes while she rechecked to make sure his cabinet drawers were empty. She packed a few other leftover pieces of his clothing: a pair of stained, threadbare boxer shorts; a short-sleeved, starched, striped shirt he'd had since working as a manager at Brake-All; and a couple more Mr. Rogers–like cardigans.

"An old man can't ever have enough cardigans," Jakob had said when he'd opened the box from Nel at Christmas.

A young girl dressed in purple scrubs that hung off her thin frame pushed a wheelchair into the room and pulled an empty cart behind her. Silver piercings jutted out from the side of her nose, the right corner of her upper lip, and her left eyebrow, in addition to the rows of rhinestone studs outlining one ear. She hardly looked old enough to work. Her name tag flipped backward, and a photo of a baby with a giant daisy headband bigger than her head smiled from it.

"Hi, I'm Karrie," she said to Nel. "Heard it's moving day for Big Jake here."

"You better believe it, missy." Jake winked.

She patted Jake's shoulder. "You ready, Big Jake?"

"Ready as I can be, except for leaving you. And I mean that in the most respectable of ways. You're a special lady, Karrie. Don't you let those dirty young men take advantage of you, hear? And lose a couple of those pierced things. You're too pretty for those."

"Yes, sir. I will." She kissed Jakob's cheek, then put her arms, like thin ribbons, around his thick body and squeezed him hard. A tear fell down her cheek as she backed away. "I wish they still made gentlemen like you."

Karrie and Nel packed up the cart and helped Jakob into the wheelchair.

"Let's get this show on the road."

Like a macabre parade of strangers thrown together in a side-show for the aged and decrepit, the troupe made their way past the recreation room, where fuzzy-headed women sat with blankets over their shoulders picking at yarn and needlepoints, hooked-rug and macramé projects. A few waved their hands. Most didn't seem to notice. Heading for the front doors, the three of them passed the cafeteria, where a few straggling residents poked at frothy remnants of their pureed lunches.

"Bye, Big Jake." The receptionist put a finger in the spot she'd been looking at in her magazine and closed it as Jake and his procession passed.

Jake raised his hand in a gesture of good-bye but never looked away from the glass doors and the trusty Crown Victoria beyond them.

CHAPTER 26

Nel breathed a sigh of relief. By the time she and Jakob arrived back at the house, David's pickup truck was already parked in front, and he and Mattie were standing in the front yard waiting for them. David came alongside the car, opened Jakob's door, and helped him out. He stayed next to Jakob, helped him unfold his walker, and held a hand loosely under his right arm as they shuffled toward the house. Although steady now—a marked improvement from where he'd started before rehabilitation—Jakob moved slowly, and any sort of large rock or dip in the terrain could buckle his leg and break another bone.

"Nice to see you, David." Jakob coughed between steps.

"You too, Jake."

"Well, well, well. Look who else has come to welcome my old bag of bones home." He nodded toward Mattie, who was waiting for him at the top of the bright, clean wood of the new ramp David had built to the front door.

She blew him a kiss. "Made you some meat loaf."

Jakob plodded harder and faster. "C'mon you two. I'm not dead yet."

But his determination didn't last long. A couple dozen stone steps led from the drive to the front door, and each one proved a near-mountain for Jakob, as did the ramp, despite the gentle incline David had designed. With each lurch, Nel wondered whether or not his hip would hold him up. Tears threatened as she questioned yet again what she might be getting herself into.

The meal Mattie made for Jakob's homecoming rivaled Thanksgiving: her special meat loaf (better than turkey any day) smothered in gravy; homemade, smashed red potatoes; green-bean casserole; and yeast rolls filled the center of the old, round oak table in the dining room. Pumpkin pie, blueberry cobbler, and carrot cake on a cut-glass pedestal lined the antique oak sideboard in the dining room.

"Mom and Dad's wedding china." Nel picked a dinner plate off the top of the stack she'd pulled out of the matching oak glass china cabinet to begin setting the table and stroked the painted, tiny pink roses and gilded rim entwined with delicate ivy.

"She always said it doesn't do anyone any good tucked away in a cabinet," said Mattie.

"No, it doesn't. Plus, in a way, having this out makes it feel like she's welcoming Dad home too." Nel turned toward the living room, where David sat reading the newspaper next to Jakob in his recliner. Jakob's chin bobbed against his chest as he appeared to fight a nap in vain. "I'm worried about him, Mattie. As much as he's improved, I can't shake the feeling he's not much longer for this world."

Mattie came alongside her and put an arm around Nel's shoulders. "You never know. But either way, that's why it's good you brought him home. When I die, I don't want to be hooked up to a bunch of tubes with doctors pounding on my chest, or alone in a cold room at a nursing home, no matter how nice the place is. I want to be home. And I'm pretty sure he does too." Mattie kissed Nel's cheek.

"Think we should skip the fancy table settings and eat out there? I could get the TV trays out so he doesn't have to get up. He's so comfortable there."

"That's a good idea," replied Mattie, giving her another squeeze.

The four of them sat and ate in the living room, the sound of *Wheel of Fortune* on the television in the background.

"It's good to have you home, Dad."

Jakob didn't respond as he struggled to get a piece of blueberry cobbler into his mouth. His hands shook much of the time now, something else that bothered Nel, who'd always been amazed at how steady her dad's hands were as he created his gem and cabochon designs. He wiped a glob of blueberry off his chin and worked at getting another bite on his fork. Either he hadn't heard her or he was too preoccupied with his cobbler to pay attention.

Mattie, sitting next to him, patted his knee. "Jakob."

"Yeah?" He peered over the top rim of his glasses at her. It sounded like half the cobbler was stuck in his throat.

"Nel said she's glad you're home."

"Nel?"

"She's right there." Mattie nodded toward Nel, who sat on the couch across from him.

"Well, well, well. So she is." His face brightened as he looked at his daughter, as if realizing for the first time that she was there.

Nel supposed he might've been realizing it for the first time—at least the first time in the last five minutes. And yet, as many times as she'd been through repeating herself and listening to him repeat himself, as many times as Jakob had called her Catherine, hearing his lapse in short-term memory in his own home—her childhood home—was more than she could bear in that moment. She stood so fast she nearly knocked over her TV tray. "Is anybody else finished? I'll start clearing plates."

"I'll help," David said, following her to the kitchen.

She stood at the kitchen sink and watched three blue herons soar across the horizon without hardly moving their wings.

"Here." David came behind her and wrapped his arms around her, handing her a clean dishtowel to wipe her tears. "It'll be okay."

"I know he can't help it. It's just so hard to see him like that. Especially here at home."

"Give him a few days. The doctors said there'll be an adjustment period, right?" He gently kissed the side of her face.

She leaned back into David's chest and sighed. "They did … Did you see how his hands were shaking?"

"Yeah … I imagine moving took a lot out of him."

"I suppose."

David swept her hair away from the side of her neck and kissed her below her ear. "It'll be okay."

"Will it?"

CHAPTER 27

Jakob had sat in his recliner and drifted in and out of a nap as Nel and Mattie cleaned up the meal and unpacked Jakob's belongings, throwing most of his clothes into the washer. A hospital bed had been delivered that morning, and they'd set it up in the den, which was closest to the bathroom. They made it up in new flannel sheets and several quilts and afghans Catherine had made so it would feel as much like a "normal" bed as possible.

"Whew," Mattie said, untying the apron from around her waist. "Now that all that's done, let's get some fresh air."

After putting on her own windbreaker, Mattie helped Jakob with his jacket. As he stepped outside, the breeze off the lake made Jakob's eyes fill with tears, not from the chill, but rather from the crisp freshness of the outdoors he'd always loved. He tried to ignore the pain in his hip as he settled himself on a sturdy chair on the back deck.

The sun prepared to sink into the far edge of the lake, the yellow orb accenting the edges of the lawn, the trees, and the escarpments tumbling to the shore below. A black squirrel darted across the lawn as the two of them sat together in silence for a while, the way friends who know each other well can do without awkwardness.

Mattie pulled a chair up beside him and tucked a striped wool Pendleton blanket around them both to ward off the chill of the evening. Jakob welcomed the feel of her thinning, aging body pressed lightly against his for warmth.

"You really scared me this time." Mattie sighed, then tilted her head back to find the first stars of the evening sky through a break in the pinking clouds. "Losing Catherine was hard enough. I don't know how I'd stand losing both of you."

Jakob fiddled with the cuff of his Brake-All jacket.

"Some nights when you were so sick in the hospital I didn't know whether you were dead and I ought to be saying the Kaddish for you, or if I should be reciting a blessing that you're here yet another day, so every night before I got in bed, I knelt down and said both." Mattie pushed back a stubborn wisp of her curly, gray hair sticking out from beneath her red, boiled-wool hat.

"Why bother?"

"Why bother what?"

"Why bother saying either? I'm not sure prayer makes a lick of difference." He thought about the first chapter of Ecclesiastes again. *The sun rises and the sun sets, and hurries back to where it rises.*[1] Over and over again. No matter what anyone does. *Meaningless!*[2]

"You're a stubborn, stubborn man."

"Yes, well …"

"Never mind. I have enough prayers for the both of us."

"I have no doubt."

She turned to face him, gripping both of his thick, gnarled hands in hers, clad in soft black-leather driving gloves. "Jakob Stewart. God has returned you to the land of the living so many times. Do you really not believe? Do you not see how He has repaid you for the years the locust have eaten? That He restores and renews you even as you've wandered around in your pain and anger all these decades?"

"You have no idea what I lived through." Jakob dropped his head. "Just let me live out these last days in peace. I am too old to be preached at about redemption."

"I know something's haunting you. That Catherine tried for years to get it out of you. That your nightmares are more than just scary dreams." She sat back in the chair again and followed his gaze out onto the lake in time to see a shooting star sweep across the horizon. "You're not the only one to have suffered pain, to have seen things—horrific things—in this life. Our family ran for our lives out of Germany, if you'll recall. I raised those five children of mine alone after Jack left us. I didn't want to follow God either, if that meant turning the other way while my husband had an affair."

"And then you found Jesus." Jakob hadn't intended to sound condescending.

"No. Well, yes, but that's not what I was going to say. Don't sound so impudent. I've seen plenty of times your faith in Jesus guided you—or at least guided Catherine, who guided you."

"So I'm having a faith crisis."

"Look. No one's trying to spoon-feed you the gospel. Gratefulness is a choice. One I have to make every day. One that wouldn't hurt you to choose either."

"That'll do, Mattie."

"Don't tune me out yet. I did a lot of thinking while you were away. Wouldn't it be wonderful to leave this world without heavy burdens?"

"Let me sink into death like an old slab of granite out there." He waved his hand out at the great lake. "After that, no one will care. Dead. Done. Belly up like a floating muskie. Worm food. Kaput."

"Nel will care ... and I will care too."

He turned toward her, eyebrows raised, pale cheeks pink from the cold as much as from the conversation.

"Nel will find her way without me. She already has."

"I don't think so." She paused. "Forgiving ourselves can be harder than forgiving our enemies. But holding on to the past, well ... if your hands are full, you can't accept anything else, even the good that life might have for you. Whatever you went through, let go of it. Tell Nel. She deserves to know. And if you can't start by telling the bad, start by telling the good. There had to have been some good."

The screen door creaked as Nel and David came outside. "We're going for a walk on the beach."

Jakob smiled at them and nodded.

"Don't mind us. You go and have fun now. And don't worry," Mattie said to Nel, "I'll stay until you get back."

"Thanks, Mattie. Love you, Dad."

The two of them tromped toward the stairs leading to the beach, and Jakob was glad to see David grab Nel's hand. He'd succeeded in not leaving Catherine alone in the world. It would be a relief to know Nel wouldn't be left alone when he died too.

Jakob and Mattie were silent then. The cardinals and mourning doves, finches and sparrows sang, joining the chorus of frogs and the lapping of waves on the shore below them. He looked at the flower beds Nel had been tending back into shape and recalled how beautiful they'd been when he and Catherine had been able to tend them as they should be tended, freshly mulched, weeded, and thinned. The peonies would burst open soon, Catherine's favorites, their giant blooms like scoops of ice cream overflowing and cascading to the ground in delicious pastel heaps. They'd researched and taken great care over the years to plant perennials that didn't have to struggle against the often-cruel Michigan springs, and to plant enough varieties so something would be blooming all season long.

"Sunflowers," Jakob said so suddenly Mattie startled. "There were sunflowers in Chudniv."

Jakob described them to Mattie, how the sunflowers grew, golden waves of them like an ocean stretching all the way to the edge of the world. He and his siblings ran as deep as they could into the fields and could never find the end. They had played hide-and-seek among them, giving up only when they reached the main road laden with honeysuckle. From there they'd trek to the creek, where they waded and caught frogs to hide at the feet of Peter's and Zahava's beds—their oldest two siblings "too big" to join them anymore.

One day, the summer before the pogrom, when Jakob and his siblings returned from playing in the sunflower fields, their arms overflowing with fresh-cut flowers for Mama, they caught a glimpse of how much their sister Zahava's interests had shifted from child's play. Though the rules of the matchmaker said she wasn't allowed to choose a suitor for herself, everyone knew she had her eye on Taras, the son of the local milkman and bread maker. That day Taras had been making his usual delivery for Mama, and Zahava made sure to be outside sweeping the front path so she could talk to him without Jakob and the rest of the younger siblings hearing. She didn't know that the three of them were crouched in the tall grass behind the fence bordering their property. Neither did she know that Papa had come in from the fields through the back of the house, and when he saw the two teenagers blushing and giggling together, he ran out front with a pitchfork and chased poor Taras, cow in tow, back toward the village. Zahava ran to her room sobbing, and Papa came back into the house grinning from ear to ear, sending the rest of the children into convulsions of laughter. Mama scolded Papa severely before heading to Zahava's room to console her.

The days had been glorious, golden halos of sunflowers set against the azure blue of the summer skies; bumpy rides in the oxcart across wheat fields, where it seemed the entire village had come out together to rake and bundle the sheaves; and always the storks—with their white heads and chests, black tails, and the flash of their long, orange beaks—perched high on outbuildings, where the owners fastened wagon wheels for the birds to build their great nests. Legend said if a farm had a stork's nest, the farm would have peace, prosperity, and good health. And Papa had told many stories of how storks helped people. But the storks migrated in the fall all the way to South Africa, long before they could have helped the Maevskis, or anyone for that matter, in the village of Chudniv in the winter of 1904.

"Thank you for telling me about your family," Mattie said.

Jakob exhaled and hung his head so Mattie would not see the new moisture in his eyes.

Mattie rose and held his head between her hands and kissed him on the center of his forehead. Her lips reminded Jakob of the delicateness of the first peony petals of spring. He wished he'd had the energy to reach back toward her, but his age and memories of Catherine, still thick in his mind, kept him still. Instead, he patted the side of her soft face in a grandfatherly way more suited to his wasted frame.

"I love you, old man," she said as she walked down the steps of the deck toward her backyard. "And I won't give up on what we've talked about. I'll pray for you tonight, as always."

CHAPTER 28

Jakob lay on his side, his hip aching from the commotion of the day. He decided he didn't mind having a bed in the den, surrounded by his beloved books. The moon reflected off the dogwood blossoms—the most vibrant show the tree had put on in years—outside the window. He and Catherine had planted the tree when Nel was born, after Catherine had read in Genesis about Abraham planting a tree shortly after Isaac was born. Jakob's mind drifted to the old stories of Abraham and Isaac, his namesake Jacob, the wandering of the Israelites, and the things Mattie had said about hanging on to pain.

What if she was right?

She probably was right.

She was always right.

But that would mean he'd wasted his life, wouldn't it?

He hadn't though, not completely. After all, he'd provided for Catherine. He'd loved her deeply. He loved Nel. He loved his brother, the Stewarts, and his family.

And yet, he'd loved conveniently, and with boundaries—walls so tall and so reinforced with pain and fear that whatever he allowed himself to feel was more contentment than passion. More resignation than peace.

His eyelids grew heavy as the argument continued within him, and the shimmering moonbeams shifted, illuminating another landscape ...

"My znaÿdemo sposib."[†]

Peter's confidence did not convince little Jakob, who ached for Mama and Papa. He longed to sit at Papa's feet, for the warmth of the fire, for the soft hammer of Papa's voice as he spoke and bantered with Sasha the priest late into the night, and the way he whispered into Mama's ear and made her giggle when he came in from the fields. Jakob's heart throbbed, and the journey since they left the shtetl had become only more horrifying the farther west they raced toward Austria-Hungary.

Peter said evil men wanted them dead because they were Jewish—even though they had accepted Messiah Yeshua. Their conversion didn't matter to the pogromshchik. Nothing mattered to those madmen. They made up stories about the Jews being set against the tsar, when all the people—any people— wanted was to live in peace in the beautiful countryside. The land of Ukraine was like a Siamese twin, pulled between its own independence and Great Mother Russia. Young men in their twenties caught on fire with zeal from propaganda leaflets

---

[†]   We will find a way.

thrown in the streets, telling them to put down anyone who resisted. What they resisted did not matter. And so they picked the Jews, whose differences were most obvious. None of it made sense to Jakob.

"Like the cloud and pillar of fire for the Israelites, God goes before us, and He comes behind, Jakob."

The sky hung above the two boys as they traveled, a curse of clear-blue cold biting through their fur and sheepskin coats. Jakob thought Peter referred to the story of Moses leading the Israelites, that God had led them with the clouds and fire of which Peter spoke, one of many stories he recited to help distract them from the freezing air. Even Galya seemed to long for warmth and a place to stay and rest. He had quit fighting the bit and reins. Around his muzzle, frozen breath formed a ring of snow, and frozen spittle dripped into icicles.

Tears froze on Jakob's face even as they rolled out of his eyes, so fierce was the wind and so brutal was the cold. He could not have guessed how long Peter had been racing Galya across the flat and snowy fields, only that the moon rose higher and higher as they rode. The moon and stars shone on the snow and ice, which shimmered and glowed, making everything—trees, shrubs, abandoned oxcarts, and plows—along the horizon look like ghosts chasing them. If Jakob had to run from them, he knew he couldn't; his legs were numb and nearly frozen stiff.

Crack!

Galya bucked at the sudden burst of sound, and Peter, who had jumped as well, pulled hard on the horse's reins. "Shhh, shhh, now, Galya. There now. Hush." Peter guided Galya toward a patch of naked birch trees. He reached forward and ran his hand along the gray horse's neck, Galya's frenzied eyes nearly popping out of his head.

More cracks of gunfire pierced the air. Jakob felt fear hastening his brother's breathing, and for the thousandth time, he prayed Papa was right—that whoever held the guns would see they were just boys and in no way a threat to the tsar … that they might not assume they were Jews, but simply orphans, like so many others in the land, all running from something, starving flesh stretched tight over their ribs.

It was a wonder they survived that night—or any of the others—when Peter had done his best to carve a shelter out of the several feet of snow on the ground. They dared not light a fire. The sounds of gunfire mixed with memories of the guttural screams of his mother and sisters that would not leave Jakob's ears, and as he crawled into the little cave in the snow, he was once again stuck in the cupboard, hiding and too afraid to help or cry out or even try to defend his family. Screams and cries and shotgun blasts. On and on and on it went.

Until finally the night fell silent.

Silence thicker than the several feet of snow around them.

Silence darker than the sky above.

And Jakob knew then that if there were a hell, it would be full of silence.

When Peter and Jakob awoke in the morning, they ate the last of the near-rancid beef and raw beets they'd found in the cupboards of the homes of the last abandoned shtetl they'd passed through. Peter set Jakob on Galya's sagging back, and they set off again, staying far from where they thought the gunfire had come from the night before. But then they stumbled upon it, the snowy road, trampled flat by what must've been hundreds of human feet. Peter stopped Galya, who whinnied and stamped his hoof as though he was annoyed to have another crazed ride cut short. Peter walked closer to the newly trampled path, following it into the dense groves of pine, where it disappeared.

Jakob tugged on his brother's coat, pulling at him, begging him wordlessly not to go on.

"Shhhhh—wait here."

Jakob was too afraid to wait alone, and the gap in the trees swallowed them, the thickness of the evergreens darkening with each step they took. The snow-packed path narrowed as the ground inclined heavenward, where a half-dozen hawks, wings as wide as ship sails, floated on the sky above. The muffled moan of an infant echoed the bitter cry of a mourning dove overhead. Part of Jakob wanted to run back to Galya, but the better part of him stayed close to Peter as he kept walking toward the sounds. Finally they came upon a steep ravine, and the sight below caused everything in Peter's belly to come rushing out of him, splatting against the crushed snow at their feet.

Jakob peered over the edge as Peter heaved behind him, and he was greeted by the stare of an unmoving girl, about the age of their sister Ilana. Her jaw was slack, and a trickle of blood ran down the side of her ashen face. Next to her lay a dead infant, and under the infant, a man and a woman, still clutching each other, half their heads blown off.

There were hundreds of them.

All naked, dead. Twisted and unmoving.

The gaping hole steamed with the warmth of their lifeblood rising and disappearing into the cruel, clear sky.

Was this the pillar of clouds Peter had meant?

The boys didn't stay to find which infant still made sounds, but ran, as they had run from their parents and sisters, back to Galya.

Jakob ran, but his legs wouldn't work. He fell and lost sight of Peter. Arms and hands reached up out of the ravine for him, and he screamed at his legs, begging them to move, but still his legs lay limp beneath him.

"Peter! Help me! Peter!"

"Dad! Wake up. It's a dream. It's just a dream."

Jakob trembled, still fighting the darkness and the feel of blackness, of voiceless corpses reaching for him. He pushed against whoever held his arms down.

"Dad, it's me, Nel. It's a dream. You're having a dream."

He heard a click and light filled the room, nearly blinding him. He squinted as the face before him came into focus, then he grabbed at the person. "Help me ... my legs, they won't work—"

"Dad," the face said. "Wake up, Dad. You're home. You're safe. You're home."

"Catherine?"

"No. Nel. It's me. It's your daughter."

He felt the arms around him, rocking him as if he were a child, wiping the sweat off his face and neck. Then he burst into tears. "I'm sorry. I'm so sorry."

"It's okay, Dad. You're safe. Let it go now. It was just a dream. Let it go."

CHAPTER 29

"Mind if I watch?"

Nel grinned at her dad's question as she leaned over the worktable and used pliers to twist the heavy silver wire. "That's usually my question, isn't it?"

"Used to be."

She didn't take her eyes off the wire as she bent and wrapped, twisted and turned it around the newly shined and tumbled piece of jade. At the same time, she listened to the thump, drag, and shuffle of her dad and his walker as he hobbled into the workroom. It'd been a good couple of weeks since he'd had the night terror, and both of them were feeling more at ease, even in a routine. Nel took to sleeping late, as had Jakob, whom she knew had been relieved to be away from Lakeview's strict rehabilitation schedule. Up at 6:30. Breakfast at 6:45. First round of physical therapy at 7:15, then occupational therapy at 8:00. There might've been time for a nap between occupational therapy and community exercise hour at 9:30, but that had been rare. Though the Lakeside staff tried to cluster their tasks, especially at night, to allow residents regular sleep schedules, she'd learned from the memory-care doctors how even a couple of unnatural interruptions were too much for the fragile rhythms of a geriatric, causing exhaustion, adding to confusion, and compounding tendencies toward anxiety and depression. So much of that heaviness had lifted off her father after he'd come home, and Nel knew this was one reason for what everyone—she, Mattie, and even David—felt was a new brightness, even an extension, of his life.

"Do you remember all I taught you about reflection and refraction?" His question applied to faceting, which he preferred to talk about over cabochons, tumbled rocks, and metalworking. Those subjects were too easy for him intellectually, although he had enjoyed doing some of that work too. He simply preferred the intricate calculations of angles and measurements, the exactness required to bring out the most brilliance in a gemstone.

Nel didn't have to think hard to answer Jakob's question. Everything she'd watched him do and listened to him say had stuck with her. "The angles on the outside reflect the light. When the light bounces off the angles on the back of the stone, that's called refraction. It's what gives the stone its brilliance and shimmer."

"That's my girl."

Nel paused her work on the bracelet and glanced at the rock Jakob had poked around his containers for and now held in his hand.

"I always liked this tourmaline," he said. One end of the stone was a pale green, which blended gracefully into the other end, which was pink. When heated, it would turn any number of solid colors, depending on the time and temperature used.

"Prettier heated, I think."

"Me too," Jakob said as he poked around some more in a box of old agate.

"I remember those." She referred to the oval pencil marks on the surface of the agate where Jakob had long ago identified where to make the first cuts to the stone. If he made cabochons, agate was especially fun to work with, vignettes and scenes hidden within the striations and patterns of the stone. She pointed to the image isolated by one penciled-in oval in particular. "That one looks like little blackbirds, or eagles, maybe, soaring over snowcapped mountains."

"I thought the pattern on this one looked like the outline of sea grass on the shore." He pointed to another.

"The storyteller's stone, you always called it." Nel turned off the brightest light glaring on the worktable and set her wire and tools aside. If she was ever going to talk to him about his past, this was as good a time as any. But she'd start with Mom. "I miss her."

Jakob appeared startled by the mention of Catherine. They didn't avoid talking about Catherine, necessarily. It had simply become easier to let the days go by without bringing her up. He sat down heavily on the chair across from her and rubbed his knees.

Nel continued. "I miss her cooking. The way she smelled like lilacs and night cream."

Jakob inhaled deeply. "The way she sang when she folded and ironed the laundry."

"To Pat Boone," they said in unison, laughing.

"Yeah—and that time she tried to teach me to sew," Nel said. "And when I wore the skirt to the market, it fell apart."

"Homemade fried chicken on the beach. Homemade gingerbread men at Christmas."

"Gingerbread girls. She always made girls, not men ... for me, she said."

"Only the good die young," Jakob said, joy on his face falling as he nudged his bifocals farther up on his nose.

"That's not true, Dad." Emotion welled up in her. "You're good, Dad. And you're all I have."

Jakob responded by reaching out and patting her hand.

She squeezed his back, then reached across the table to the box where she kept the kiddush cup and aquamarine since she'd found them, as well as Catherine's research. "Speaking of Mom, I found this when I was going through some things."

She pulled each item out of the box, and the moment Jakob saw the aquamarine, his whole countenance changed, filled with emotion she didn't recognize. She handed the stone to him, and he sank back into the chair and turned it in his hands.

"Does any of this have anything to do with your brother? With Peter?" The only way she was going to find out anything was if she came right out and asked him. She'd heard nothing from the correspondence she sent to Ukraine and had resigned herself to never hearing from them. "Dad, I don't want to upset you, but I'd love to know more about him, and about your past. Where you—where we—came from. Peter must've been important to you, for you to keep these things all these years."

She watched as her dad struggled with a response, opening his mouth to speak, then closing it again as if having a silent argument with himself about what he would and would not say.

He held the stone up to the sunlight coming in the window, and the facets caught the light, sending dappled bursts of reflections across the walls of the room.

"I will tell you my story."

CHAPTER 30

Once Jakob began, the words flowed from him like the ripples he used to make while tossing pebbles into the pond behind his childhood home in Chudniv. He told Nel everything, starting with Mama and Papa; his sisters, Zahava, Tova, Ilana, and Faigy; and his brother Peter. He told her about the colorful floral scarves all the girls and women wore, and about listening to the songs of fiddles and bayans as people danced at festivals and at the break of Sabbath. He told her about the wooden churches and synagogues, the sashes of shtetl homes painted pure white, and the doors painted turquoise. He told her about market day, when the peasants came to town, and how the commotion of shopping and playing and bartering felt like a carnival every week. He told her about Sasha the priest coming to visit, and how they learned about Yeshua Messiah from him, and how it made many of their neighbors very angry, but many other neighbors believed in Yeshua Messiah too.

Then he told her about his journey with Peter. About Raisa and the maniac in the barn. Peter losing his fingers. Finding the hundreds murdered in the woods. The cold. The hunger. The burning villages. The kindness of the old and wrinkled Luda. The hospitality of Russie and Chaim. How Peter sold Galya to Zsófia and Makár in Austria-Hungary. About the man who'd tried to rob him on the train. Parents selling their daughters in the shipyards. Two weeks on the ship in steerage. Ellis Island. John and Harriet Stewart. Saint Stanislaus. Mr. Grünfelder. The Battle Creek Sanitarium.

And finally Faigy. Faigy and what happened the night Peter left, the same night the pogromshchik came to the shtetl.

Nel stared at him. "Faigy? Your youngest sister?"

"Yes." Jakob exhaled, pondering whether or not to go on.

He began with Peter leaving home on Galya.

"Sometimes I wish Peter had never come back."

Peter always said God had told him to turn back, and that after a day of riding, he couldn't ignore the constant prompting in his soul telling him to return home. At first, Jakob had thought the sound of horse hooves against the hard-packed snow was another rider from the pogromshchik returning to kill him. And so when Peter found him in the cupboard, Jakob had screamed and screamed until Peter covered his gaping mouth with his gloved hand, then lifted Jakob and pressed his small head against his broad chest.

"Be quiet, brother," Peter said, swaying for a moment like Mama did whenever Jakob cried. "You must be quiet."

Jakob sniffed back a sob and his body slackened, if only slightly, as Peter held him on his hip and began to search the home for something—anything—to salvage from the scene of carnage before them. Mama lay half naked on the kitchen table. The arms of her dress sleeves were nailed to the wooden tabletop so her arms stretched out wide, like when she ran to greet Jakob, he thought, as he walked home on the afternoons spent learning Talmud with his siblings at a neighbor's. Her face was blue, her neck twisted at an impossible angle. Her skirts were torn off at the bodice, her pregnant belly rising into the air like a camel's lopsided hump. Blood dripped onto a round puddle on the floor through the cracks on the table. Ropes pulled tight around her ankles and secured around the table's legs had torn clear through to her shinbones.

Faint orange coals burned in the hearth, where remnants of the Bible Sasha had given them and Papa's Talmud smoldered. Above on the wall, a cross painted with blood spelled out "Die, Jews!"

Choked rage gurgled in Peter's throat, and he reached for Jakob's face, as if hoping to shield his eyes and protect him somehow from the gruesome scene. But Jakob brushed him aside, squirmed out of his arms, and walked up to his mama. He placed his hand on the side of her cold belly where he'd felt the kicks of his unborn sibling. Then he moved toward her ashen face and kissed her on the lips. Hot tears ran down the young boy's face and fell onto hers.

Grasping Jakob's hand, Peter moved toward their sister Zahava's body that lay curled in a ball at the base of the potbellied stove. In the center of the room, nails pierced the wooden floor in the shape of her arms and torso, resembling the crucifix-like shape of their mother. Chunks of fabric from Zahava's dress were still attached to the nails where she had managed to pull herself free.

In minutes Jakob seemed to age ten years as he helped Peter with Zahava. Jakob lifted one of her legs, caked with blood, as Peter lifted her limp body under the arms, and together they dragged their oldest sister to her bed, where they found two of their other sisters, Ilana and Tova, curled around each other like a pair of forgotten rag dolls, heads bashed in at the temples, gunshot wounds in the sides of their necks. Then they loosed Mama from the table and lay her beside her daughters, their sisters.

"Where is Faigy?" Peter asked.

Jakob's already pale face whitened, and he couldn't meet Peter's eyes.

Peter grabbed him by the shoulders. "Did you see? What did they do with baby Faigy?"

Still, Jakob could not meet his eyes.

Peter tilted his chin up gently, and it trembled as Jakob replied, *"Vony yiyi zabraly."*†

Peter didn't ask for details and instead took his hat off and ran his hands through his hair. He searched the room for something they could cover their mother and other sisters with, since they couldn't stay to bury them. The only thing they could find that the pogromshchik didn't take was their six prayer shawls, strewn across the bedroom like rags.

"Where is Papa?" Peter asked Jakob, barely whispering the question.

Jakob shrugged. He didn't know that answer either. He had clambered into the cupboard by the time the men had finished with his mother and sisters, and he stayed there even as the house quieted, the pogromshchik taking their laughter and glugging of alcohol with

---

†   They took her.

them. He had only seen what happened to Faigy because the one man in the black robes had returned.

Peter searched the house quickly for anything of value they could collect before leaving the house to look for their father. Meanwhile, Jakob left his side long enough to wander back to the kitchen, where Mama had prepared Shabbat so many times, twisting and separating the challah dough, making the kugel, mixing pepper and matzo flour for gefilte fish. From inside a slightly open cabinet door, an object gleamed—one of the family's silver kiddush cups the pogromshchik left behind. Josef had etched a scene replicating the village of Chudniv onto each of the family's eight cups and had been working on a ninth for the new baby. Jakob stretched onto his toes to reach the cup and knocked it to the ground, causing both boys to startle severely.

"What was that noise? Are you hurt?" Peter ran into the kitchen and followed Jakob's gaze to the cup. "Good job, Jakob. We'll take this cup with us."

As Peter started to tuck the cup into his coat, a piece of folded parchment fell onto the floor, startling them both again. Wary, Jakob crouched on his haunches, unfolded the paper, then held it toward his brother, who came and crouched next to him. The boys recognized instantly their father's squared-off penmanship. Words and numbers described precise instructions for faceting the Star of David aquamarine. Papa's penmanship was precise, as were the design and measurements on the thin, unlined parchment.

Peter stood quickly, as if suddenly realizing once more the precariousness of their situation, indeed the dire danger of allowing grief or fear or emotion of any kind to cause them to linger.

"Come on, Jakob. Papa must be outside."

Peter refolded the paper and stuffed it, along with the cup, into a spare satchel. He slung the satchel over his shoulder, then helped Jakob put on as many pieces of clothing as he could wear and one of their sister's larger coats over the top. Together the boys walked out the back of the house to begin the search for their father, which didn't take long. Blood-soaked clothing, broken lamps, pottery, and books, pages torn out of some of them, others half burned, bindings curved and charred—all of it littered the snowy ground.

They discovered Papa's fate near the ancient oak by the barn. There was nothing they could do to bring dignity to his grizzly death. The murderers had decapitated him and stuck his head high upon the broken end of the house broom. His arms and legs had each been severed from his body, his torso dragged and dumped near the side road that ran past their home. Peter pulled the pole down and laid it gently on the ground, then turned away and vomited.

Jakob's eyes locked upon his Papa's torso by the road, ribs sticking out, the white *tallit katan*[1] and the frayed strings of Josef's tzitzit stuck against the ground, bloodied and ruined. Peter walked over to the corpse, took a knife from the belt beneath his coat, cut a single tassel from the garment, and tucked it into the satchel next to the silver cup.

Then he picked up Jakob, held his trembling body against his shoulder, and took him to the front yard, where Galya waited, eyes wild, front hoof stomping with impatience. Puffs of frozen air escaped rhythmically from Galya's giant nostrils as Peter placed

Jakob on the front of the saddle. He climbed on behind, pulling on the reins to steady the horse long enough to sear the sight of the little cottage into his mind, onto his heart forever.

Finally, with a flick of the leather and a kick of Peter's heel, Galya seemed happy again to run, frenzied and insane, across the cruel, white countryside toward the west.

"Faigy would've lived if it hadn't been for me," Jakob said to Nel when he finished telling her the story.

"But, Dad, you were only four years old."

"That's what Peter said. But I should've been able to scream or do something when the man came back. He took the rest of Papa's stones too."

"You were a baby. What do you think you could've done?"

"I don't know. But I've never forgiven myself."

"Dad—"

Jakob held a hand up to stop her. "I've often wondered since then if Lot's wife, as she turned to stone, felt the same when she saw Sodom burning as I did leaving them behind and failing my sister Faigy."

CHAPTER 31

Nel stayed on the couch that night, afraid to be far from Jakob in his new makeshift bedroom. She heard him sleeping fitfully and attributed it to the hours he'd spent telling her everything. She could hardly sleep either, visions of her grandparents, aunts, and uncle she'd never met, their faces gray and solemn like the old portraits of shtetl Jews she'd seen throughout her research.

By morning, Jakob had developed a high fever. He was more than his usual confused too. She was tempted to call David or Mattie or both of them and take her dad straight to the hospital emergency room, but the visiting-nurse service was already scheduled to come that morning, so she waited to see what they would recommend.

"We'll take some blood and a urine sample and see if he's got an infection. In the meantime, let him rest."

The kind nurse's calm words didn't reassure Nel, who flipped nervously through Catherine's old magazines and tried to busy herself dusting the first floor so Jakob wasn't left alone. She tried to do a little work on her jewelry, but any creativity she might've had that day was now doused with worry over her dad. Thankfully, she'd been able to assuage Sandra and her buyers by completing orders and commissioned work so that she was, as she'd hoped to be, ahead of schedule.

The phone rang and it was David.

"How was your night?" .

"Not the greatest. I hardly slept worrying about him having another night terror, trying to get up by himself, or both. And now the nurse thinks he might have a urinary tract infection—she called it a 'UTI'—which would make sense. The doctors at the hospital told me how those can really mess with elderly patients, making them all confused, sometimes being the underlying reason for a fall. Whatever it is, Dad's snowed. He hasn't been up yet, and I'm not sure that he will be today."

"I'm sorry. Can I bring you some burgers or something for lunch? Maybe your dad would take a milkshake? I'm working at the old Thompson place just down the road today, so I'm close. I'm finishing up their kitchen cabinets this morning, and was planning on bringing some things by your house today to get things ready to start on the roof."

"That'd be amazing—burgers and shakes for both of us."

"And a large cup of coffee?" Nel heard the smile in his voice on the other end of the line.

"Extra large, if they have that," she replied.

Frustrated with trying to calm her nerves with busyness, she settled herself onto the couch and flipped on soap operas and drifted off to sleep. She awoke to the side door creaking open and David carrying his red toolbox and a nail gun with one arm and lugging an air compressor behind him with the other. "Hey there, beautiful—"

"Shhhh—Dad's sleeping."

"Oh, sorry," he whispered, setting his tools down and kissing her on the cheek. "Looks like someone else might've been napping too. I'll be right back with the burgers."

God bless him, Nel thought, hungry for lunch but more relieved to have someone with her when her dad was feeling poorly. Nel sat up, ran her hands through her hair, and tried to smooth her rumpled clothes before he came back. She blew the dreads falling over her eyes away from her face in exasperation.

"Let's eat out back," she said when he returned with the bags of food and the carrier full of shakes and coffee. "We can talk out there without disturbing Dad."

They settled on the back deck, and Nel brought the baby monitor with her. She'd picked up a set last-minute so she could hear Jakob if she was busy in another room, and she was glad she'd thought to do so. The similarities between caring for her father and what her friends described to her about caring for a young child were striking.

"Lumber company's delivering the roofing materials this afternoon," David said through a mouthful of cheeseburger.

Nel played with the straw in her milkshake.

"Aren't you gonna eat?" David asked.

"I will … It was a rough morning, is all. Dad woke up confused. Incontinent, which isn't unusual. But he was talking out of his head like when he was at the hospital with his broken hip. That's how I knew something was wrong besides his normal, everyday loopiness." Nel hesitated, searching for the right words to tell David the worst. "He tried to hit me. He just got so agitated when I was cleaning him up."

"He tried to hit you?"

"Yeah. I ducked." She looked at David sheepishly and grinned. It wasn't funny, but if she didn't try to make a little light of it, she'd burst into tears.

The phone rang and Nel jumped. "Maybe it's the doctor's office with the lab results." She ran inside to grab the call.

"You look relieved," David said to her when she came back several minutes later.

"I am. He has a bladder infection, but it's not too bad yet. They're calling in an antibiotic. They said he should be back to himself in a couple days."

"That's good news."

"I'm afraid I pushed him too hard yesterday." She told David the major portions of the story Jakob had told her the day before.

David looked stunned. "That's incredible. And he's carried that around with him his whole life? He never told anyone? Not even your mom?"

"No. All she knew was that he and Peter were from Ukraine and that the Stewarts had adopted them. No wonder she'd been determined to figure out what his story was, if she'd been living through his nightmares and all that. Maybe since Ukraine gained their independence in 1991, she thought she'd finally have the chance to know the whole story, where he'd come from and such."

"Makes sense." David stuffed their sandwich wrappers back into the bag. "But you haven't heard anything back from what you sent to Ukraine?"

"No. I doubt I will. It was a long shot. But now that he's told me the story, I don't feel like I need to know more. Not really."

Nel ran to the drugstore while David stayed with Jakob and waited for the lumber. After she returned and gave Jakob his first dose of antibiotics, he drank part of his milkshake. Then he fell asleep again.

"Hope you don't mind," David said when Nel came back to the living room. "I called Mattie to see if she'll sit with him a bit so we can take a walk."

"Mind? That sounds like heaven. How do you know what I need before I know myself?"

He shrugged, and she threw her arms around him and kissed him.

"Thank you, David, for everything you've done for me since I've been home, since all of this."

Mattie arrived, and Nel and David walked down to the lake, which was unusually placid. A group of blue herons flew overhead, so low they could hear the sound of their wings beating against the wind.

Nel pulled the rough piece of tourmaline out of her pocket, the same stone she and Jakob had been talking about the day before. She sighed, holding it up to the sun hovering over the lake. "The stone that can't decide what it wants to be."

David looked at her quizzically.

"That's what I call it. It's tourmaline. Turns to a solid color when it's heated up. Otherwise, it stays two-toned like this." She turned the stone between her fingers. "Ever since I've come home, I feel like that. Like God's heating me up. Trying to teach me who He wants me to be."

David picked up a flat beach stone and flung it across the smooth water, where it skipped half a dozen times. "He has a knack for that, that's for sure."

Nel glanced at him and wondered what he was getting at.

"Have you noticed anything curious about me since we've met?" David asked. "Or re-met, I should say?"

"Hmmm. Let me think. You talk with a lot of clichés. You love takeout. You're a fantastic kisser, which makes me mad all over again that I never got to find that out at the senior prom."

"You really bury the hatchet, don't you?"

"The handle could come in useful. Like today."

They laughed, and then David got serious again. "No, really. Think about it. What's missing?"

"Seriously? I have no idea what you're getting at."

"Your dad finally told his story. I guess I ought to tell you mine."

"David, you don't have to …"

He stopped, turned to her, and brushed her windblown hair away from her face as the sun gleamed down on it. "I want to. Maybe I need to. There was a reason I left Florida. I lost my wife. Lost everything … I killed a girl."

Nel stepped back instinctively. "What?"

"Not on purpose. But it was my fault. I started drinking in high school. All those bonfires we used to sneak off to? Turned into a big problem for me. Got worse in college. But everybody drank back then, so my fiancée didn't think twice about marrying me. Turns out she should have."

"What happened?"

"She couldn't handle my drinking. Especially when I'd start up about noon every day."

"No, I get that—you were an alcoholic. I mean what happened to the girl?"

"First of all, I *am* an alcoholic. Always will be."

"Okay, you *are* an alcoholic."

"I was driving drunk along the ocean-side road during the time when all the college kids come down for spring break. I'd already racked up three, maybe four DUIs." He hesitated. "Sunny day. Not a cloud in the sky. I didn't even see her and her friends crossing the road. It was the middle of the afternoon. They were heading to the beach, a whole group of them. She was the last one to cross, and I barreled right over her. She died instantly."

"Oh, David."

"By that time, my marriage was over except for the paperwork. The judge who sent me to prison helped finalize the divorce for her the same day."

"How much time did you serve?"

"I was sentenced to fifteen years. Vehicular homicide. Got out in seven and served the rest on probation. Sobered up when I was in prison through an in-house AA program. Isn't a day goes by that I don't think of that girl and her family."

Nel watched his eyes fill with tears as he looked out at the horizon.

"Figured God'd be done with me then. I had nothing in that concrete cell, or out of it, for that matter. Folks came in from prison ministries and tried to tell us we were forgiven and how much God loved us, and I couldn't believe them." He held his hand out toward her. "Can I see that tourmaline?"

"Sure."

He held up the lucent stone and peered at the different layers of color. "I can't tell you for sure when God started changing me.

Maybe the day I killed that girl. Maybe in prison. Maybe before all that, but I was too drunk to pay attention. But He did. I was all mixed up like this stone too. But He changed me. Still is. I tried running from Him. Over and over again, I ran and ignored His voice. But He kept heating me up. Bringing people or a scripture or a piece of nature into my life unexpectedly, and I knew it was Him, talking to me and chasing me. I still carry a lot of shame. But at least I know I can live a better life with His help."

"Wow." Nel stared at him, disbelieving.

"Yeah." David hung his head and watched the waves lap onto the shore. "You deserved to know."

The squeak of hydraulic truck brakes, followed by the repetitive beep of a truck backing up, caught their attention.

"Sounds like the lumber's here," said Nel. "We better get back up to the house."

CHAPTER 32

Jakob's infection cleared, and soon he was back to a relatively stable routine again, even cooking eggs for breakfast now and then. On this particular morning, Mattie had brought a coffee cake for breakfast and they sat in the living room watching the morning news together while Nel ran some errands. A sharp pain had been nagging Jakob in the back of his head, and it kept him from sipping on the cup of Nel's mud-strength coffee that Mattie had poured and set on the end table beside him. He waited for the pain to pass, but soon blackness covered the entire field of vision of his right eye. He tried to dismiss the pain by focusing his still-working left eye on the tree limbs swaying outside the living-room picture window. Squirrels chattered, no doubt fighting over the corncobs and seeds that Nel had kept replenishing in the feeders. Sunlight pressed through the edges of the shutters, and Jakob's toes and legs felt cold and stiff, even though it was late spring. Catherine had always kept blankets on the arms of every chair and couch, but even with a couple of those thrown over his lap and a pair of wool socks on his feet, he didn't feel warm.

"Aren't you going to drink your coffee?" Mattie said offhandedly as she flipped through a catalog.

"I'm letting it cool a bit," he said, hoisting himself up out of his recliner and heading toward the bathroom. "Excuse me a moment."

Jakob hadn't told anyone about the changes in his vision. It wasn't like he'd never had the strange eye spells before—he'd had them lots of times. Even before he broke his hip. But it was only one eye at a time, and they always passed as this one finally did too. Still, a chill he hadn't felt before crept deep within his limbs as he fumbled for his walker and trekked to the bathroom even slower than his usual slow.

"At least I kept my pants dry," he mumbled to himself after dropping his drawers to the floor. He grabbed onto the newly installed steel bar on the wall as he lowered himself onto the commode. David's additions and renovations pleased him, and he was truly grateful Nel had been there to orchestrate all the updates to the home. He and Catherine had always gotten by on what they had and didn't believe in fixing anything unless it was broke, but Jakob fully admitted the work needed to be done if he was to live out the rest of his days at home. He hadn't realized how neglected the place had become until he saw it fixed like new again.

When he was finished, Jakob let the water run in the sink until it steamed, then splashed his face with it, most of it ending up on his shirt and the counter and floor. He was still weak from the infection, and every bend of every limb felt clumsy. He debated whether or not he should try to shave, since he hadn't for several days, and decided he would. Dark age spots on his saggy cheeks and hands reflected back at him as he lathered up his shaving brush.

Fresh-shaven, he headed back to the couch, but before he could sit down, Mattie stopped him.

"This is the day the Lord has made. Might as well rejoice and be glad in it, eh?"

"Humpf."

"I'll get your pills out. Then let's go for a short walk, shall we? Grab the paper, maybe walk down the street a bit. It's still nice and cool outside. Besides, who can nap with all the racket of the trim and roof work going on?" David had hired a couple of helpers, and the roof renovation was well underway.

Though Jakob's vision was back to normal, the back of his head still throbbed. He considered asking to skip the walk, but maybe the fresh air was exactly what his weak arms and wobbly knees needed. If nothing else, surely being outside would raise his spirits. "Fine. Let's go."

"Don't be grumpy with me," Mattie said playfully.

"Sorry. I have a bit of a headache."

"The fresh air should help that too."

Mattie was right. The sun massaged his joints and warmed his cold hands. As they neared the mailbox, a young boy on a bicycle swerved Jakob's way down the sidewalk. Usually Jakob ignored kids, figuring they wouldn't want to have anything to do with an old geezer, or fearing he'd frighten them as he had unintentionally on more than one occasion. But he noticed this one, mostly because he headed straight for him. The boy's father jogged alongside him in the grass, arm outstretched, ready to grab the seat if the boy leaned too far one way or another, separating from him only to avoid a large oak tree in the grass between the sidewalk and the street. This momentary separation, unfortunately, allowed just enough time for the boy, dressed in a bright-yellow T-shirt with a dump truck on the front and plaid shorts, to topple sideways to the ground. With a head full of dark curls, the boy sat in a crumpled ball for a stunned moment. But as soon as the blood oozed from his right knee and the palms of his hands, he let out an ear-piercing wail.

"Da-aaaaad! Why'd you let go-oooo?"

"Oh my!" Mattie gasped.

"Here, son, let me help you." Jakob kept one hand on his walker and stretched his other hand toward the boy, ignoring his creaking knees.

"Jakob, careful now—" Mattie cautioned.

"I'm fine."

The boy didn't seem bothered by Jakob's spotty, veined hand, and grabbed on tight as his father came up behind him and scooped him into his arms. Soon the boy's wails turned to sobby sniffles.

"Thank you." The young father nodded.

Jakob found the man's Chicago Cubs shirt endearing, but his khaki shorts, fringed all along the bottom, could've used a good hemming. Jakob supposed that was the style, but he didn't have to like it.

"How old is the boy?"

"Four. About to turn five. Learning to ride his new birthday bike. Figured we'd give it to him a bit early, nice weather and all."

"Four, eh?"

The boy was small, baby fat still visible on his thighs and around the knuckles on his small hands. He studied Jakob, his walker, and his jowly face as his dad gave him the obligatory parental talk about getting back up when you fall down.

After his father set him down, the boy swung his leg over the bike and looked over his shoulder as his dad grabbed hold of the back of the bike seat. "Don't let go, Daddy."

"I won't, buddy."

"Promise?"

"I promise."

Only then did the boy put one foot on the pedal and then push off with the other foot, a trickle of blood running down his pudgy, unsure leg. The two of them headed away, the young dad hollering wahoos and yahoos and attaboys.

"What a cutie. Too bad about his knee," Mattie said as she pulled the mail out of the mailbox.

The boy pedaled pretty well, smiling even as he headed back their way again. His father still had hold of the seat, as promised.

"I think you can let go now, Daddy," the boy hollered.

"You sure, buddy?"

"I'm sure!"

The father gave a little extra push, and the boy was off on his own. He grinned ear to ear, though his knee still shone siren red.

"That's a way!" Jakob clapped his hands to applaud, and Mattie joined him.

Four years old—the same age he'd been during the raid in Chudniv—with a father who kept holding on.

Jakob and Mattie walked back up the driveway to where David stood taking stock of the roofing supplies and plans for the day.

"Let's go sit on the back deck awhile," Mattie suggested to Jakob then turned to David. "Care to join us for a bit?"

"Thanks, but you two go on. I've got my hands full here and want to get as much in as I can before the rain they keep talking about settles in. S'posed to pour for a week."

They walked around the side of the house, past the rounded and newly mulched beds outlining the home's foundation, past the oak tree sheltering Nel's bedroom window, past the rounded beds of knockout roses and hydrangeas, the beginning mounds of hyssop and coneflowers, lupine and foxglove. In front of the viburnum and chokeberry bushes stood a pedestal topped with the crazy blue gazing ball Catherine had insisted they purchase at a patio show a couple years back. Only now it wasn't crazy as much as it was endearing, as most things become that belong to someone who's passed on.

"Only a few more yards, and we're there," Mattie said, encouraging him.

"I see it, I see it." Jakob feigned more annoyance than he felt. Mattie had been hypervigilant with him ever since he came home, and he knew the help she'd given him and Nel was a big reason why he hadn't kicked the bucket yet. He pushed himself up the incline of the ramp leading to the deck and settled himself onto the bench he and Mattie'd sat on most often since he'd come home.

"Look there." Mattie pointed out at the lake. "I think they caught something."

Jakob's distance vision was about the only part of him that hadn't failed him completely. The eighteen-foot aluminum Tracker bobbed softly in the slow-rolling tide near shore. Two men gathered at the front of the boat, one of them reeling hard against an acutely bent rod. At last he yanked the fish onto the boat deck, and even from where Jakob sat he could see the reflection of the fish's golden scales.

"Got themselves a nice yellow perch."

"Yes they did." Mattie smiled, holding on her head the hat that the breeze seemed determined to blow away.

Papa Stewart came to Jakob's mind, and the days he devoted to Jakob while they stayed at the lake house when Peter was sick in the sanatorium. Papa Stewart worked in Chicago during the week, then came to join Jakob and Mama Stewart, who lived there full-time, except when school was in session. Papa Stewart had taught Jakob how to make his own rod, and they sat on the shore whittling and shining the slender wood, wrapping the metal eyes in place with colored thread, even notching out a ruler to measure whatever they caught. As the last step, Jakob had painted his name on the base: *JAKOB STEWART*.

"Have you spoken to Nel yet about your past?"

The discomfort of another one of Mattie's well-intentioned lectures approaching tightened like a knot in Jakob's chest. "I have."

"Good."

The fishermen on the lake continued to catch and release several more fish.

"So?"

"So what?"

"What'd she say?"

"She was glad, I suppose." He turned toward her with a grin so abrupt and wide and exaggerated Mattie startled. "Satisfied?"

Mattie threw her head back and laughed heartily, and soon Jakob joined in, holding his belly and praying his parts wouldn't leak.

And in that moment, his hardened marrow shifted like the sun lighting on the yellow perch's side, a creature held firm in the fisherman's hand and let go just when it thought it might never breathe again. More memories—good ones—surfaced like a buoy held under currents and finally let go. Memories of his sisters and frogs and honeysuckle. Of leaning against the curve of Mama's soft breast as she rocked him and sang prayers of thanksgiving in the mornings and evenings; of Papa finishing his stones and letting Jakob help polish them with his own piece of cheesecloth; of crystal white snow on white birch branches in patches of forest around Chudniv; of Galya's strong withers; of the taste of milk fresh from the milk cow's udder; of Sasha the priest, Russie and Chaim, Luda, Zsófia and Makár; of Papa Stewart warming a quilt by the stove and wrapping him in it and carrying him up to bed; of Mama Stewart praying outside his bedroom door; of the first time Catherine and he made love; of lunch hours spent laughing with the guys at Brake-All; of fishing; of sunflowers.

Later that evening, David brought in a catch of his own perch he'd caught with some friends that day. Jakob's hands, still steady enough to scale a fish, rubbed the edge of an old spoon backward over the iridescent flesh, the tiny, razor-like pieces flipping all across the counter. He remembered a nun from Saint Stanislaus, wrinkled face framed by the white hood of her habit, as she recited the story of Saul on the road to Damascus, how he became blind when he met his Savior, and how the scales finally fell from his sightless eyes.

CHAPTER 33

"Hey, Dad. David." Nel hopped off her mom's bike that she'd cleaned up and walked it toward where Jakob sat in a lawn chair under a tree in the front yard. He hadn't seen her yet, and she slowed her pace, taking in every bend, curve and wrinkle of his aged form. He lifted a cup of coffee to his mouth and dribbled half of it down his chin without seeming to notice. Nearly ninety-five and yet when she lost him, she knew it would still be too soon.

"Find anything good?" David hollered from his spot on the ladder.

She pulled off her glasses and cleaned them in an attempt to be discreet about wiping the tears off her face, then she cleared her throat and waved up at David. "Got enough rhubarb to make a couple of pies, a bunch of mixed greens, brown eggs, and a new hosta I don't think's represented yet in our garden." She pulled the hosta out of the bike basket and set it in front of Jakob.

David pried another piece of rotten trim from the second-story eaves. He let it fall, and it splintered into dozens of soggy, mildewed pieces on the ground. He climbed down the ladder.

Nel helped him gather an armload of debris and toss it into the large, steel waste container they'd rented.

David brushed his gloved hands together, shaking away the rotten flakes of wood. "Whadda you say we go fishing later on?"

"Is that all you do all spring and summer?" Sweat trickled down her neck and the small of her back as she shielded her eyes from the morning sun already blazing. David's Michigan State T-shirt clung to his sweaty chest and accented his broad shoulders, and she found it more and more difficult to look him in the eyes when his mouth was always slightly upturned, as if he were waiting to kiss her. She used her arm to wipe the sweat off her own forehead.

"It's a bad habit, that's for sure. Don't you like to fish?"

"I like it plenty. Could probably out fish you, in fact."

"Is that a challenge?"

"Do you want it to be?"

"This afternoon. Black River. I'll pick you up around four thirty. You can use my rods."

"I have my own, thank you." She was proud of the fact she not only knew how to fish, but she could hold her own against most any man, most any day. No matter that she hadn't been in awhile. She'd been fishing since she was old enough to hold a rod.

"Four thirty, then."

"Sounds good."

Nel pulled her fishing rod off the rafters where her dad stored all the rods in the garage. She ran her finger over her name and fishing measurements notched in the wood, still shiny and smooth after all these years. She'd chosen pink thread, which Jakob had helped her wind perfect and tight around the metal line guides to keep them in place.

"You ready?" David said, leaning against the front of his truck.

"I'm ready. The question is, are you?"

The drive to the Black River Bridge wasn't far, just across Interstate 196 along the Kal-Haven Trail. They passed an occasional chippy, clapboard house that gaped at them, cracked and dingy windows sighing at the unusual sight of a car passing by. Many of the rolling hills and fields were striped with rows of blueberry bushes, many fully blossoming, and Nel breathed in their sweet scent through the open windows of David's truck.

Once they arrived at Kal-Haven, they found a side trail leading to the river, and David spread a blanket out along the shore, where they laid out their gear and a basket of snacks. Nel's thoughts wandered as she attached a new hook and sinker to her fishing line and baited the hook with the worms they'd stopped to buy, then cast it far into the middle of the river. As her line grew tight floating along with the current, she grew silent.

"Penny for your thoughts?"

"Wow, who even says that anymore?" Nel chuckled.

David shrugged.

"I'm not thinking of anything, really. Sometimes it's nice to think of nothing." She watched her bobber sway with the current and felt for a nibble on the hook, then pulled back hard on her rod as something yanked her bobber beneath the surface. The tip of the rod bent as she began to reel, until the end of the line came near the shore, and she saw that the line was empty. "Stole the bait."

"Stripped it clean too." David headed for a patch of grass where they had set up their tackle. "Mealworm or night crawler?"

"Night crawler. Thanks."

Nel folded the long worm onto the hook and cast it back out into the river. "You wouldn't want me, you know."

"What do you mean?"

Nel focused on her bobber again, determined not to look at David. "I know we're beyond the point of being 'just friends.' That you want more from me. That's why you trusted me with your story, and I'm so, so grateful that you did. But trust me, you don't want me."

"You're being pretty presumptuous." David shook his head. "I can't have more of someone who won't give me a chance." He threw his line into the river as well, closer to shore, near a clump of fallen trees. "You know what I think?"

Nel spun the reel, not answering him.

"I think you're afraid."

She stopped spinning her reel and glared at him.

"You are, aren't you? Beautiful, brilliant, talented girl like you … never married …"

"You think you know so much, do you?"

"I know those same tendencies in other people, same as mine were for a while, especially after the accident. I didn't want to let anyone close to me. I didn't deserve to have anyone close to me. And they certainly didn't deserve me."

"Well, you're wrong. About me, anyway."

"Whatever you say. You don't have to tell me anything." David's rod bent severely, and he reeled back hard against the fish pulling at the end of his line. He landed the fish, dark green with a speckling of pale-yellow spots, and orange front fins. He held the fish in his hand, smoothing back the fins, and worked the hook out of the side of its mouth before throwing it back. "A fine example of a brook trout."

He threw the fish back, then wiped his hands off with a rag from their pile of tackle. He walked to where she stood, put his arm around her tentatively, then strong and unyielding as he kissed her on the temple. "You've been through quite a bit since fall."

"It's not just that," she said in barely a whisper, her voice quaking. "I can't have kids."

Instead of slackening his arm as she'd expected, he pulled her closer.

"It ends with me, Mom and Dad's legacy. I can't have kids." She pulled away from him and walked to the edge of the river, tears falling freely. "All these years, I've been filling my life with my art, creating things that will outlast me, somehow, since no one ever will. Maybe I am afraid … afraid of what's left for me in the future. Maybe that's why Dad's story, his past, matters to me so much."

She told him everything, then, about Tom and the miscarriage and the subsequent hysterectomy. About her breakup with Sam and all the breakups before that. How she'd become so involved with her art, she'd lost track of what was most important, which was family. Family and home.

"Here's your glasses." David centered them on her nose for her after she'd taken them off to wipe her tears, then put his other arm around her and kept holding her, strong and consuming as the full moon cast long shadows all around them. Like gypsum, the alabaster that held Mary's perfume, the moon gleamed, pouring out light as the cicadas sang and the river ran and the pain in Nel's soul receded.

CHAPTER 34

The postman had tucked the shoebox-sized package between the door and one of the two matching pedestals of geraniums blooming crimson on the front porch. Nel almost didn't see it in the shadows as she and David walked up to the front door later that evening.

"David, look." Nel picked up the box and wiped away bits of potting soil stuck to the bottom. The penmanship of the address appeared stiff, as if the sender struggled to make each letter, compared to the return address written in flowing Cyrillic.

"It's gotta be from them, don't you think?"

"Maybe ..." She hugged the box to her chest as if to quell the excitement rising inside her. "But I'm afraid to get my hopes up."

They found Mattie sleeping on the couch with a *Midwest Living* magazine across her lap, and Jakob in his recliner snoring heavily.

"Shhhh." Nel raised a finger to her lips as she and David tiptoed to the kitchen. She grabbed a pair of scissors from the junk drawer and cut through the taped edges of the box.

On top of the contents was a rag doll, pieced together with embroidered fabric, with ribbons on her skirt and shirt and a scarf around her head. The plain face was probably white once but was now yellowed and stained from age. She picked it up and startled.

"Where did you get that?"

Nel and David both jumped at the sound of Jakob's voice. His eyes were locked on the doll, and his face was nearly as pale as the flat, empty cloth face.

"Jakob, what on earth are you doing? How'd you get past me?" Mattie tumbled into the kitchen behind him, bleary-eyed and pale herself, appearing frightened that she'd slept through Jakob scooting by her. She came alongside Nel and David.

"Dad, I … this box came in the mail today."

He appeared more lucid than she'd seen him since his fall as he scooted toward her. He reached out and took the doll from her hands, then ran his fingers along the red cross-stitching of the blouse; the tiny, red, beaded necklace around the neck; and the tassels and stitching on the skirt; then he gently adjusted the scarf on the doll's head. "Faigy," he whispered.

"What, Dad?"

His eyes, puddled with tears, met Nel's. "Faigy had a doll like this. And the sisters. All my sisters had dolls like this. But this one … Faigy's was just like this."

Nel pulled a stack of old and fragile photographs, several papers, an old bound book, and a large, white cloth with blue stripes and fringe on the edges out of the box, along with a note addressed to her.

Mattie picked up the cloth. "This is a tallis."

"A tallis?" Nel asked.

"A Jewish prayer shawl," she replied.

"Where'd this come from?" Jakob asked again, shifting his weight and approaching the box on the table.

"I know about as much as you do—that's what we're trying to find out, what this all means." Nel unfolded the note and began to read. "Dad, I think you'd better sit down."

Jakob waved away David's hand as he offered an arm to steady him and instead fell heavily into one of the dining room chairs.

"What's the note say?" David prodded.

She hesitated. "Dad … do you remember I told you Mom had been researching your past?"

He nodded, not moving his eyes from the doll, still running his fingers across every detail.

"Well …" She hadn't told him about her research and letters to the church in Ukraine. She truly didn't think at that point anything would come of it, or that they would ever hear anything back; it had been so many months. Besides that, so much weight had visibly lifted from his shoulders when he told her about his past, she hadn't thought it mattered anymore. "I did a little more of my own research."

Jakob did look up then, and the emotion in his eyes overwhelmed her. Was he angry? *Please, Lord, don't let him be angry with me. Let this be something good. Let this be something that will help Dad see that You work all things together for good.*

Mattie nudged her. "Maybe it will help if you read the note."

"Okay. Yes. I think it might." She cleared her throat and began to read:

Dear Miss Stewart,

My name is Ira Levchenko. I run orphanage near Chudniv, and receive your letters. I knew your aunt, Faigy. She started this orphanage

with help from the church. The things in box will explain how we know
she your aunt. The diagram and photo of the stone you sent matches
Faigy's stone. And we found records of Josef and all your brothers and
sisters, and your father, Jakob, in our church records. Copies of these
papers are in the box, along with pictures of Faigy and Sasha and the
orphans. We did not know what to do with her things when she die. She
thought all her family die in pogrom. But now we know. And now you
know too.

    Maybe you visit us sometime? See where your father from. See the
children in orphanage.

    (Forgive my English is not so good. I had help of translator.)

With love,
Ira Levchenko

By the time Nel finished, Jakob had started sifting through the
stack of photographs.

"Sasha," he gasped.

"Sasha? The priest you told me about?"

Jakob nodded, his eyes fixed on a photo of a bearded man in
black robes with a little girl standing beside him.

Nel knelt beside Jakob, put her arm around him, and
searched every detail of the photo he held. The girl appeared
to be three or four. She had the plump little wrists of a toddler,
round cheeks, and dark braids in her hair. The man stood tall
and appeared stiff, but a kindness in his eyes softened his whole
countenance. His robes appeared thick and heavy, except for a
white collar at his neck. "Dad, you said a man in black robes took
her—could it have been Sasha and not the pogromshchik?

He set the photo on the table and began to sob, years of shame pouring out of him. His shoulders shook as he buried his face in his hands. "Faigy. My baby bird. Forgive me."

Nel embraced her dad with both arms. "Dad, it looks to me like there was nothing ever to forgive."

He sobbed harder, and Mattie joined in the embrace.

"Guys …," David said gently. "Sorry, but I think there's something else here you need to see."

Jakob pulled a handkerchief out of his pajama shirt pocket and blew his nose, then wiped his face as David handed him a wooden box painted shiny black and detailed with exquisite, colorful flowers. He opened the lid and the facets of a large aquamarine beamed from within, reflections dancing across the room.

Nel hurried to retrieve the aquamarine in the old kiddush cup on their worktable, by then, her own tears falling as she compared the Star of David pattern on the crowns of both gemstones. "Look, David, Mattie … Dad, they're same."

CHAPTER 35

Jakob woke early the next morning, still smiling from the images of Faigy and Sasha in the old photographs, how she'd grown strong and beautiful. Jakob thought Faigy resembled their mother when she'd become an adult, especially in photographs of her playing with the orphans she so clearly adored.

The four of them had stayed up until the early hours of the morning sorting through the photos, flipping through the journal (although none of them could read Cyrillic—they would have to find someone to translate that), and laughing as he told more stories of Sasha the priest's visits and all he could remember about his family.

Sasha had come back.

Faigy had lived.

And she had lived well, saving the lives of children who had no homes, who'd lost parents and brothers and sisters, just as she had. Of course, she would have assumed he and Peter died. In hindsight, they should have, two boys wandering without so much as a compass through across the Carpathian Mountains and Eastern Europe. He thought again about all of the people who'd helped him and Peter. Of all the times Yahweh never let them go.

Who are You, indeed, Abba, that You've been mindful of me all these years? The springs and components of the hospital bed cracked and groaned almost as much as his joints as he rose and made his way to the bathroom. He shuffled to the kitchen, where he scooped heaping tablespoons of coffee into the filter and held the open can to his nose to smell the earthy, bittersweet grounds. The morning paper thudded against the front door and silenced the songbirds for a moment, as did the squeak of the screen door as he scooted himself out to retrieve the paper, then took it to his recliner, where he ran his fingers along the brown-and-orange, matted-down plaid fabric of the arms. He'd worn the right side down markedly more than the left from all the evenings he'd reached across it to the couch to hold Catherine's hand as they watched TV. How many times had they watched *Ed Sullivan, Father Knows Best, The Adventures of Ozzie and Harriet, I Love Lucy,* and later *Lassie, Perry Mason,* and *Andy Griffith* as they took turns letting Nel fall asleep on their shoulders? And who could forget Rod Serling's *Twilight Zone* and Ronald Reagan Westerns? TV had to be the best invention of the century, he thought.

He opened the paper to the weather, then the op-eds, then the obituary section. Used to be a time when he recognized at least one name every day of someone who'd kicked the bucket. After he turned eighty-five or so, familiar names didn't show up so often. And now he rarely recognized a name, except an occasional adult child of an old friend or neighbor. Even so, Catherine and Mattie had always kept him from feeling lonely, as had the comfort of filling the bird feeders; tending to the squirrels; soaking in the subtle changes in buds and leaves, trees and grass; watching the shift of the tides and the patterns in the sand as the lake resculpted it every night.

He wondered if his grandfather Dedus had felt the same way as he plodded through the billowing wheat fields of Chudniv with a cow's lead in one hand and a scythe in the other, his deeply creased, sunburned face worn like leather. He could taste the thick milk Dedus had ladled out of the bucket for him on hot summer days, even as he pulled gently on the great beast's teat.

Thank you, El Shaddai.

Thank you, Messiah Yeshua.

Jehovah-Shammah.

Jakob shuffled to the kitchen and plunked a couple ears of corn and a bag of suet and sunflower seeds, and another bag of thistle seed, in the pouch of his walker. Outside, a black squirrel and her three babies ran across the yard as he lumbered toward the feeders. They were placed close, but not too close, to the house, so Jakob could see them all from the windows, except for three bluebird houses on high poles on the southwest corner of the property. The bluebirds took care of themselves and preferred to be left alone.

One black squirrel, in particular, had been coming to the feeders for corn so often, he didn't scurry away from the tree as Jakob approached. Nel had helped him mount the stands decades ago, and a long, rusty nail held the cob in place. Another one of their father-daughter projects, Jakob had suggested they build the stands one summer when she, sullen and distant, was home from college. Seemed like nothing at the time, looking back to that summer, but well, maybe those feeders had meant a lot to her. Maybe that's why she always kept them full since she'd been home. It's a grand shame most of us don't know the impact of what we're doing with a person until it's too long past or too painful to revisit, Jakob thought. Then again, maybe it's better not knowing and having done the thing anyway.

The black squirrel chattered as Jakob moved between the feeders. He sprinkled sunflower seeds on the seat of a flat feeder that hung from the old sweet-gum tree. Then he filled two more hanging feeders on the pole nearby with thistle. The back of his head began to throb, but he tried to ignore it as he poured the fine seed, then glanced up at the window where Catherine used to watch him and wave while she washed dishes at the kitchen sink.

"Peace and a song" is what Catherine had said about the birds. That's why she'd wanted them close to the house too. Sometimes she sang to the mourning doves, and she'd laugh and laugh as they sang back.

One of them cooed as darkness seeped across the field of vision in Jakob's left eye. He figured it'd pass like all the other times. But instead, his left leg buckled. He lost his grip on the walker. Felt himself crumple to the ground. The world felt blazingly hot and icy cold all at the same time. He tried to holler for help, but all that came out was a weak cry.

Adonai, help me.

Jakob tried to cry out again, but no sound came from his thickened throat. Not even a movement from his lips.

The rest of the world grew black.

Jakob smelled familiar chemicals and heard beeps of the IV and hissing of oxygen in the hospital room.

"*Slova zalyshylysya u Vashomu sertsi, Yakob, tak?*"† Peter sat at the foot of his bed.

"Yes. Yes, they did. But it took me a while to believe them."

"*Vy zavzhdy viryly. Vy til'ky tikaly. Vin znaye, chomu vy tak dovho tikaly.*"‡

"I don't want to run anymore. Will you forgive me? Will Yeshua, will Adonai forgive me?"

"Dad, I'm here. It's Nel. Can you hear me?"

"Nel?"

"Yes, Dad. It's me. Please don't leave me." She tried and failed to stifle a sob. "I need you."

"No." Jakob's tongue hardly budged and felt thick and dry as an old rag in his mouth. "You don't … you … need to love … love and let … yourself … be loved."

"No, Dad."

He felt her wet cheek pressing against his.

The thick scent of honeysuckle overwhelmed him, and he found himself walking on a dirt road he'd seen long, long ago. Beside him, fat carpenter bees and wide-winged butterflies bobbed along a vine-covered fence, fields of sunflowers billowing as far as he could see below the sapphire sky. A family with four young children passed by him, the father pulling an oxcart, and the mother smiling hello.

---

† The words remained in your heart, Jakob, yes?

‡ You always believed. You have just been running. He knows why you ran for so long.

Beyond them where the road began to bend, a man waved, and Jakob could hardly wait to greet him. The man's eyes enraptured Jakob. And when they at last reached each other, the man's embrace, swift and fierce, intoxicated Jakob with joy.

"Welcome home, My child. All is grace. All is forgiven. Welcome home."

"Yeshua." Jakob sobbed and laughed at once, soaking the shoulder of his Savior's shirt.

"Laskavo prosymo dodomu, brat."§ Peter came up beside Yeshua, and Jakob clung to their hands as together they crossed a great river, the light of the place shining, reflecting against the ripples of the water like millions of diamonds stretching to the opposite shore. As the three men crossed over, thousands of people along the riverbank waved and sang hymns. And in front of them all, waiting for him, stood Catherine and Mama, Papa and Zahava, Tova, Ilana, and Sasha the priest.

And next to them stood his sister Faigy.

Jakob stood on the golden shore in the arms of Yeshua and his loved ones, and he sang.

He sang, and he sang, and he sang.

---

§   Welcome home, Brother.

... a little more ...

When a delightful concert comes to an end,

the orchestra might offer an encore.

When a fine meal comes to an end,

it's always nice to savor a bit of dessert.

When a great story comes to an end,

we think you may want to linger.

And so, we offer ...

AfterWords—just a little something more after you

have finished a David C Cook novel.

We invite you to stay awhile in the story.

Thanks for reading!

Turn the page for ...

- **Book Club Questions**
- **The Inspiration Behind the Story**
- **Notes**
- **About the Title and Cover**
- **About the Author**
- **Suggested for Further Reading**
- **Acknowledgments**

BOOK CLUB QUESTIONS

1. In this story, we are privy to an overview of Jakob's nearly century-long life. In what ways did Jakob change or not change over the decades? What things prevented or contributed to his ability to change?

2. Nel, on the other hand, was less than half a century old and received the benefits of a safe upbringing. In what ways did she change after going home to South Haven? In what ways did she stay the same? What were the contributing factors to these changes (if any)?

3. Many Americans find themselves part of the "sandwich generation," caring for aging parents while at the same time trying to care for their own children. Are you able to identify with Nel's struggles to understand and care for her father of deteriorating health? In what ways?

4. Nearly twice as many Jews as were killed in the Holocaust—some estimates are as high as eleven million—were massacred in Eastern Europe and especially Ukraine in the decades leading up to World War II. How do you think the pogroms did or did not eventually contribute to the Holocaust?

5. As the group ISIS invaded the Middle East in the summer of 2014, heinous reports emerged about the genocide of Christians. Darfur,

Rwanda, Bosnia, and Cambodia are other regions where people groups have been targeted over the last century for genocide based on their ethnicity, religion, or both. How has society learned—or not learned—from history as it relates to the advancement or prevention of genocide?

6. Which character in this novel do you identify with most? Why?

7. Many references were made to Jewish traditions throughout Jakob and Peter's escape to America. Did any of these traditions resonate with New Testament teachings and practices?

8. How do you see the promises of the Old Testament reflected in Jakob and Peter's journey? Do you think Jakob saw evidence of these promises by the end of the story? Why or why not?

9. Nel was so preoccupied with her own busyness that she didn't fully realize the decline in her parents' health. Share a time when your own preoccupations prevented you from being as "present" as you wish you had been.

10. Mattie was a lifelong family friend. How did her own life story help Nel and Jakob?

11. The metaphor of how rocks and minerals are discovered and shaped runs throughout the story. How have you seen this process unfold in your own life? Can you think of another hobby or tangible

process that parallels the way God works in our lives? If so, share it with the group.

12. Think of an event in history—your own, your ancestors', or humanity's—that you've learned from.

13. Nel eventually became more open to a relationship with David. What factors contributed to these changes in her?

14. Read Isaiah 43:18 and Deuteronomy 4:9. Compare and contrast what God says about memories in these verses. Are there other scriptures that you have turned to when faced with guilt and shame or the fear that God has abandoned you?

15. Read Psalm 13. Describe the differences in the author's thoughts between the first and last stanzas. What does this tell you about how we can talk with God?

16. This novel begins with a quote from Charles Spurgeon about "Jehovah-Shammah." How has this novel impacted your belief—or disbelief—in the characteristics of this name (one of many) for Yahweh?

THE INSPIRATION BEHIND THE STORY

*Ritual allows those who cannot will themselves out
of the secular to perform the spiritual, as dancing
allows the tongue-tied man a ceremony of love.*
Andre Dubus, "A Father's Story"

Three important parts of my life inspired this story, the first of which is an organization called Mission to Ukraine (www.missiontoukraine.org). Through our interest in and support of Mission to Ukraine, in 2009 my family began to sponsor—and fall in love with—a boy in Ukraine named Peter Predchuk. As we learned through blog posts of friends who live near and travel to Zhytomyr, Peter was like many thirteen-year-old boys—happy, funny, tenderhearted, and kind. He loved cars and he liked to sing. But Peter was different too. Abandoned by his mother because she could not care for him and his degenerative muscular dystrophy, he was alone, filthy, and regularly beaten in an orphanage. He was losing hope and growing weaker by the day. But God had special plans for Peter. He was rescued and adopted by a man named Yuri Levchenko (who has nine biological children and a tenth on the way as of this writing). Peter was deeply treasured and loved until he passed away July 1, 2014. Peter was a hero to many, and I had the privilege of finally meeting him in January 2013, in what has been proven to be one of the most pivotal moments of my life.

The second inspiration for this story was my paternal grandfather, Joseph Kossack, a savant hobby lapidarist who died at the ripe young age of ninety-four, a month shy of his ninety-fifth birthday. Up until a month before he died, he was vibrant. He lived in his own apartment, enjoyed life with his friends and neighbors, told the same stories over and over again, and yes, he still drove a car. I discovered through genealogy research that his grandparents—my paternal great-great-grandparents—were Jewish immigrants who escaped to the United States from Eastern Europe—most likely near the edge of Ukraine near Belarus, from what I can tell from my research—during the first waves of pogroms in the Pale of Settlement that occurred in the 1880s. This is where his last name (and my maiden name), Kossack (a variation of "Cossack"), originated. The story goes that my great-great-grandfather's true last name was too difficult for the Ellis Island intake administrator to figure out how to spell, so they assigned him a new one: Kossack.

Learning of my significant Jewish heritage compounded my adoration for the plight of the people of Ukraine, and I was compelled to write a story that not only reflects the deep pain and struggles within the region, but also the ways in which Yahweh is with us throughout all of our sojourns: Jehovah-Shammah. Indeed, there is no place where we can flee from His glorious love, grace, and presence (Psalm 139).

In addition to writing from a Jewish perspective, for some time I have wanted to incorporate the work of a lapidarist into a novel. All my life, my grandfather brought his shiny rock and mineral creations with him on his visits to our home. The brilliant gemstones and cabochons—as well as his lengthy stories of what each stone was made of and where he found it, and the details of gemstone conventions he attended—mesmerized me. The metaphor of a rough and unsightly rock or mineral being faceted and polished into something beautiful, and how Yahweh does the same thing with us is one that never grows old or cliché to me.

The third inspiration for this story was my work as a registered nurse on a busy medical unit where I currently care for aging patients every week. I see how families struggle with end-of-life care decisions, and how exhausting and discouraging the process can be for everyone involved. When an elderly person suffers a fall as the protagonist, Jakob, did in this story, that often sets off a cascade of difficult decisions and recovery processes. But this season of life is not without hope—far from it. While some of the elderly patients I care for have succumbed completely to dementia and Alzheimer's disease, a good number of them have minds still as sharp as yours and mine. They love to tell stories about their youth, how they met and courted their spouses, the war years, you name it. They love to tell stories about their *lives*. And we are wise to listen.

For more information about some of the unique themes and background inspiration for *Then Sings My Soul*, visit: www.AmySorrells.wordpress.com/Then-Sings-My-Soul

NOTES

Prologue

1. Small Jewish towns or villages formerly found in Eastern Europe.
2. "The Pale of Settlement ... was the term given to a region of Imperial Russia in which permanent residency by Jews was allowed and beyond which Jewish permanent residency was generally prohibited. It extended from the eastern pale, or demarcation line, to the western Russian border with the Kingdom of Prussia (later the German Empire) and with Austria-Hungary.... It included much of present-day Lithuania, Belarus, Poland, Moldova, Ukraine, and parts of western Russia.... Jews were [also] excluded from residency at a number of cities within the Pale, while a limited number of categories of Jews were allowed to live outside it. With its large Catholic and Jewish populations, the Pale was acquired by the Russian Empire (which was majority Russian Orthodox) in a series of military conquests and diplomatic maneuvers between 1791 and 1835, and lasted until the fall of the Russian Empire in 1917.... Because of the harsh conditions of day-to-day life in the Pale, some 2 million Jews emigrated from there between 1881 and 1914, mainly to the United States" (Wikipedia, s.v. "Pale of Settlement," last modified September 17, 2014, http://en.wikipedia.org/wiki/Pale_of_Settlement).
3. Traditional Ukrainian fur coat.

Chapter 3

1. "Holodomor Facts and History," Holodomorct.org, accessed September 20, 2014, www.holodomorct.org/history.html.

Chapter 8

1. Ecclesiastes 1:18.

Chapter 9

1. Fringe tassels tied to a small cloak worn under a shirt.
2. A stylus used to achieve the design on the painted wooden eggs.
3. Traditional colored eggs of Ukraine, made by some Jewish children for Passover and Orthodox families for Easter.

Chapter 13

1. Traditional embroidered Ukrainian shirt.
2. Traditional Russian felt boots.

Chapter 21

1. Luke 12:7 NKJV.

Chapter 24

1. Traditional Jewish prayer said during times of mourning.

Chapter 27

1. Ecclesiastes 1:5.
2. Ecclesiastes 1:2.

Chapter 30

1. Small cloak worn under a shirt and on which the fringe tassels called *tzitzit* are tied.

ABOUT THE TITLE AND COVER

When I converse with readers, a common question is how book titles and cover designs are determined. For my first novel, *How Sweet the Sound*, lyrics to the song "Amazing Grace" appear in one of the chapters. Not only is it one of my favorite hymns, but the phrase "how sweet the sound" made the editor and me misty-eyed enough to know it was destined to be the title of that book.

Then Sings My Soul was a bit more of a challenge. Although it is a phrase from "How Great Thou Art"—also one of my favorite hymns—I was hesitant to use it because there isn't much reference to the actual song within this novel. However, I believe it truly captures the theme of the novel. Moreover, once I heard the story behind the hymn, I knew "Then Sings My Soul" had to be the title. Stuart Hine, an English missionary to Ukraine, stumbled upon the Russian text for "How Great Thou Art" and translated it into English. His travels and missionary work across Eastern Europe, and the beauty of the Carpathian Mountains, prompted him to write the hymn's fourth and final stanza. Indeed, the entire hymn speaks to the steadfast, enduring beauty of God and His faithfulness to us throughout the ages—a truth that Jakob eventually realizes.

All of the credit for cover design goes to the amazing graphic artists at David C Cook. However, *Then Sings My Soul* was a bit unique. The designers came up with the cover pretty much as it appears here, but initially they didn't know where they would be able to find a usable graphic for the blue gemstone. Although I had access to the thousands of gemstones faceted by my grandfather, the stone featured on the cover was discovered in a plastic bag tucked in a corner of a manila file folder that was stuffed in a binder full of faceting designs. The only reason the folder even caught my eye was because it was marked "Star of David," which of course was a wonderfully perfect match for this story.

The actual Star of David stone my grandfather designed and faceted appears on the cover.

ABOUT THE AUTHOR

Amy, an Indianapolis native and graduate of DePauw University, lives in central Indiana with her husband, her three boys, and a gaggle of golden retrievers.

After writing and editing for her college newspaper, Amy combined the knowledge from her nursing degree with journalism and creative writing. This unique combination of skills led to her editing and publishing a wide array of medical and nursing multimedia and writing projects over the past twenty-one years, including a weekly column for a local newspaper.

Amy has since become a two-time semifinalist for the ACFW Genesis Awards and the winner of the 2011 Women of Faith writing contest.

When she's not reading or writing, Amy enjoys spending time with her husband and three sons, walking her dogs, digging in her garden sans gloves, and up-cycling old junk.

SUGGESTED FOR

FURTHER READING

A lot of research went into this novel, and like me, you might be interested in reading more about some of the themes in this book. Listed below are the names of books that I found to be both helpful and interesting.

Eastern European/Ukrainian History

- *The Golden Age Shtetl: A New History of Jewish Life in East Europe* by Yohanan Petrovsky-Shtern
- *Wonder of Wonders: A Cultural History of Fiddler on the Roof* by Alisa Solomon
- *Borderland: A Journey Through the History of Ukraine* by Anna Reid
- *Forgotten Fire* by Adam Bagdasarian
- *The Chosen* by Chaim Potok
- *Erased: Vanishing Traces of Jewish Galicia in Present-Day Ukraine* by Omer Bartov

Lapidary Arts

- *Gem Cutting: A Lapidary's Manual* 2nd edition, by John Sinkankas
- *Smithsonian Handbooks: Rocks and Minerals* by Chris Pellant

Aging and Dementia

- *Still Alice* by Lisa Genova
- *No Act of Love Is Ever Wasted: The Spirituality of Caring for Persons with Dementia* by Jane Marie Thibault and Richard L. Morgan
- *Not Alone: Encouragement for Caregivers* by Nell E. Noonan

ACKNOWLEDGMENTS

To all those who made this book what it is through your support, encouragement, patience, wisdom, and expertise: Sarah Freese, who did triple duty as my agent, editor, and therapist for this project; Nicci Jordan Hubert and Jennifer Lonas for your incredible, patient (but fierce!) editing and encouragement; and to Don Pape and John Blase for the chance to write this book in the first place. And to all the professionals at David C Cook for making it happen.

To Robert Vukovich and his assistant, Mary, for spending an entire evening capturing the photograph of my grandfather's gemstone for this cover.

To Sergei Marchenko, for early read-throughs and gracious help with the Ukrainian language elements, and to Becky Gluff, also for help with the Ukrainian language.

To Jon Lieberman, for your time and invaluable input into the Jewish aspects of this story, and for encouraging me to research my Ukrainian family history.

To Dr. Ken Ney and Jill Kendrat and everyone who helped me travel to Zhytomyr and Chudniv, Ukraine, in January 2013, thank you for not taking no for an answer! And to all the people of Mission to Ukraine (www.missiontoukraine.org) on both sides of the Atlantic: я тебе люблю.

To Pastor Peter Levchenko for your legacy of unwavering faith in the midst of dark and seemingly unreachable places. I miss your smile and laughter.

To Peter Predchuk—I can't wait to see you running in heaven.

To Grandpa Joe, whose hard work and storytelling "faceted" my life.

To my great-great-grandparents, who survived and escaped the pogroms so that your children, and now my children, could live freely.

And to Scott, Tucker, Charlie, and Isaac: my soul sings because of each of you.

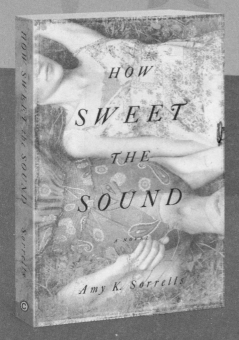